Follow
Where he
Leads

Follow Where he Leads

MISTY MONCUR

Eden Books   Stansbury Park, Utah

Published by Eden Books, Stansbury Park, UT

ISBN-10: 0-9898959-7-1
ISBN-13: 978-0-9898959-7-2

Moncur, Misty Leigh, 1978-
Follow Where He Leads/ Misty Moncur
Summary: Olivia runs away from her father's wicked friends, and Shad rescues her.

ISBN: 978-0-9898959-7-2

Library of Congress Catalog Control Number

2015951735

"In memory of our God, our religion, and freedom, and our peace, our wives, and our children."

Alma 46:12

With special thanks to Alyssa

CHAPTER 1

The darkness was overwhelming, and there were things in it—scratching, scampering, biting things—that made it nearly unbearable to sit silent and still.

"In here." The whisper was so soft and unexpected, I thought I imagined it, but then three shadows crept through the doorway of the decrepit old house.

I froze. I was already fearful—tucked into the back of the darkest corner of the room with the rats and spiders and snakes—but my heart beat so loudly when the men came in, I was sure they would hear it.

They paused inside the doorway, adjusting to the deep darkness. After a moment, two of them went to their heels under a hole in the wall that had once been a window. The third remained near the door, with its torn and shabby mat that covered little and offered no protection from the outside world. He lifted it with two fingers and peered out into the night.

All was still and silent but for their soft breaths, and then I heard it—the reason they were hiding.

The Nephite patrol was approaching.

As the glow from the soldiers' torch swept across the

room, I saw the outline of the two men huddled under the window.

And the man near the door saw me, huddled like a waif in the corner.

One of the soldiers spoke and the others laughed, raucous and cruel, and the sound of their laughter made my blood run cold. This was not the Nephite patrol, and they were not simply keeping the city curfew that had gone into effect after the murder of the Chief Judge. These were the men I had been hiding from for a week.

They were still looking for me.

"What did they say?" one of the men whispered after the footsteps and laughter had faded. "Something about dogs?"

When the answer came, I realized the third person hiding in the darkness was not a man but a girl, one who knew the Lamanitish words of the traitorous men of Gadianton's band. "They don't like this part of the city," she murmured.

"Come on," the man at the door said, giving no indication to the others that he had seen me, and they stole out of the ramshackle building together.

I didn't know who they were, but I wished I was with them.

I waited in the heavy silence until the rodents started moving again. Something scampered past my foot. I closed my eyes and let slow tears roll down my cheeks, but I would not make a sound. I would not make a move. I could not be found here.

I didn't know how long the shadow had been in the doorway before I noticed it. When I did, I betrayed myself with a soft intake of air. It seemed to be the confirmation he needed that I was there in the darkness.

"Are you okay?"

It was a man. His voice was soft, but he wasn't whispering.

Something scampered past when he moved through the door. I tried to bite back another gasp, but I flinched, my fancy sandal scraping across the dirty floor.

"Come here," he said.

I shook my head jerkily, then realized he couldn't see it. "N-no."

He stilled. "Do you live here?"

"N-no."

He was silent for a moment. "Can I help you home?"

"No!" I couldn't go there.

"I see." More silence. "Are you hungry?"

I wanted to say no, but I couldn't and my silence spoke for me.

"Come on." He was moving closer. "I have food. You don't need to stay here with the lizards."

Lizards? They were rats! Gigantic, disgusting, terrifying rats!

He went to his heels in front of me, and I could see the reflection of light in his eyes and on his hair. He was handsome. But when he reached out for me, I flinched again.

His hand stilled before it touched me. "I'm not going to hurt you," he said. "I saw you when I was here before with my friends. I took them to safety. I'll take you to safety — if you'll let me." When I didn't say anything, he said again, "I'm not going to hurt you."

I pressed my lips together. Go with this stranger — trust this strange man who dodged the patrols in the middle of the night — or stay here with the rodents.

"Okay," I said. I hardly recognized my voice, I hadn't used it in so long. "But don't touch me," I said when he reached out for me again.

He stood and stepped back. "I only want to get you out of here."

I got to my feet. My muscles were aching. The man didn't reach out for me when my knees buckled and I nearly dropped to the ground again. He just stood there, large and silent and still, until I had my feet under me and I was steady.

He paused at the door, searching the dark street. Then he said, "Follow me," and he slipped out into the night.

We kept to the shadows. He moved slowly, and I thought it was deliberate so I could keep up. He didn't say anything, didn't try to ask me what I was doing in the derelict part of the city, only gave me terse instructions as we made our way through the streets. We moved generally west until we were in the very nice part of the city, the part where I had lived until a week ago. Inexplicably, I looked down at myself in the sparse moonlight and felt embarrassed at my appearance. Not that the man had yet looked at me. But he would. And when he did, he would exact a price for his protection.

There was only one way left for me to pay, and I was so hungry I thought I would pay it. I had held out as long as I could, but I would have to pay it. I was starving.

Finally, he ushered me into a small hut. I stood in the darkness until he lit a lamp, and then I stood trembling as he turned to look at me. I watched his eyes as he took me in. I was a sight, I was sure. Ragged, filthy clothes, flea bitten skin, unkempt and tangled hair, and frightened eyes blinking in the warm glow of the lamp.

After a moment he gestured to a stool. "Sit. I will prepare

some food. It will be simple, but it will nourish you."

I nodded slightly and sat as he instructed.

"I haven't money to pay you," I said.

He glanced over at me, his slight flush clearly betraying what he was thinking—but it was only what I had implied.

"But I will. Pay you, I mean. Do you have a basin I can clean up in?" I knew I looked disgusting and smelled worse.

He looked fully at me then, his eyes very hard.

"I don't want that," he said, but after a moment he suddenly flushed again. "Or anyway, it is not mine to take."

I felt very foolish for offering, and if possible, I felt even dirtier than I was.

"The basin is there." He pointed. "I will haul in some water."

He left the little house abruptly and did not return right away. I closed my eyes and let my head fall back against the wall. I didn't intend to, but I fell asleep there in the stranger's home. But it was clean—sparse actually—and rodent free, and despite how frightened I was, I somehow felt safe enough to sleep.

I woke alone in the morning on the lone pallet, and it was well past dawn, but the water the man had promised was in a pitcher beside the basin along with a cloth, a comb, and some opaque salve in a little jar.

I had finished with the basin and I was sitting stiffly on the bed when the man returned. In the light, I could see he was younger than I had imagined, not much older than me. He had hair the color of roasted chestnuts that fell into his eyes, and his eyes were dark like charcoal.

"I should go," I said.

"Do you have a home?"

What could I tell him? He had found me hiding in squalor. Would I have been there if I had any other place to be?

"Yes," I said, deciding on honesty. "But I can't go there." I wouldn't.

He didn't ask me why, just leaned back against the little table that was in the room and looked down at his sandals.

"We'll go into the market."

"No." I couldn't go there. I might be seen.

"Would you be safer outside the city?"

How did he know it was a matter of safety? And didn't he know it was not possible to get out of the city? Not with the Chief Judge murdered on the judgment seat and the army patrolling and enforcing the curfew and the sealed gates.

"I have a place I can take you, but I can't stay with you there." At my wary look, he added, "It's with my mother."

I shook my head, not to refuse the offer, but because I couldn't believe he had made it.

"She won't view it as an imposition, if that's what you're thinking."

I shook my head again. "I couldn't ask that of either of you. You don't even know me."

He regarded me for a long moment. "I know you have a need, and I know I have the ability to fill it."

But why? I wanted to ask. What could I possibly give him in return. I had less than nothing now.

"Get some more rest." He motioned to his face with a finger, I guessed to indicate I had dark circles under my eyes. "How long were you hiding in that—?" He stopped, took a breath. "I'll go into the market alone," he decided and came off the table. He paused at the door. His back was to me, but he turned his head. "Will you let me take you somewhere safe?"

He didn't even know my name. And I didn't know his.

"I will." What choice was left to me?

He was right. I needed help. I needed food and shelter and a place to disappear, to hide.

And he was right about me being exhausted, so I lay back down on the pallet, curled up tight, and fell asleep.

I thought he might come back with the Nephite guard to haul me to the prison, but he came back with a sarong and a soft new pair of longboots.

"I can't take those," I said.

I would owe him.

"Put them on," he said as if he hadn't heard me, though I knew he had. "You'll draw attention to us if you don't, and getting out is going to be tricky as it is."

"How do you plan to get out of the city?" The gates were locked. No one could get out.

"You're not the only one with secrets."

I guessed I deserved that.

He cleared his throat. "I'll wait outside while you change."

"I'm Olivia," I said before he could go through the door. "Livi."

"Get dressed, Olivia. I want to get on the road."

The frustration of the past week caught up with me and I very suddenly wanted to scream that I didn't care about what he wanted. I cared about what I wanted, which was to go home, to have everything back to normal—but that didn't even exist anymore and was no longer an option for me.

Dutifully—because up until a month ago I had been nothing if not dutiful—I dressed in the clothing he had bought me and prepared to leave.

If he could just get me out of the city, I determined, I could go anywhere. I would not have to impose upon this stranger's mother. I had never been outside of the city. I didn't know how to care for myself out there—and as it was now abundantly clear, I didn't know how to care for myself inside the city, either—but that didn't mean I couldn't learn. I would watch the stranger, and I would learn.

As we walked along the road in silence, I stole glances at the boy beside me. He was large like a man—tall, strong, and dangerous. Either the muscles in his arms were very large or his tunic was very small. I felt slight next to him—frail and helpless. I had taken my safety for granted my whole life. Why was I trusting him?

He had not hurt me yet.

And besides the rats and lizards, I didn't have any other options.

For a time, I thought he was taking me back to where he had found me, but he didn't take me to the crumbling shack. Instead he turned north and eventually cut back toward the west. I could hardly reconcile what we were doing—sneaking out of Zarahemla—with the beauty of the day. The sun was bright, the air was calm, and the birds were chirping in the trees.

I didn't see it until we were on it, and even then, I did not believe it. We walked over a place where the city wall simply did not exist. It had been neglected to disrepair around what looked to be perhaps an ancient mudslide.

The boy gave me his hand to help me up onto it, but after that he did not offer any more assistance or explanation.

When we were outside the city wall, heading west, I wanted to thank him. I wanted to share my relief at being at least temporarily safe from my life, but I said, "What was so complicated about that escape? Anyone could have walked over the wall."

He snorted softly. "Very few people know about that area of the wall, and fewer would dare walk over it."

"Ha!" I nearly laughed. "And why do they not dare?"

"It is guarded by…" He thought for a moment. "Some very dangerous men."

I hadn't seen any men. "Whatever you say."

"If my way out of the city does not please you, I can take you right on back," he said, clearly annoyed.

"No."

I couldn't go back. Not unless I wanted to live the way he had found me, and in that condition, I wouldn't live much longer.

He stopped walking, took a deep breath and let it out, and surprised me by saying, "Sorry."

I had walked a few steps past him, but I turned when I heard the sincerity in his voice.

He caught my eye, looked away, then made himself look back. "Sorry, Olivia. I didn't mean to make your safety conditional upon…upon anything." He adjusted his satchel. "You are safe with me. You don't have to agree with me, be kind to me, or even like me."

I didn't believe that for one moment. At the first sign of his temper I would be gone, I would run from him, but until then, I really did need his help.

"What is your name, please?" It was something I had been wondering for hours and had been too afraid to ask.

He was squinting into the distance, but he looked back at me. "Shad. Let's stop for a short break."

We stepped off the road together.

"And how far away is your mother, please?"

"My parents live outside of Orihah. You've heard of Melek?"

"You've a father?"

"Of course I have a father," he said, affronted. "Don't you?"

I opened my mouth to speak. Then I closed it. What to say to that? So I glared at him and raised an eyebrow.

"Okay. Dumb question," he said under his breath.

I sighed. "It wasn't dumb. It's only, when you said you were taking me to your mother's, I assumed she was alone."

"All right." He cracked his knuckles, and heaven help me, but he noticed when I flinched at the sound.

Shad stared at me for a moment. Curious. Confused. Then he raised his hand and, to my humiliation, I cowered when all he did was wipe the sweat from his brow with the back of his forearm.

"Oliv—" He shook his head and reached for his water skin, the only water we had between us, and held it out to me at arm's length. "Drink," was all he said.

With shaking hands, I took the water skin.

"I'm sorry," I said when I passed it back.

He didn't reply. I couldn't tell if he was angry. His frown was very severe. He hesitated before he took the water skin, and in that moment, I had a vision of him hitting it from my hand in a rage. But in the end, he took it almost gingerly and replaced it at his belt.

I backed away—slowly, so maybe he wouldn't notice.

"Is it time to go?" I asked into an awkward silence when all he did was stand there and do nothing.

He gave a curt nod and moved back into the road.

We spent much of the rest of the day in silence, which was fine by me. I was afraid and alone and had great pity for myself.

I had heard of Melek, but I had no idea where it was or how long it would take us to travel there. When Shad had offered his mother's home as refuge, I had assumed it was a small abode within the city or in one of the outlying villages. But we had passed the villages and this was starting to look like real travel, like a lengthy journey.

With a boy I did not know.

When we finally stopped for the evening, he was careful not to touch me. He didn't even come near me. If there was something to hand to me, like the water skin, he set it down and moved away. He was so deliberate about it, I almost smiled.

Almost.

"Sit," he said when he had pushed a log up to our cook fire for me. "Have you been eating?"

He had been giving me things to eat all day. I hadn't been throwing them on the ground.

He must have seen my confusion because he said, "I mean before today."

I looked into the tiny flame. "I left home a week ago." He was silent, so I said, "I took what I could."

"How old are you?"

"Seventeen."

He frowned.

"How old are you?" I dared to ask.

"Older than that."

Something about his answer made me smile.

"You're not married, I take it," he guessed.

"No."

"Not betrothed?"

"No. Not exactly." I had disappeared before that could happen. Had Shad noticed my hesitation?

"I see."

He had noticed it, and I was afraid he did see. What he must think of me, cowering away from nothing, apologizing for things that were not my fault. I was pathetic and I knew it, and now he knew it. But I thought of the way he had found me, and of course he had known from the first how worthless and pathetic I was.

I had allowed my fear to overcome my honor, and I was sure that even if Shad could not read my dishonor on my face now, he would be able to if he looked at me for very much longer the way he was.

"Why did you leave home?"

Couldn't he guess? There was really only one reason a girl might run away. A hundred words for it, but one reason.

"Olivia."

"An unwanted betrothal."

He scoffed. "Is that why you flinch from my hand?"

"No!" I protested.

"Your father thought he would force your obedience."

I was reluctant to admit it, but I nodded.

"He has hit you before."

I realized what he thought had happened. "Oh, no. Father didn't hit me. He wouldn't." But then, he hadn't stopped it from happening either.

Shad scoffed again.

"You don't have to believe me," I said. "My acceptance of your help is not conditional upon that."

A quick smile split his face.

"Okay. I guess I'm prying. I just need to know if there is someone who will be coming after us."

"Apparently not," I said, wishing my father would come. I looked up at Shad. "I mean, no one will suspect that I am not still inside the city. It is impossible to leave."

He raised a brow. Obviously, it was possible to leave.

"Maybe you better just tell me why you were hiding in the worst part of the city and who you were hiding from."

It hadn't taken me very many days without shelter, food, or money to realize I needed help. Shad was offering it. I was afraid, but I had to trust him.

"When I refused the betrothal, the man my father wants me to marry got angry." I took a breath. "He hit me with his fists. A lot. And my father did not stop him."

"I see."

And now I was sure he did see.

CHAPTER 2

It turned out that the journey to Orihah was to take us four days. Though we passed a few small settlements, there was no way I would have been able to blend into any them without notice. And as we continued through the forest, I knew no amount of watching Shad was going to teach me how to survive in the wilderness. He could build fires so fast I couldn't tell how he was doing it. It was almost as if he conjured them like the priests of Noah I had read about in the city's official scrolls. It wasn't like he just used a smoldering stick from the main hearth like we did at home. He might have conjured the food and water, too, because they also seemed to appear out of nowhere.

"Why do you put the fires completely out each time?" I asked him after I watched him meticulously conceal the evidence that a fire had ever burned on the ground between us.

He glanced back over his shoulder as he brushed over the ground with a dead branch and tossed some stones randomly about.

"We should probably stop building the fires. I can't shake the feeling we're being followed." He looked at me apologetically, as if he had somehow failed me.

"I've been feeling it too. Not eyes, but something."

He let his gaze run over me, reassessing me, perhaps.

I bristled. "I can feel when something is wrong. Such things are not reserved for the devout."

I watched as he picked up his travel gear and his weapons, wishing I didn't have to pick up mine, too, though he was carrying ever so much more than I was. He might be a little brusque at times, but his kindness kept showing through.

He waited while I picked up the bag he had given me to carry and pulled it over my shoulder. "We should keep moving," he said and turned to go. A bird flew low in front of us, the flutter of its wings startling in the quiet forest. Shad stopped mid-step and held out a hand, silently bidding me to be still as well.

"What are you doing?" I asked quietly.

He was scanning the forest around us, but he glanced over his shoulder at me.

"I'm looking for anything that might have spooked that bird."

I remained quiet, thinking of the concealed fires and of the feelings of warning we had both been experiencing, the feelings that had made our steps quick. But it was only a few moments before he gestured to me and started to walk again.

For anything that might have spooked that bird.

A shiver went up my spine, despite the hot sun on my skin and the longboots that made my legs sweat. I thought of complaining about the boots but knew Shad had purchased them with this journey in mind. He certainly hadn't purchased them for fashion, though I guessed they were tolerable to look at.

He interrupted my thoughts. "Are you a believer in Christ then?"

"Oh!" I was thinking about the prettiness of my boots and he was thinking about Christ. "Because I can feel the warnings of the Spirit, you mean?"

He grunted in response as he pushed back a branch and held it for me.

"Yes," I said. Admitting it to him somehow seemed okay. "But I do not advertise it about."

"Are you ashamed?"

"My belief is private." I paused. There was no reason to be dishonest. Not out here, not outside of the city and away from Father and his corrupt friends and colleagues. "But yes, a little, I guess. It is not a popular thing to believe—in a Messiah that may or may not come."

He didn't say anything. Probably judging me. Well, let him—so long as he fed me. That was the thing I was ashamed of now—my hunger, not my faith. I took all the food he offered me and wanted for more. I was greedy for it, having had the unfortunate experience of being without for the first time in my life, and I still would do almost anything for it.

After a long time, he veered off the main road and led me through a thick forest. It was nearly twilight anyway, and it was even darker beneath the trees and among the foliage. My uneasy feelings intensified, and I wondered if he did not indeed intend to hurt me.

"Shad?" My voice came out on a shaky breath.

"There is a spring here. The water is sweet. You'll like it."

But when we knelt at the spring, my heart began to pound. I felt like I should run away.

"We should go," I said.

"I agree."

We stood, but before we could move, a man appeared

17

from among the trees. Shad breathed a sigh, and I could sense that he relaxed.

"Hello," he called across the short distance.

The man approached and returned the greeting. His eyes flicked to me, but he spoke to Shad. "I'm surprised to see you here. I heard you had work in Zarahemla. How is your family?"

"I am on my way to see them now," Shad told him. Then he turned to me. "Olivia, this is Lib, a friend of my family's. Lib, this is Olivia, a friend of the Chief Judge."

My eyes shot to Shad. Did he know who I was?

"A dangerous allegiance just now," Lib said. "But one that I share."

"Are you camping nearby?" Shad asked him.

Lib's chin lifted. "Aye," he said.

"We've come for water, and now that we have it, we have to be moving." Shad put his hands on his hips and looked around us. "I don't think it's safe to stay here. You should consider moving if you're camped nearby."

"Do you have reason to think it is unsafe here?"

"It is always unsafe near water sources," I interjected. Even I knew that. "Anyone could stop here."

Lib turned his gaze on me. It was sharp and assessing, but not unkind. "We are camped far enough away, I think."

"Do you travel with Ethanim?" Shad asked him, angling himself toward the west. He was ready to go, already moving away.

"No. With Miriam."

Shad stopped dead in his tracks. "Alone?"

I didn't know either of them, and I didn't know who Miriam was, but I knew she meant something to them both.

Lib gave a small nod. "Aye."

Shad glanced in the direction we were headed, toward his home. "We have to go. We have to move farther along tonight before full dark." He turned to leave, gathering me in a glance. "Take care of her," he called back over his shoulder.

"Who's Miriam?" I didn't wait to ask. Why should I?

He surprised me with his candor. "A girl I used to court."

"Oh." We were moving very swiftly through the trees now, the soft sound of brush and leaves accompanying us. "Is she pretty?"

"Yes."

Of course she was. She wasn't the one who had been living in a den of filth.

Shad kept walking long into the night and not slowly. He stopped once to make camp, but looked at me for a long moment and then threw the tinder he had gathered back into the brush, hefted his pack back onto his shoulders, and continued onward. I sighed, but didn't complain as I followed him. When at last he rolled out the thin bedroll for me, I collapsed into it and fell asleep before he could conjure food. I awoke to the sound of hushed whispers.

"Two men at the spring. They're after the girl."

"I know. I've been dodging them all day. I think it is her betrothed or his emissaries."

"She's betrothed?" I thought it was Lib's voice that came out in a harsh whisper. "You cannot help her leave if she is promised to another man. You're breaking the law."

"Her home isn't safe," Shad whispered. "But I do not think she is betrothed. It's…I think it's complicated."

"Either she is or she isn't."

"As far as you're concerned, she isn't."

A long pause. "I hope you know what you're doing."

"My father taught me what is right. She's not married. She doesn't even like him."

Another long pause. "Did he give her the bruises?"

How had he seen those?

"So she says."

"Well, wake her up. We'll circle to the south and you can both camp with us."

"Wouldn't want to intrude," Shad said snidely, even as I felt his hand shaking my shoulder. I feigned wakening and followed the men into the night again.

Though my new longboots were soft and comfortable, my feet were swollen and aching. I did not want to go out into the night, to travel when I could have been sleeping. But one thought of the men my betrothed might have sent after me made me keep moving my feet until at last we arrived at Lib's camp.

Startling me, Lib let out an animalistic cry.

I nearly jumped out of my skin. Lib didn't seem to notice, but Shad said in a low voice, "For Miriam's safety and ours." We walked for another minute, and Lib let out a lower call just before we entered a small clearing where I could see the dim embers of a fire and a form kneeling next to it.

"Shad!" The form rose and came toward us. She went into Shad's arms, greeting him as though they were good friends. "Who is your pretty companion?" she asked, looking to me.

Quite often other women and girls spoke with a note of jealousy when I was around their men, but I didn't hear it in this Miriam's voice, though I could clearly see she had some claim to Shad's acquaintance. But there was something. Awkwardness? Confidence? Perhaps it was nothing more than our meeting under these strange circumstances.

I stepped forward. "I'm Olivia," I said for myself.

She stepped toward me. I could see that her arm was in some kind of splint. "I take it you have been traveling all night," she said. "Sit here and rest. I will prepare some food."

Lib stepped to the two bedrolls, bent, and returned with Miriam's water skin. For all he had been kind to us, he barely even acknowledged Miriam before he left again through the trees.

"I should go with him," Shad said uncertainly. He turned to me. "We're out of water, too."

"Of course you should," Miriam coaxed. "Go on."

They exchanged a look I did not understand. Then Shad nodded to me and left me in Miriam's care.

"I'm Miriam," she said.

"Yes. They told me."

"You look tired."

"We've been traveling since early morning. We meant to camp, but no sooner had we gathered tinder for a fire than Shad caught sight of pursuers. He thinks we're being followed."

"Are you in some kind of trouble?"

I didn't know how to answer her, or rather, how much to tell her. Before I could decide, she gestured to her bedroll.

"You need sleep more than you need food, I think. Be at rest." And then, as if she knew I was worried about it, she said, "Neither Shad nor Lib will let any harm come to you."

"Do you know Shad well then?" I asked carefully as I lay down on the bedroll.

"Yes." She took a breath and paused. "Shad has been courting me for several years now."

Shad had said as much, but he had made it seem like it was far in the past.

21

She touched my arm. "He withdrew his courtship."

"Ah," I said and added, "When he said he meant to take me to his mother's, I thought it meant he was unattached."

"As far as I know, he is. Except…"

"Except what?"

"Well, the reason he gave for withdrawing his courtship was that he meant to live in Zarahemla and take a job which required him to be free of attachment."

I was too tired for this conversation. I didn't care if Shad was or was not courting this girl. What did it matter to me?

"How fortunate for me that I am not seeking an attachment," I said as I snuggled down into the blanket. "I am withdrawing from an unwanted courtship myself."

At that statement, she went quiet. Good. I was exhausted.

"Have you known Shad long?"

Couldn't she see I was trying to sleep?

"No." I sighed and decided to just tell her my story so she'd leave me alone. "I ran away from my father's home, but I had nowhere to go. Shad found me two nights ago and offered his help. He gave me food to eat and clothed me and offered me shelter at his mother's home."

It was embarrassing to say it all out like that, but after I did, she remained quiet and I quickly fell into a deep sleep.

The others were ready to leave when I woke. I knew I was the weakest one there, unprepared for travel, unfit to do it. The farthest I ever walked was from my home to the Great Plaza to the shops in the market.

I wished we could stay in the little clearing longer, but the fire had disappeared — completely — and Shad and Miriam appeared anxious to get on the road. The other man, Lib, was nowhere to be seen, but neither one of them mentioned it, and in fact said very little to each other that was not necessary. I decided not to mention Lib's absence either. Either they would tell me where he had gone or they wouldn't.

But after we had been traveling a while, I became so bored with their silence — it was not at all like traveling alone with the handsome Shad — that I asked about him.

"He's gone," Shad said. "He figured since we were heading to the same place, we might as well take Miriam with us."

Something about that seemed strange. "Where did he go?" I asked.

"He lives by the sea," Miriam said. "Up north."

"A dangerous road, I've heard."

Miriam tucked her hair behind her ear. "A little."

Shad snorted.

I turned to him. "It's not?"

Shad hooked a thumb into the strap of his satchel. "It can be dangerous," he allowed, the hint of a smile on his lips.

"Have you traveled north then?"

"Me? No. All of my brothers have."

"How many brothers do you have?"

"I have three, and they are all older, stronger, and wiser," he laughed.

"But surely there is not one so handsome as you."

"Then you've met them already." He laughed. "Ugly dogs, all of them. Isn't that right, Miriam?"

"Hmm? Oh, um, yes that's right."

"You don't sound very sure," I said, but I could tell she was distracted and not interested in the conversation.

"It's true," she said with a roll of her eyes. "Shad is the

most handsome among them by far, and the friendliest. The others are not very personable. Except Jashon, maybe."

I turned back to Shad. "Ugly and unfriendly. How very unfortunate."

He grinned. "Only for their wives."

I had to laugh at that, and it felt good and strange to laugh again. Even Miriam, distracted as she was by Lib's sudden absence, laughed at Shad.

When we stopped for the night, Miriam quickly whipped up some food over a fire that Shad quickly put out, even though I thought we could use its warmth during the coolness of the night. I was exhausted from both the travel and the worry, so I curled up in the blanket of my bedroll and listened to the sounds of Shad helping Miriam with hers.

"Here," he said, his voice low, and then, "She's asleep...long day...not used to travel."

He was making excuses for my weakness. If either Shad or Miriam were someone I wanted to impress, that might hurt my feelings.

"She's like a princess," Miriam whispered.

"Yeah."

"I hope you don't get your heart set on her."

"That would be hard to do since it's already set."

"I thought it was set on Zarahemla and your secret job."

I didn't miss the emphasis Miriam put on the word *secret*, and I knew she didn't hold his job in Zarahemla in very high regard.

"It is. You didn't think I meant you, did you?"

Was he flirting with her? Blech.

"Of course not. I only meant you would be her servant for life if you marry her."

"Miriam, she's in trouble. I'm taking her home to my mother's care. That's all. Then I'm going back to my work."

"Well, I'm just saying you were flirting mighty hard…"

I heard him shift, but he didn't reply otherwise.

"Never tell me that was to make me jealous," she said.

"Would it?"

"Of course. I haven't forgotten all we were to each other. Have you?"

Another long silence. One of them was getting into their bedroll.

"I shouldn't have kissed you," Shad said at last.

To which her only reply was, "I'm sorry. For it all."

I thought of their hushed conversation for a long time the next day as we traveled. Maybe his relationship with Miriam wasn't as in the past as he had made it seem.

After we left Miriam at her family's stinky bird farm, the likes of which I had never before experienced, Shad finally led me to his mother's home.

"We're not going through the town?" I asked, disappointed when I saw it through the trees as we passed it by.

"There's no need."

I guessed he was right. "But I haven't seen people in days," I complained.

"The less people who see you here, the better. And don't pout, princess. If you've somewhere better to be, you're free to leave."

He didn't mean to be harsh. I could tell. But I knew there must have been some truth to his words. Miriam had been the one to call me a princess when she thought I was sleeping the night before, but Shad hadn't disagreed. And if he truly did know who I was, if he had somehow figured it out, their

25

assessment wasn't completely off base. Shad wasn't rich enough to be in my father's circle of friends, but my father was very well-known among all the classes of people.

Shad kept his distance from me and though he did not make it obvious, he was still very careful not to scare me. Even so, when he threw up an arm to point to his family's farm in the distance, I jumped back.

"S—sorry," I stammered. "I didn't mean to—"

"Don't say you're sorry. You've done nothing wrong."

"But I know you're not going to hurt me. At least, I'm relatively sure you're not."

"Relatively?"

"Well, you haven't so far."

"Your confidence in my decency honors me," he said sarcastically.

"I'm sorry."

"I told you not to say you're sorry."

"Okay," I said quietly, studying my longboots as I walked.

"Well, you could stand up for yourself."

I sighed. "Which is it? May I say what I wish to say, or shall I say what you wish me to say?"

He sighed too. "Say what comes naturally."

"But if I do that now, is that not submission to your wishes?"

His laughter was nice. He grabbed my neck in the crook of his elbow and ruffled my hair. Our eyes met, and we both stilled. We were so close together. I could smell the venison on his breath. I could feel the strength in his heavy arm. I could see where his nose had been broken, where his lip had been split.

But then he let me go and stepped abruptly away.

"Sorry," he mumbled.

His touch—his embrace—had been playful. It was something he might have done with one of his friends, perhaps even with that Miriam. It was not intended to be nor taken as rough or harmful. But somehow, I didn't think his apology was for the touch alone. I could still feel his chest breathing next to mine.

"Come on. We're almost there," he said.

He took off walking again, and I had to put a skip in my step to catch up.

I looked up at the sky, at the clouds floating across it. There would be rain tonight, and I thought of being stuck in a home with strangers while it rained outside. But I would be dry, and my stomach would be full. Would they be kind like their son? Of course they would. How could that gentle, decent person come from cruel parents?

After a long silence, Shad said, "Shortcut," and he led me through the open fields that surrounded several buildings near the center of them.

"Why is your home not protected in the trees?" I asked.

"I have often asked myself the same question. I think my family likes to tempt fate."

"And this is the safe haven you have brought me to?"

"You will be safe from your would-be betrothed."

"Will-never-be-betrothed," I clarified. "As if I would tie myself to a man like that. I'd rather starve."

"You were on your way," he said quietly.

"Don't remind me." But I would never need a reminder. Every step I took away from Zarahemla, from my family, my self-important father, and the despicable Kishkumen was a step in the right direction.

27

CHAPTER 3

Shad led me to one of the largest buildings, a home of stonework with a thatched roof. Two women sat in the yard. One was folding linens and the other bouncing a baby on her hip while she sorted clothing with the other hand. When they noticed us entering the yard, they stopped what they were doing, glanced at each other, and grinned at Shad. The older woman, obviously his mother, enfolded him in her arms, into which he went easily. The younger woman offered me a smile while she awaited her turn. Shad bent to them both, but allowed a much longer embrace to his mother.

"Mother, Keturah, this is Olivia, a friend I have met in the city. Olivia, I present you my mother, Naomi, and my brother's wife, Keturah." He indicated each of them in turn, though the distinction was not necessary. "And Gabriel, my nephew," he added.

I noted his proper introduction and greeted his mother and sister with a proper hand on their shoulders.

When Naomi returned the greeting, my sarong shifted from my shoulder, and I saw her notice the greenish bruise there. Her eyes shot not to mine, but to her son's.

Shad folded his arms and met her eyes with silence.

I glanced at Keturah, but she was looking at the baby.

"Do you plan to stay long?" Naomi asked her son, letting her questions about the bruise drop, which I was grateful for.

Shad had told me he'd arranged to be away from his work—whatever that was—for a sennight, but he hesitated before he said, "I don't know."

"Well," she smiled at us both. "We'll take you while we have you."

I sat quietly while Shad talked to his mother and sister. He told them things about the city and they told him all about people from the village. It sounded like he had not been in the city long but planned to stay there.

I sensed they didn't want him to live in the city, but they seemed to be resigned to it.

Keturah offered to take me to the stream to wash the dirt from the journey away.

"There is a small canal that runs through the fields," she said. "But I prefer the seclusion and privacy of the stream in the trees."

"Have you lived here long?"

"A few years."

"Do you spend all your time with Naomi?"

"A good deal of it. I like Naomi."

"Where is your husband? Is he always gone from home?"

"Today he is working at the timber mill with his cousins. But there was a time when the city called to him, too."

"Do you mean like it calls to Shad?"

"Yes."

"I take it he is not content here on the farm."

She laughed. "No, he is not. He seeks intrigue and danger. We did not expect him home for quite some time."

I could see the stream now. It was shallow but flowing quickly, and when I knelt next to it and put my hand in the water, it was very cold.

"We get our water from the cistern in the city, and it is not nearly this cold."

"It will feel refreshing. How did you get the bruises?"

"I guess it was too much to hope you wouldn't notice them."

"I'm well-acquainted with bruises. Those look about a week old."

I splashed the water over my face and hair, wondering what she meant by *well-acquainted*.

I felt a warm hand on my back. "I am a healer," Keturah said gently. "Let me look."

I jerked away, but her hand remained on my back until I said, "O—okay."

Slowly, methodically, she pulled my sarong aside and found the various bruises and wounds.

"This cut is deep," she said. "Let me wash it."

I shifted so she could have a better angle, and while she ministered to my wounds, I told her, "Shad gave me some salve before we left Zarahemla, but I've used it all. He didn't know about the cuts."

"Is this why he brought you here?"

"Yes."

"He did the right thing. These wounds need to be treated—at least these deeper cuts do."

"I think he intends to leave me here, to make me his mother's problem."

31

Keturah's feminine laugh rang out again, mingled with the sounds of the stream. "That may be his intention, but I do not think he will be able to just walk away from a pretty girl like you."

I knew I was pretty. That was why Kishkumen wanted me for his wife. Only the best for him. Only the prettiest. Only the richest. In the past months, I had come to resent my beauty, as well as my father's wealth and my every advantage that made me appealing to men, but the way Keturah said it made it seem silly to resent being pretty.

"Olivia, who inflicted these wounds?"

"You do not suspect your Shad of inflicting them?"

"Of course not."

"You sound very sure."

"I know the woman who raised him. I know his father and his brothers. Shad could not inflict these wounds even if he was very angry with you."

"What if he was drunken with wine?"

"He would not be."

I nearly rolled my eyes. She could not know that. Perhaps he did not overindulge in drink at home, but what about when he was with his friends? Drinking with friends was probably just the sort of danger he was seeking in the city.

"He is frightfully strong. I can see his muscles even through his tunic. I...I sometimes cower when he lifts his hand to point out landmarks or offer me water."

Keturah lifted my damp hair behind my shoulders and began to comb through it for me. "He is made strong to protect women, not hurt them."

"Forgive me if I have a hard time believing that right now."

She made no reply to that. "Your hair is very pretty," she said after a moment.

"Thank you," I managed to say.

She combed it for a few minutes more. The long, smooth strokes calmed my nerves.

"Do you want to know a secret?" she asked. "When I met Gideon, the muscles were the first thing I noticed, too."

A sudden giggle escaped, and Keturah laughed with me.

"Besides," Keturah said, a smile still on her lips. "I don't think you're the kind of girl who would stay around someone who hurt her."

"The obedient kind?"

Her smile faded, but she just dabbed again at the cut on my shoulder. "You know," she said, "I was supposed to marry someone else."

"Not Shad's brother?"

She paused a moment to retrieve something from her satchel. "A boy from my village. My best friend. A very good boy, and handsome."

"What happened?"

"I joined the army. It kept us apart long enough that we both came to see we didn't belong together."

This was the girl who had been in the army? I had heard of her back in Zarahemla. Everyone had.

"You didn't love him?"

Melancholy crept into her voice. "Oh, I loved him."

I frowned and glanced back over my shoulder. "I don't understand. Didn't your father arrange your marriage?"

She dabbed something that stung onto the cut. "Sorry," she murmured when she saw me wince. "My oldest brother," she continued. "He saw that my heart was elsewhere."

33

"I wish my father could see that."

Keturah moved to my collar bone. "You cannot convince him to forestall the wedding?"

"No. Well, I think it is more complicated than that. The man who did this…" I nodded to the cut she was cleaning. "I think he holds something over my father. Something valuable. Something that would ruin him. My father cannot simply forbid the wedding."

She was quiet for a time as she worked.

I had never told anyone I suspected Father was being coerced. What did they call it? Blackmail? It was the same kind of corruption he used in his work, and I suspected he had been on both sides of it many times before. I wondered why I had revealed it to Keturah. But she was there, and she was kind, and I needed kindness.

"Has there been an official betrothal?" she asked as she began to work my long hair into a plait.

"Of a sort," I said carefully.

Slowly she wrapped the plait around and around until it coiled at my neck.

I sighed. These people were harboring me. I should tell them what they were getting themselves into. "I do not think it was legal. I wasn't even there."

"Well, then you have nothing to worry about."

"Except survival!" I laughed. "And anyway, it will be made to look legal." I worried a thumbnail. "My father can do that."

"I see," she said. She secured my hair with two slender sticks from her bag. "I think I have some beads," she said as she rummaged in her satchel again. "Yes." She held out a hair clip on her hand for me to inspect. It was a barrette of sorts, fashioned from polished wood and what looked like obsidian. A cluster of pretty stone beads hung from the clip. "This red will set well against your dark hair," she said.

Probably the same way it set against her own.

"It fastens like this." She showed me, and then she flipped out the pin that held the hair tight and grinned. "It can also be used as a weapon." She adjusted it in her fisted hand, and I watched her move it through the air in a demonstration. The pin was thick and sharp like a small blade. I didn't think I would need it as a weapon, but I let her fasten it into my hair.

When I moved my head, I could hear the beads clink lightly against each other. "I don't need the beads," I told her, leaning over to try for a glimpse of them in the water.

"You want to look pretty don't you?"

"Well, I hadn't…I suppose…Looking pretty has not been first on my mind of late."

She smiled as she got to her feet and assisted me to mine. When I was facing her, we were eye level with each other. "I take it you have been without your pretty things for a while."

I bit my lip and nodded.

She reached out and caressed the beads. "Take comfort in these."

Comfort in material possessions? I had spent a lot of time trying not to covet beautiful things, but in the lavish world with which my father surrounded me it was often difficult to have perspective.

"A gift," she clarified. "They will help you feel safe. Every girl should carry some kind of protection with her."

"But I've nothing to give you in—"

She put a hand up. "No need, Olivia. Your gift to me can be what you do with them."

"I'm not sure I understand," I admitted.

She looked at me for a long moment. Then her eyes fell to my shoulder, and I felt her adjust my sarong to conceal the bruise. "I hope that you never do. Now, let's get back. The men should be home soon."

Two men were already standing in the courtyard when we returned, so our arrival was more like a grand entrance at one of my father's parties. Keturah gave me an encouraging smile before she retrieved Gabriel from Naomi's hands and went to her own home across the fields where she met a third man who waited there for her. Keturah's husband was a handsome man with muscles larger than Shad's, and I watched him touch his son affectionately on the head. Shad was by far the more handsome of the two. I didn't want to notice such things, but the comparison made me smile.

Naomi returned my smile with a knowing one of her own. I blushed and quickly looked away. She was a mother. She knew her sons were handsome and strong. But Shad could as easily have been an ugly old man with a battle-scarred face, and I still would have accepted the food he had offered.

"Sit," Naomi beckoned. "It is time you ate a real meal."

I looked at myself. I hadn't lost that much weight, had I? It had only been a little over a week since I had been eating the best food the Zarahemlan market had to offer. Even with the lockdown after Pahoran's death, many fine foods had come in with supplies, though, admittedly, many of those foods never made it beyond my father's table. The things that made it to the common classes were basic grains and dried meats. I wasn't so naïve as to not be aware of that.

"Can I help?" I asked as I watched Naomi moving busily about. I didn't know how to help fix a meal, but I did have two

36

idle hands. I had often wanted to assist with meal preparation, but Father forbade it. He insisted it be left to the servants he so generously employed for me. "You remind me of our cook," I said impulsively, and blushed furiously when Naomi straightened and gave me a somewhat startled look.

But her calm and pleasant demeanor returned when she handed me a bowl-shaped vessel and a large stirring spoon. "I've cooked many a meal," she said simply.

I looked at the bowl and the mushy grain inside it and the long handle of the spoon.

"You can do it with your hands if you prefer," Naomi said as she laid some kind of meat on a grate over the coals of her cook fire. "This won't take long to cook. I want to serve it warm," she went on.

Do what with my hands? And what exactly was I supposed to do with this dish of grain? Eat it?

I glanced up at her and then brought a spoonful of it to my nose and sniffed it. The large dish held much more than I could eat myself. I glanced around to see if there were similar dishes. There weren't. Were we all to share this one? How much should I take?

Shad caught my eye for a moment as he talked to the man who must have been his father, but he did not indicate what I should do with the bowl.

"It just needs to be stirred." Naomi had seated herself next to me, and my eyes shot to hers.

"Like this?" I asked her as I looked down at the grain in the dish and began to stir it.

"Just like that." But I must have been doing it wrong because after a moment she asked, "Have you never mixed up corn cakes before?"

Reluctant to admit I hadn't, I shook my head. How could I explain it all to her? Father did not think it appropriate for me to mingle with our servants in such a way. I had no idea how to mix this grain, and I had no idea what a corn cake should look like. Martha, the woman who cooked food in my father's house, had never made anything called corn cakes.

The grainy flour began to stick together and soon formed into a ball. I couldn't stir it with the spoon anymore, and that was when Naomi quietly took the dish and set it between us. She scooped some of the meal into her hands and showed me how to flatten it. Tentatively, I reached into the dish and withdrew some of the meal. It felt grainy, but it was moist and stuck together easily as I formed the flat cake like she had.

Though I knew she had many unasked questions, there was a warmness in Naomi's smile, and soon we had the dish emptied. She showed me how to set the cakes onto an odd-shaped flatstone which she then placed into a hollow that was built into the fire round. It was an oven much like the ovens I had seen in Martha's kitchen and very cleverly made.

"There is a basin inside where you can wash up," she said and nudged me toward her house.

It didn't seem polite to go into her home without her. When I resisted, Naomi called for Shad.

He broke away from his father and gestured me ahead of him into the house, seeming to understand what she wanted, though she didn't tell him. The house was large, but I could only see one other room besides the one we stood in. Shad led me to a corner where there was a basin and a vessel of water beside it. I stared at it for a moment, waiting for him to leave, but when I did not reach for the vessel of water, he picked it up and poured water into the basin for me.

"Some don't like the feel of the dough on their hands," he said. He seemed to be avoiding my eyes, but he still did not leave me to wash up on my own.

"Your mother doesn't want to wash?"

He smirked. "She'll have her hands into something else by now. She's well used to it."

The dough *had* dried on my hands. It *was* cracking and uncomfortable.

"I don't need to wash," I tried to tell him and backed away from the basin.

There was that smirk again, hidden as he turned to retrieve a drying cloth from a high shelf.

"I'm not some princess who can't get her hands dirty."

"Just wash up. It will be time to eat soon," he said as he placed the cloth near the basin. Then he finally turned to go.

As soon as his back was turned, I trailed my fingers through the water. It was cool, so I dipped my hands in and gently removed the dough from them.

"I know you're not familiar with the work here."

I jumped nearly to the ceiling. "I thought you left!"

Was that the smirk again or a mollifying smile?

"Here, it's not work. It's life. Everyone helps. I know the adjustment will be hard, and I'm sorry for it, but there is enough work on a farm without an idle pair of hands and an extra mouth to feed." He looked down and up again, and his eyes tempered the harshness from his words. "I should have given you a little more warning."

"I didn't refuse to help!" I snapped as I dried my hands.

"You looked horrified when Mother handed you the bowl of grain."

"You were watching me?"

39

His mouth opened, but he had no reply.

I smiled coyly at him. "I've never stirred anything before," I said and gave a teensy little shrug.

He found his voice. "If that's true, I feel sorry for you."

"You've been feeling sorry for me since the first moment you saw me."

Again, he didn't say anything, but the whisper of a smile touched his lips as if he knew something I did not. He backed toward the door. "Come out when you're ready."

I was ready to leave the house immediately. I was ready to go back to Zarahemla. Clearly both he and his mother thought I would be a burden on them. I sighed. Returning to Zarahemla just now was not really an option for me—not a good option—so I turned back to the basin. This time I listened carefully for the mat to fall against the door frame. When it did, I turned and searched the room.

It was large but not grand. The furniture was plain. A table. Some chairs. Sleeping pallets lined the walls. Two small windows provided the only light, and it wasn't enough. The dimness of the room was probably the reason Shad's family cooked and spent their time outdoors. Another mat was pulled back from a doorway that led into a second room. I wondered if Shad had slept in this room as a boy or in the room beyond the door.

I sat on one of the chairs, put my head into my hands, and felt sorry for myself. I knew I should feel lucky, feel blessed for the hospitality of these people, but it felt like charity, and I was too proud to be comfortable with charity. Maybe I was no better than my pious father after all.

CHAPTER 4

I let myself wallow in self-pity for quite some time, but gradually I became aware of more voices in the yard and male laughter. They were probably laughing at me, the girl who did not know how to mix a corn cake. But they were justified in it if they were. I was pitiable.

When I slipped the mat aside and stepped through it, the sudden light hurt my eyes. I squinted to see the new arrivals. In addition to Naomi and Shad's father, whom I hadn't yet met, Keturah's husband was there with Keturah and Gabriel. Another man who looked completely unrelated to the family, probably a friend, leaned against a table. His arms were crossed over his chest, and when he noticed I had emerged from the house, his eyes came slowly to meet mine.

There was something dark in his eyes. He reminded me of Kishkumen, and I had the sudden feeling to run to Shad. I breathed a sigh of relief when he came instead to me.

He led me with the softest touch on my elbow toward his father. I smiled nervously at the man, and he nodded his head.

"My father, Liam," Shad said. "Ket's husband, Gid." He indicated the man I had seen with Keturah earlier. "And my brother, Lamech," he finished as he gestured to the man with the dark eyes.

How could that man be his brother? Shad had dark hair and eyes too, but he looked like goodness itself. This man, this Lamech, looked to be all the dark things of the world.

Not one of them greeted me with the traditional hand on my shoulder, and I knew Shad had advised them not to. I was grateful and embarrassed at the same time, but I made myself look them each in the eye. I would have to get over my embarrassment if I was to stay here for any amount of time. So what if they all knew what had happened to me? So what if they knew my father had so little regard for me? Those were facts, and ignoring them or hiding them would not make them go away.

"It is nice to meet you all," I said.

Naomi and Keturah began to serve the food, and Shad gestured to a bench where I could sit.

I shook my head. "I would like to help with the food."

"You're a guest."

I shook my head again. "I'm not."

The others eyed us curiously, but none offered a word. Neither did Shad. He looked uncertain, so I ducked around him and approached Naomi. She smiled and offered me two dishes filled with food. It was plain fare, but plentiful and hearty, and it smelled good.

"For Shad. And this for Lamech," she said.

I accepted the dishes and took the first to Lamech who nodded his thanks and didn't bother with me beyond that. He glanced at Shad and then set to eating his food.

"Thank you," Shad said as I passed the other dish to him.

I turned to retrieve a dish for myself, but Keturah stood

behind me with one at the ready.

"Pretty beads," Shad said when I was seated next to him on the bench.

"They're Keturah's."

I caught the glance Gideon sent to his wife, though she didn't seem to notice it—or she ignored it if she did—and I wondered if the unique barrette with the sharp, pointed clasp had been a gift from him.

"What part of Zarahemla do you live in?"

I looked up to see Lamech leaning forward with his elbows on his knees, his empty dish already set aside.

"The affluent part," I said, not knowing what else to say. I hadn't thought to come up with a lie. I looked to Shad to see what he thought of my giving this information away.

He read the question in my eyes. "It is safe to tell my family everything. It is important that they know."

I nodded. How much had he already told them? Should I offer information or wait to be asked? It was so different here— I didn't know how to act.

"You are safe here," Gideon assured me.

"My father's influence is far-reaching." He could find me here. Kishkumen could find me here.

"You didn't take her through Orihah, did you?" Gideon asked his brother.

"Shad knows better than that," Lamech said.

"Of course not," Shad replied. "No one has seen her with me, but two men tracked us from Zarahemla. We lost them when Lib came to warn us."

"Lib and Miriam saw us together," I pointed out.

"Oh? You met Miriam?" Keturah asked.

"They know the importance of keeping your presence a

secret," Shad said. "We discussed the danger."

"Wait. What was Miriam doing with Lib?" Lamech asked.

Everyone fell silent.

Lamech looked slowly from one family member to another, his eyes finally resting on me.

"You think I know?"

"Lamech," Keturah jumped in. "Shad decided not to pursue a betrothal with Miriam. Her heart is with someone else."

"With Lib?" Lamech looked back to Shad. "That's ridiculous. You and Miriam wanted to get married."

"Just because you're getting married doesn't mean the rest of us want to," Shad joked, but his laughter did not reach his eyes.

"Who are you to wed?" I asked.

"No one you'd know."

"Lamech!" his mother reprimanded.

"Her name—"

Lamech put a hand up to stop Gideon. "Her name is Sarai," he said, and the way he said her name made me almost wish I was her. Who was I kidding? I *did* wish I was her. Despite his brooding looks and unfriendly personality, Lamech had to be better than Kishkumen.

I nibbled on my thumbnail for a moment, a habit I couldn't break. "Sarai is lucky," I said to him, and his brothers teased him when he blushed.

"Does young Sarai know you blush at the sound of her name?" Gideon asked.

"Hush," said his wife as she served them both more food, but there was merriment in her eyes, too.

"He's been blushing at the sound of her name since he was fourteen," Shad informed me with a grin. "Since he first saw her at Gid's betrothal in Ket's village."

Lamech kept his eyes on his food and ate it like there would never be any more, but I thought I caught the hint of a smile between bites.

"I think it's sweet," I said. "I know Kish—" I took a breath. Should I say his name to these people? "I know Kishkumen would never do such a thing."

He had no soul. There was no way he could do something as innocent as blush, and there was probably nothing left on the earth that would make him do so.

The table fell silent again when I stumbled over his name. It was Naomi who spoke at last.

"Is Kishkumen your betrothed then, dear?"

"Of a sort." I looked to Shad, and he returned my gaze steadily. "As far as the law is concerned, yes. But I was not present, and I did not give my consent." I looked down at my own food. "I would never give my consent to him," I added quietly.

My father could betroth me to whomever he saw fit, but the law did require me to agree to the arrangement in the courts, even if it was unwillingly.

Speaking for the first time, Liam asked, "Is he likely to look for you?"

I turned my attention to him. "Until he is dead or I am."

He took in the seriousness in my voice. He looked like he might say something more, but he didn't.

Naomi put a hand over mine on the table. "I'm sorry that happened to you."

At her motherly touch, tears formed in my eyes, and to

my embarrassment, they began to stream down my face. I tried to wipe them away, but they couldn't be hidden. Everyone saw them.

Naomi pulled me into her shoulder and said, "Shad, go prepare a pallet for Olivia. I think she needs some good rest."

It wasn't time for sleep, not even close to dark. They wanted to get rid of me so they could reprimand Shad for bringing me there, or they wanted to discuss their options. Where could they send me that would keep them safe?

But I feared that if Kish found out they had harbored me at all there in the barley fields, Shad's family would never be safe.

Naomi walked me inside her home. I didn't see Shad until I looked into the second room. He was kneeling by a large pallet on the floor, but when he saw me, he stood quickly. He caught my eye and nodded as he passed, but other than that, he didn't acknowledge me.

"Through this way," Naomi said. She held out a hand toward the room.

I shook my head. The more I thought about it, the more I knew it was the room she shared with her husband.

"I can't take your room," I said.

She kept her hand out. "You're a guest."

I shook my head again. "I'm not." I would have to earn my keep here. Everyone else did.

She looked at me with pity. "You are. Now, right in here."

She spoke as to brook no argument, so I preceded her into the room. She took one look at Shad's work, harrumphed, and redid it. "It's like I never taught them anything," she said.

I looked at the low pallet. It was a lot better than what I

had been staying in with the sharp-clawed and snaggle-toothed rats, but it was not nearly as nice as my bed in my father's home at Zarahemla. But I had to forget about that. Leaving my father meant leaving his wealth and all that came with it. This bed was clean and would suit me fine.

Naomi turned back the blanket with a final satisfied hum. Then she retrieved some clothing from a shelf on the other side of the room.

"These are yours now," she said as she passed them to me. "And we will make you some more of your own."

After she left, I inspected the bundle. It contained a night dress, under things, and a length of cloth I could tie into a sarong on the morrow. The threads had been dyed indigo, and it was much softer than I had expected to find out here so far from the city's markets. As I fingered it, I suspected it was Naomi's finest.

Hospitality was one thing, but her finest clothing? She must have thought very little of me, thought that I would turn up my spoiled city nose at her everyday items. But I feared that two weeks ago, she might have been right.

I put on the night dress and lay down on the pallet, and I was asleep long before dark.

I was almost surprised to find Shad still there when I woke very early the next morning. He was asleep on the floor of the main room. I stopped for a moment before I passed through the door into the gray pre-dawn. I tried to keep my eyes away from his parents, who slept on the far side of the room—it did not seem right to see them in repose—but I watched Shad's chest rise and fall until that too did not feel right, and then I turned and slipped through the mat at the door.

It was dark. It had rained while I slept. I could still smell it in the air. The moon was falling below the hills to the west. I stood silently, my arms folded against the chill of the air, and watched it until it slid completely away.

"What are you doing?"

I jumped and muffled a startled scream with my hand. Squinting into the darkness, I tried to make out the man who stood in the shadows. "Lamech?"

He came closer, moving from the direction of the fields. His eyes were holes of blackness, and looking at him increased the chill I felt.

"What are you doing?" he repeated.

"I fell asleep early. I couldn't sleep anymore." When he didn't bother with a reply, I asked, "What time is it, please?"

"The start of the fourth watch."

"Thank you." I could hear the breeze in the plants of the field. I could hear a little chime that hung from the house. "What are you doing up before dawn?" I had already seen the rest of the household did not rise this early.

"I always take the fourth watch," he said, surprising me with an answer. "It would be Shad's, but I..." He hesitated a moment. "But I like to watch the sunrise."

The way he said it made me doubt the shadows in his eyes.

"I do too," I told him. "Though I admit, I generally do not rise before the sun."

He grunted in response. Apparently, he did not have a high opinion of sleeping late.

I rubbed my hands over my arms, realizing suddenly that I was in his mother's nightclothes.

"I didn't expect anyone to be awake," I said.

"Clearly." His tone was sarcastic, but surprising me again, he stepped forward and handed me his cloak.

Stunned by his kindness, I just held it in my hand.

"Put it on, or I'll take it back."

I quickly slipped it over my shoulders. It still held the warmth from his body! My eyes closed at the deliciousness of it.

"You are full of contradictions," I said to him. "I can't tell if you are a nice person or a mean one."

"Mean," he said immediately, but I thought I heard a smile in his voice.

"Can you make a fire?" I asked. I was dying for a little light.

"I usually don't this time of morning." But he took my elbow and led me to a stool where I could sit. Then Lamech knelt, and soon he had conjured a fire just as Shad was able to do.

"I am amazed at how you do that," I told him when he had a small blaze and its warm, flickering glow was chasing the darkness away.

"Everyone lights fires this way. You talk a lot."

"In my home, we light fires from another fire."

"Extravagance," he said and added, "You won't find that here."

"I'm not looking for extravagance." My words came out sharply. "Safety only," I said more softly.

He rolled back onto his heels. "How long have you been on the run from your Kishkumen?"

"Two months, and he is not mine, nor would I ever want him to be. You talk a lot."

That made him laugh softly. "What has Shad been feeding you?"

"Venison. Rabbit. Roots. All manner of wild things he conjures from the forest."

"And your stomach handles these things without trouble?"

"Yes."

"You were without food for two months?"

"Oh no. I took plenty with me when I left my father's household."

"You stole it."

"No!"

"You told Shad you had been gone a week."

"I didn't want him to pity me. I didn't even know him."

"You have developed a habit of saying what suits you."

"You would too," I shot back, "if you lived where I do."

"Honesty will do you better here."

"Thank you for the warning. I shall take it into counsel. But I think Shad does his share of deceiving others, as do you."

He was quiet for a moment at the insult. "It is Shad's work to deceive. It is my nature."

"What is that supposed to mean?"

"It means you talk too much. Enjoy your fire."

It wasn't a moment before he had disappeared into the darkness. I whirled, staring into the darkness after him, but it was no use. He was gone. I turned to the fire he had built for me. It was small, but it was bright and it chased the shadows away.

As the morning light slowly began to rise, I noticed the hills to the east. Shad's home was in a small valley that could be seen from many vantage points. I understood why Lamech said he did not light the fire in the darkness. I felt completely inept for asking it of him, but I wondered why he had complied. Though his manner was gruff, he had shown me much in kindness I had not expected. I had judged him on his looks alone, and it shamed me.

I did not like when men judged me on my looks alone. I had fended off many unwanted advances from my father's disgusting friends and even from my own friends. Men took one look at me and thought they could touch me, handle me, and own me, but I had grown skilled at playing their game.

It was always a game.

I thought of Shad bringing me the clothing from the market. I looked down at the longboots, simple but feminine. I felt the warmth of his brother's cloak around me, and I knew the game here would be different. But I could learn it. I could win it.

I looked up at the sound of a large yawn. Shad stood in the doorway of the house. His arms were stretched over his head, one bent at the elbow. His hair stuck up in several directions, and he smiled at me, sheepish and sleepy. Perhaps Lamech took the fourth watch because Shad did not like to rise early, though a glance to the east proved it was not particularly late in the day either.

I stood, but he shook his head as he approached the fire, gesturing me to sit back down. He hooked another stool with his foot and sat across from me. After a moment, he grunted, pushed the stool away, and simply went to his heels as Lamech had.

"You look tired," I said.

He rubbed his eyes with the heels of his hands.

"And you look pretty in my brother's cloak."

CHAPTER 5

So. It was to be a game then. Or perhaps a simple transaction. I eyed him across the fire. What would it cost me to stay here for a time, until I figured out what to do next?

"It is not for you to look at," I said.

"Anyone may behold your beauty," he said easily, but then he lowered his voice. "As I have many times before."

I stilled inside. What did he mean? Did he know who I was, then?

He chuckled low when I had no response to that. "I've seen you before, Olivia."

"Not possible," I said, panicking a little when he used my name like that. "Zarahemla is too big, and you have not been there long enough." I had seen where he lived. It was not terrible, but he certainly did not have the high connections he would need to be in the same crowded halls as I was made to be in.

He leaned forward and said, "I work for Helaman."

I nibbled on my thumbnail but stopped immediately when I noticed I was doing it and clasped my hands in my lap. "You are in the prophet's employ?"

His eyes narrowed a little. "Something like that."

If he worked on Helaman's grand estate, there was a slight possibility our paths had crossed before.

"Is that where you have seen me?" I inquired. "On the Estate of Alma?"

He rubbed his chin as if he were thinking on it deeply. Despite the terrible circumstances I found myself in, I giggled.

Shad's teasing eyes sparkled up at me.

"If you've a mind to be useful, young Olivia, I could use some help with the morning meal."

Embarrassed to be caught laughing with her son, I looked up to see Naomi already bustling around the yard with her arms full of linens.

I stood and smoothed down my—I cringed—my night clothes. "I do," I said as I pulled Lamech's cloak tighter around me.

Having given me a quick once-over, she had already noticed the nightclothes, but she just said, "After you've changed, bring out your travel dress. It's wash day." She jostled the items in her arms. "I will show you how to clean it properly."

I nodded to her and hurried inside.

I stopped short in the doorway when I saw Liam kneeling on a pallet in the far corner, apparently offering up his morning prayers. He didn't appear to notice me, didn't move, so I darted into the other room.

I scrubbed my face with water I found in a vessel near the basin and combed through my hair until it shone. As I tied the silky sarong behind my neck, I again wondered that Naomi would give me of her finest. I didn't know all the work I would be required to do here, but if we were to work that day, she must know the dress would get dirty.

Feeling nosy, I stepped to the shelf wherefrom she had

selected the garment. There were many clothes in various types of fabrics. I was surprised to find the one I wore was among the finest but was certainly not her only pretty sarong.

I felt better about wearing it, but when I entered the yard again, and everyone stilled to look at me, I wanted to turn right around and put my soiled clothing back on.

Lamech stopped chewing. Some of the color drained from Shad's face. Liam noticed his sons and looked up at me too.

Naomi paused briefly in what appeared to be admiration, but then came directly to me. Her smile eased some of my misgivings. She put a motherly arm around me and led me to the table.

"That color suits you," she said into my ear. To Lamech she said, "Close your mouth before your food falls onto the table."

Shad laughed, and Lamech slugged him in the arm.

Naomi tsked at them as she placed a bowl filled with some kind of cooked grain in front of me. Ignoring the boys' scuffle, I looked at it a moment, wondering if I was to make cakes from this too. But before I could put my hands into it, she slipped two wedges of fruit into the bowl and poured milk onto it.

"It's barley," Shad said quietly.

"It will keep you full all day," his mother added.

She really did remind me of our cook back home. Though I had to sneak down to see her, Martha had always given me the little mothering she could, and I had yearned for that much more than I had yearned to know how to cook a meal.

But as I looked at the meal Naomi had made out of thin air, I wished I had spent more time learning the art of it. Well, I thought, here was my chance.

Once she had food in front of me, Naomi gave a satisfied

noise in the back of her throat and bustled off to join her husband near an outbuilding as he strapped strange looking gear to his belt.

Shad and Lamech had resumed their conversation, so I pulled my dish toward me and began to eat. I took a bite and found the milk to be warm. Sighing at the lovely flavor, I put another bite into my mouth. I hummed and let my eyes drift closed. If Naomi could teach me to cook like this, perhaps I could find work in a kitchen. Perhaps there were large estates in other cities that needed cooks who could conjure such delights as this barley.

"Are you doing that on purpose?"

My eyes drifted open to see both boys staring at me again.

Shad slugged Lamech in the arm. I could see it was playful, but I flinched inside.

"Doing what on purpose? Eating?"

"Eating like *that*," Lamech said and shrugged away from another of Shad's fists.

I licked the sweetness from my lips. "It, um...tastes good." I ran my tongue over my teeth. Actually, it was a little crunchy. "Is yours not sweet to the taste?" I asked Shad, confused.

"How would he know? He inhaled it. He didn't stop to taste it," Lamech said of his brother.

I giggled. "Lamech?"

"What?"

"You talk too much."

Shad burst into laughter. "No one, and I mean no one, has ever said that to one of my brothers. It must be Sarai getting to you. You need to take a trip and go flirt with your own girl."

Your own girl. The words echoed in an awkward silence. Of course he didn't mean it how it sounded, like I was his girl and Sarai was Lamech's. He didn't have to explain it away. He needn't be as embarrassed as he looked.

I pulled my dish closer and gripped my utensil. "How does one inhale barley?" I asked them.

They both shifted, the awkward tension broken. Shad picked up his empty dish and tilted it toward his face to show me how it was done. I glanced at Lamech who had a skeptical glimmer in his dark eyes. He didn't think I would do it.

I set the utensil down—it didn't appear as though I would need it—and I brought the dish to my face. Tilting slowly at first, I let the grain slide into my mouth. It was fun, and it accomplished the task so much faster. The boys egged me on, and I tilted the bowl farther and farther until I had eaten it all. I set the dish down and grinned with my mouth still full.

Shad slapped his hand on the table and leaned back, laughing. Lamech was amused, too. I giggled and wiped the mess from my face with my hand.

"It's like I never taught you two anything," Naomi said as she approached us. "Olivia, don't let their terrible manners rub off on you."

"Oh, I'm sorry. Was it terrible manners?" I hadn't meant to offend, only to ease the awkwardness.

She chuckled. "I would hardly know." She turned to the boys. "Your father is ready to leave. You'll have to come back for the noon meal because I've not packed one."

After they each said a quick goodbye to me and kissed their mother, Naomi turned to me.

"We've work to do as well, and I'm glad for the extra pair of hands."

I looked at my small hands. "I am not sure they will do you much good, but I am ready to try."

She hefted half the linens she had collected that morning into my arms and led me around the back of the house. A small structure with a roof but no walls, just four posts, sat between the two homes in the clearing. I noted a table and several large basins near a fire that burned in a stone round. Several large vessels had been placed into the fire. It was all tidy and ready for use.

"Keturah will be along soon, but we can make the first trek for water."

I set the linens on the table, took the bucket she handed me, and followed her to the stream that ran through the fields. As I bent to fill my bucket, I noticed she carried two. She hauled them easily as I struggled with my one, but I was determined not to spill a drop. That proved to be impossible, but I did my best. When we poured the buckets into the basin, the water hardly seemed to fill it at all.

Naomi took a breath. "More," she said and started again toward the stream.

Three more times we did this, and still the basin was not full.

"I may sound very dumb," I said. "But could we not carry the linen to the stream and wash it there?"

She didn't laugh at me. "That is one way to do the laundering. But I have always preferred to use hot water to wash."

"Oh. I had not thought of that. How will you heat the water?"

"In a kettle over the fire. When we add boiling water to our cold stream water, it will feel just right for washing. I've already got the water on to boil. Lamech brings it up during his watch."

"What does he watch for?"

She was silent as she bent to fill another bucket. "Those who would harm this farmstead," she said after she had set the heavy bucket on the grassy bank.

I bent to fill my bucket. The water was swift and deep, but clear. It was more than enough to water these fields and provide for this family. But I had never seen water moving this fast, and I had to hold the bucket tight as the water filled it.

"It seems anyone could view this farm from those ridges," I said and pointed. Hills surrounded the valley, except on the west border, which was protected by thick wilderness.

"That's the West Road." Naomi pointed toward the largest ridge to the east. "We are very visible here, but the water is abundant and minor inconveniences can be forgiven."

I frowned. That was a strange choice of words. *Forgiven.*

"God's gifts come in many packages."

And *God's gifts.* What gifts was she talking about?

"Why do you give me of your finest things?" I asked her. "Surely this sarong will get dirt on it during a day's work."

She lifted a hand to pat me on the shoulder, but she kept the touch brief, and I wished Shad hadn't told Naomi not to touch me. She reached for her buckets instead and stood.

"I would just look ridiculous in that," she said. "I'm old, and my shoulders are made big with work."

She said it with a smile, but her words did not match it. My eyes went straight to her shoulders. She was muscular, but she most definitely did not look like her menfolk.

"A little dirt will not harm it. If something is too nice to use, it is too nice to have."

How different that was from my father's philosophies on material possessions!

"It's a pretty dress, a gift from my Liam," she went on. "It should be worn." Then she cast me a wonderfully devious grin. "You nearly knocked both my boys clean off their stools."

"I don't like being exploited for my looks." I clamped a hand over my mouth at my impulsive words.

Her steps stopped, and she turned to look at me.

"I hadn't thought of it like that," she said, her eyes wide. "Forgive me."

I shook my head. "I'm sorry I said that."

She set her buckets down. Then she took mine from my hand and placed it by hers. Putting both of her hands on my arms, allowing herself to hold me, she looked me in the eyes. Hers were green like the ivy that grew near my window at home, streaked with hints of yellow and flecked with white.

"I know what it is to be used that way, for your looks and your body, and I am deeply sorry if I've hurt or offended you."

Her sincere apology touched my heart, but how could she understand? She was pretty—perhaps in her younger days she had been very pretty—but I doubted she had dodged the men in the grand halls of Zarahemla.

"I only meant to jostle Shad a little. When he accepted that job in Zarahemla, he was running from a girl." She smiled apologetically and turned to retrieve her buckets once again. "A pretty one like you. I hoped...I guess I had hoped to see that light in his eyes again." She stepped back and put her hand on her heart. "It brought joy to my heart when you made him laugh this morning."

"I knew about Miriam," I confided, surprising her. "But I didn't know she broke his heart." I had been so sleepy when I had conversed with Miriam, but I was sure she hadn't made it seem as bad as that.

"Hurt his pride, is more like it. But still, a mother wants to see her children happy."

"You can't think I can make him happy. My life is a mess. I'm a mess."

She picked up her buckets again. "While you are here, if you can make that boy smile once a day, you will have well-earned your keep."

"He's going back to Zarahemla," I pointed out. *And leaving me to be your problem.*

"Then your work will be done."

"I'm not free to—" *To what?* "To be anything to him." The words sounded silly as they tumbled out.

"A smile," she repeated, low and motherly, as we returned to the little shelter.

Keturah was holding a kettle with thick rags, pouring steaming water into the basin we had been filling. Gabriel sat a short distance away playing with a wooden toy that made noise.

"You're not free to do what?" asked Keturah, obviously having overheard the end of our conversation.

"Make Shad smile," I said, fighting my embarrassment.

"A difficult job," Keturah said with a straight face. "He has been frowning for a very long time."

Naomi hefted a bucket onto the rim of the basin, pouring expertly with one hand while steadying the bucket with her knee. "She's already managed it twice." She dropped the empty bucket and used both hands to pour the other one.

"It is not a fair trade for your hospitality," I pressed.

"Perhaps not for you. We don't have any of the entertainments of the city to offer you."

I made a frustrated noise, but laughed. "Shad said an extra mouth would be a burden."

Naomi and Keturah laughed. Naomi shook her head.

"If that boy thinks I cannot run this home single-handedly, I'll take him over my knee."

I was beginning to see that when she called Shad "that boy," she might as well have been saying, "I love that boy." It was so obvious in her voice.

"Shad's not a little boy anymore, Naomi. You are the mother of grown sons now." Keturah reached over and squeezed Naomi's arm in a way that made me think they had shared this conversation before, and in a way that showed the closeness of their relationship and made me long for a mother. Then Keturah pointed a finger in her own son's direction. "*That* is a little boy."

Naomi smiled at Keturah with a faraway look in her eyes. She sighed and went to pick up Gabriel.

Keturah watched them briefly but turned to me. "Here. I'll show you how to launder."

"Let her do her own clothing and the linens from her pallet," Naomi suggested.

I didn't wait for Keturah to retrieve the items. Sifting through the garments and linens on the table, I found mine and offered it to her.

"Toss it in," she said as she felt the water in the basin and deemed it to be the right temperature. I did and watched the water soak up into the cloth.

She showed me how to apply the soap. "Now just squeeze the water through it."

I put my hands into the warm water and did as she gently instructed. She helped me wring it out over the basin, and then I repeated the process with the linens I had slept on.

"Perfect. Now we just take them to the stream for a rinse and hang them to dry. But why don't you take Gabriel for a walk while we finish up."

"Can he walk?"

"If you let him hold to your fingers. He loves it. He'll walk all day like that. He's like his father in that." She exchanged a smile with Naomi. "You will be sorry you ever started it."

Naomi put the small boy down and he began walking toward me on his chubby little legs. It was so sweet to watch that I laughed in delight. I held out my hands and encouraged him toward me. He giggled and stopped to bounce on both legs. He was so excited bouncing that eventually Naomi picked him up and handed him to me.

"Oh!" I said. "Hello."

He smacked me in the nose.

"That means he likes you," Keturah said. "Go on. Walk him around the yard." She leaned closer and said, "Really, I don't like him around the boiling water."

I looked at the sopping wad of fabric I had just washed and thought at least in this I could be useful.

I set Gabriel down, took his little hands in mine, and off we went.

But not before I saw Keturah and Naomi pour the rest of the boiling water into the wash basin.

CHAPTER 6

"And here is the highest girl in the grand city of Zarahemla caring for a child in the country."

I had been walking with Gabriel long enough that my back ached from bending over, but every time I had tried to stop, he had begun to cry. Keturah had been right about that.

I picked Gabriel up anyway and winced as my back straightened.

"Shad, do you know who I am, please? Or rather, do you know who my father is?"

"I do."

I let out a breath.

"I have to be honest with you, Olivia. I knew from the first moment I got a good look at you, and I was nearly sure in that dark building. I knew Paanchi's daughter was missing, and I knew you had been missing for two months. I had even been out on searches for you."

I looked down, ashamed that he had caught me in what he thought was a lie about how long I had really been away from home, but I had to look up as Gabriel started squirming to get down. He let out a yelp.

Shad held out his hands. "Let me walk him for a while."

"He could have walked halfway to Zarahemla on those tiny legs already. He will make himself sick."

Shad laughed. "I doubt it."

I walked slowly at his side while Shad walked, bent over to let Gabriel clutch his thumbs.

"Why didn't you say anything?" I bit my fingernail and didn't stop myself.

"I figured you would tell me when you were ready. When you trusted me enough. And also, I didn't think you would come with me if you knew you had been recognized." He paused. "If you knew I was one of the men looking for you."

"I wouldn't have," I agreed. "Why didn't you take me back to my father?"

He was quiet for several steps. "I've met your father, Olivia. I know him. And seeing you, the way you were, the bruises and your obvious desire to stay away from him, I couldn't take you back there."

I knew the kind of men who associated with my father, and Shad was not like them. It had only taken a day on this farm to be nearly sure of that.

"I miss him," I said. "Is that strange?"

"He's your father. It would be strange if you did not miss him."

"Even if he is very bad?"

"Even so." He hesitated before asking, "Was he very bad to you?"

"I told you. No. Only in the past few months has he been acting unusual. I think he has gotten in with something he cannot get out of."

"Hmm."

"I wonder what he traded for my betrothal."

I didn't even realize I had been wondering aloud until Shad answered. "A position in the government, no doubt."

"But he might have been Chief Judge if only the people had voted for him!" I couldn't help feeling angered on his behalf. He had worked very hard to put himself into a position to acquire the judgment seat.

"Many did vote for him. Many still support him. And he may yet get the seat, with Pahoran slain."

"He seeks power."

"I know."

"But he has many good ideas he wants to implement."

Shad lifted Gabriel into his arms and straightened. "Do you believe we should have a king, then?" he asked as he stretched his back. He only seemed curious to know what I thought, not argumentative.

I shrugged and watched as Gabriel rubbed his face into Shad's tunic. He had finally tired himself out.

"I'm told the kingdom ran well under Mosiah. Do you think we should have a king?"

"Sure, if men could be trusted to remain righteous, but no, not now. Not after all I have seen of the ruling class in Zarahemla."

"Helaman is of the ruling class."

"He's a prophet, not a king."

I reached out a finger to touch Gabriel's head. He was nearly asleep on Shad's shoulder already.

"He looks like he could be yours," I said.

He shrugged with the shoulder Gabriel was not settling into. "It is a sad fact. All my brothers look very much alike."

"Except Lamech." He so obviously looked more like their mother than their father as the rest of them did.

Shad got the same pondering look on his face as he had that morning near the fire. "He doesn't look like us?"

I shook my head, smiling.

Shad sobered. "Lamech has different parentage."

I bit my nail and chewed on that information. How had Lamech come to be known as their brother, then? Had his parents died? How long had he been raised in this home with Shad and his brothers?

"Why do you do that?"

Shad was looking down at me as he held the child's head to his chest to support it. We began to circle back toward the house.

"Do what?"

"Your fingernail."

I felt my cheeks flush. "A bad habit. I've always done it."

Shad took a deep breath. "How did you get the bruises?"

"What do you mean? I already told you about my despicable betrothed."

"You've been missing for two months, Olivia, and those wounds are a week old at the longest."

"I told you the truth."

"That's a lie too. Tell me the truth."

How could I?

"The whole of it," he clarified. "Who gave you the bruises?"

"Kishkumen."

He gently, and quite naturally, moved Gabriel to his other shoulder so he didn't have to peer at me from around the boy's sleepy head. "At your father's home?"

I glanced up at him, then away. "I was staying in the cook's room. Martha. She let me, and in the daytime when my father was gone, I could sneak into the kitchen. I could see the sun and get a bit to eat. At night, Martha brought me food."

He didn't let himself laugh, but his eyes sparkled with laughter. "That whole time, you were still at your father's house? Right under his nose?"

Now that he pointed it out, it was kind of funny. I had only thought it a great inconvenience to have to stay hidden all the time. I smiled and nodded.

"And what happened a week ago? Did your father find you?"

"No."

"Stop lying to me. You don't need to."

"Kish did!" I cried. "I told you already. Kishkumen was there. In the day. One day. I don't know why. I think maybe he suspected. How else could someone like me get food? With no money of my own and no friends that would not bring me straight home? Father must have told him Martha was my friend. I don't know, but he was there when he shouldn't have been."

"Some might have said he was only trying to court his betrothed."

"Don't make light of it."

He grimaced. "I'm sorry. Go on. What happened?"

"Can you not imagine it for yourself?"

"I don't want to. I want you to tell me."

"And I don't want to tell you how he grinned when he saw me, a grin that sent chills to my bones. I don't want to tell you how he told Martha to go." When I had said that much, even more spilled out. "How he dragged her out by her hair when she wouldn't go and told her she would suffer if she hid me again."

"And then what happened?"

"He pushed me against the wall and put his disgusting lips on me," I said hollowly. "And he said if I wanted to stay and hide in the house, he would make it so I could not show my face outside." I swallowed. "He would make it so I could not leave." I looked at the trees in the distance without really seeing them. "But I did leave."

"Okay. That's enough," Shad said quietly. "You don't have to say any more."

"But I did leave," I said again. "I had to crawl from the kitchen, but I did leave."

His voice was gentle. "Olivia."

"I will have scars," I said, turning to look up at him.

He searched my eyes, and I was embarrassed for saying something so stupid, so obvious, and for wanting him to know.

"And Kishkumen will never stop looking for me, though I doubt very much he will trouble himself to do the searching himself. He has friends—cohorts, associates, followers. I don't really know what they are to him. He has many who would do his bidding."

"How many?" Shad asked, the apology gone from his tone. "How many are loyal to him?"

"I have seen him with many."

"Five? Ten?"

"Three consistently. The only three who have come to my home. But I have seen him in the city with maybe twenty men at different times."

"What were they doing when you saw them together?"

I frowned. Why did it matter?

"Attending meetings of the court. Listening to the lawyers and judges. Watching the Chief Judge like he was their next meal."

We neared the house, and as we circled back around to the front of it, I could see that Lamech and his father had also returned. Naomi was serving them a meal at the outside table.

Shad stopped and turned to me. "Olivia. This is important. Give me your honest first impression."

He waited for me to say, "Okay."

"How likely is it that Kishkumen or these men he frequents with had something to do with the murder of Pahoran?"

My uncle. Kind and wise and even quite jovial when he wasn't working.

"I heard him bragging about it," I said, detaching myself from my words, wishing I could detach myself from the memory of his.

"He said that he did it? That he was the one? Or was it someone else?"

There was an urgency in Shad's words, and I looked up at him again. His interest in the murder of the Chief Judge was burning in his eyes. The fire there was at great odds with the peacefulness of the sleeping child on his chest.

What would it hurt to tell Shad? He had done nothing but protect and care for me. Perhaps he could bring Kish to justice, as I could not.

"He told his friends exactly how he did it," I said.

"And you heard?"

"He was drunken."

"Does he know you heard?"

I made myself meet his eyes. "He made sure I heard. It was a threat to gain my obedience."

He held my gaze steadily. "One more question, Olivia."

I swallowed. "Okay."

"Did your father know?"

I shut my eyes tight, pursed my lips, and nodded quickly, trusting that he was looking at me. "I think he was the one who planned it," I said.

After long moments of silence, I heard the footsteps of someone approaching and then Keturah's words.

"Let me take him, Shad. I will put him down for his rest."

When she was gone, Shad moved closer to me.

"Was that the real reason you went to Martha to hide you?"

"I didn't know what to do. I couldn't stay. But I had nowhere to go." I finally opened my eyes to see the concern on his face. "I fear Kishkumen has hurt her, looking for information about where I went."

"Does she have it?"

I shook my head vigorously. She hadn't even helped me from the kitchen, she had been so afraid of Kishkumen's threats. I didn't blame her. I would never blame her.

He sighed deeply. "Are you hungry?"

No. My appetite was gone, but I forced out the words, "I will never again turn down food."

We made our way to the table where Naomi served us both.

"I'm leaving in the morning," Shad announced. "For Zarahemla. I must return."

"I thought you were staying a sennight!" his mother protested. "What has changed?"

I couldn't help but notice when her eyes flicked to me.

"I can't stay away that long, that's all. I thought I could, but I can't."

"When will you be back?"

"I don't know." He put a hand to his collar and straightened his tunic. "Can Olivia stay?"

His mother looked between us. "Of course she can stay."

Shad looked to Lamech. "Will you be here?"

Lamech finished chewing and swallowed. "I've no plans to leave."

"Sarai will be so disappointed," I said, teasing a little, hoping to lighten the sad mood I had caused. I didn't know what Shad's work was or exactly why he was leaving, but I knew it had something to do with the things I had told him about Kishkumen and my father.

Lamech folded his arms and said, "She will be burdened with my company soon enough."

"Where will you live?" I asked him.

He pointed beyond my shoulder, and when I turned to look, I saw a building site across the field. I had noticed it before but thought nothing of it, only that it was another outbuilding. I nodded and scooped some of Naomi's stew into my mouth. That was the reason the men had been working at the timber mill when I arrived. They were building Lamech and Sarai a home.

"It is a good site for a home," I said.

Lamech chuckled. "Not compared to where you live."

I saw his parents exchange a look. Shad didn't seem to have anything to add about the size of my home in Zarahemla, and sharing the details would make me uncomfortable.

I reached over and briefly touched Lamech's hand. It felt like the wrong thing to do, so I quickly removed it, but I said sincerely, "Where I live is crowded and unsafe and difficult to live the teachings of the prophets. This is a lovely place where there is love and the Spirit of the Lord can be felt. Your Sarai is the luckiest of girls."

The whole family was quiet as they finished their meals, but I caught a secret smile Naomi sent to Liam, and Lamech gave me a small nod acknowledging what I had said.

That evening, I waited until everyone had gone to sleep, and then I slipped silently out of the house to see if Shad was the one on the first watch. I didn't know how the watches worked or who took which one, or even why they did it, but I found Shad sitting alone on the outside table in the yard.

"It gets cool here at night," I said softly.

He craned around to see me. When he didn't say anything, I hoisted myself up onto the table to sit next to him.

"How are your wounds?" he asked.

"Keturah cleaned them again after the evening meal."

"She mentioned there are cuts. Are they deep?"

"Some of them. Thank you for bringing me here."

He shrugged.

"I know you took time away from your work, probably without pay. I want you to know —"

"The pay doesn't matter," he said. "I told you I had the means to help you."

It seemed I had touched a nerve, so I let the subject drop. He did not want thanks for what he had done.

"You have to go back because of what I said, don't you?"

"I acquired information my superiors need. That's my job. I have to report it."

"That's your job? Is that why you didn't return me to my father? So you would have opportunity to get information out of me?"

"Olivia."

"And now that you have it, what will you do? Turn me back over to Kish?"

He snorted. "I wouldn't turn a dog over to Kish."

"That's so comforting." I slid off the table and was about to say a curt goodnight when Shad wrapped his warm fingers around my arm. He pulled me back to him and let his hand slide down my arm until he was holding my hand.

"Livi." His voice was low. "Why do you think I recognized you?"

Shad's work is to deceive.

"Because your work is to gain information about my father. Because you're a spy."

He shook his head slowly. "Because your beauty is unforgettable."

He was flattering me. He wasn't done gleaning information from me. This was the game. I could stay here in safety, but it would cost me information.

"If you only want to know about my father, just ask. I will tell you all. I will tell you all I know about Kish. You don't need to pretend that you have an affection for me."

I tried to walk away, but he was still holding my hand and he gently pulled me back to him.

"Who says I'm pretending?"

I bit my lip while I thought about his words, about how he had said them. He was not like the other men I knew, the ones who came through Father's house, the ones whose flattery meant less than nothing. I thought of the predicament I was in. Being here on the farm was only a temporary solution to it.

"Well, you can't be serious," I said.

Shad looked into my eyes for a moment, trying to read them in the dark. He let go of my hand.

"Livi," he said, and I wondered when he had started calling me that. It was what my friends called me, what my father called me, and I loved the sound of it on his lips.

"I wasn't just recruited to look for you after you ran away." He ran a hand through his hair, and after a moment's hesitation, he stood up and started to pace.

"What else were you recruited to do?"

He rubbed the back of his neck and looked up at the stars. I looked up too. They were the same stars I had seen so many times when I slipped out the window of my room to walk through the dark streets of Zarahemla. The familiarity of the stars brought me comfort, but I wondered if perhaps I hadn't been as alone on those walks as I had thought myself to be.

"I saw you not long before you disappeared," he said. "In the market. The crowds were thick that day."

"They always are."

"I had never seen anything like it. I hadn't been in the city long. I had gone to Zarahemla for just that kind of thing, but I found that all the people made me uncomfortable."

I smiled. "You get used to it. In truth, the silence of the forest makes me uncomfortable."

He stopped pacing and folded his arms over his chest, and I thought of giggling with Keturah about his muscles.

"There is nothing to fear in the forest," he said.

"Then why do you watch through the night?"

He started pacing again.

"Did you only see me that once, in the market?"

He ran his hand through his hair again. "No, and I noticed you returned to the same shop a lot. So I went there myself to see what was so interesting."

I laughed softly. The only things I looked at in the market would not be of interest to him. "Was it bangles for my ankles or henna for my hair?" I asked.

He waved it off. "Adornments of some kind. Listen, Olivia, it's time you retuned to bed."

"Don't call me that," I said.

He frowned, but after a moment, he stepped closer.

"Get some sleep, Livi."

He was gone when I awoke.

I ate my morning meal quietly with Lamech, Liam, and Naomi. Though they tried to include me in their conversation, much of what they talked about were things that had nothing to do with me — the barley harvest, the weather, the new house for Sarai.

Liam and Lamech went to the timber mill again. This time, Naomi sent them their midday meals wrapped in cloth, and I wondered if she hadn't packed food before because she wanted Shad to return to the farm at midday to see to my care himself.

"I need some more of this cloth," Naomi said as I watched her wrap the food. "Do you know how to weave?"

I did not have any domestic skills. "No."

"I could teach you."

"Yes, of course. I would like to learn."

"I've had no girls to teach. I mightn't be a good instructor."

She really seemed to think she wouldn't. I smiled at her. "As long as you have patience, I'm sure you will do fine."

It did take patience for both of us, but by early afternoon, I was weaving a simple, functional cloth. Naomi stayed close to me, working her own beautiful cloth. Keturah had joined us and she worked a pattern she said was her mother's.

"I like those colors together," I said of the greens and blues in her pattern.

"You are becoming accomplished very quickly," she replied.

I looked down at my cloth. It was plain linen, the color of aspen bark, but I was moving quickly and I could not tell where Naomi had left off and I had begun. My face heated with pleasure at her compliment.

The conversation fell to domestic things, and I listened to the two women talk. Sometimes I asked a question and they explained simple things to me which, having no mother to teach me, I had never known.

"Would this not look pretty shot through with blue thread?" I asked, recalling many of the beautiful fabrics I had seen in the Zarahemlan market.

Keturah looked up to watch Gabriel playing in the grass a short distance away. She took a breath to speak, but instead of answering, she said, "Olivia, go into the house."

"Wha—"

"Do it quickly. Do not come out until I call for you."

I glanced at Naomi, but I did as Keturah instructed.

"Take your loom," Keturah said as I got to my feet.

I took it, and I went into the house. I stood in the main room wondering what to do. Had I done something to offend? Finally, I decided to go into the back room, sit on the pallet, and continue weaving. I was starting to feel confident with it, and as I watched my fingers nimbly move the shuttle over and under the threads to make the patterns, I thought how like my life it was—ups and downs, loops and lines, sometimes showing dark and sometimes light, all forming a cloth that would be useful, and hopefully beautiful, in the end.

After a time, I became aware of voices in the yard—male voices that did not sound like Liam and Lamech.

CHAPTER 7

I could only make out the rise and fall of their voices. The men seemed to be questioning Naomi and Keturah. Were these men they knew? If they were, they were not men Keturah trusted with the knowledge of my presence on the farmstead.

Finally, my curiosity won me over, and I slipped out into the main room and crept toward the door so I could hear.

"We think she may have been taken against her will from the city," one of the men said. His voice seemed familiar, but if I knew it, I couldn't quite place it.

"I have heard the city gates are closed to travelers," Keturah replied.

"How has that news traveled to these parts?" I could imagine the man looking around at the fields and the modest houses.

"My brother," said Keturah. "He has just come from there. He was not allowed admittance."

"And what was his business in the city?"

"It is no business of yours, but he lives and works in the city. The girl. Can you describe her? Mayhap I have seen her in Orihah."

"Very pretty," said another male voice, and this one I did recognize.

It was Ammon, son of Pahoran. He was one of my kinsmen. We had grown up together, but as he was a bit older, we had followed different paths into adulthood. I had not talked to him for many months, even before I had left home, though I knew him to be a friend of Kishkumen's and I did see him from time to time.

"Her hair is dark and long. Her eyes are wide and unforgettable. You would remember her if you saw her," the other man said, and I felt sure I did know him. I wanted to take a very quick peek past the mat at the door, but I willed myself to stay as still as I had in the dank old building Shad had rescued me from.

There was silence for a moment, and I briefly wondered if Keturah was contemplating telling Ammon I was just inside the door.

"I am sorry. I have seen no girl of that description in Orihah. I have seen pretty girls there, to be sure, but I am acquainted with all of them."

"You're sure?"

"Oh, very sure, though I do wish I could be of help to you." Another pause. "May we offer you some refreshment while you're here? Our menfolk will be back for mealtime. Perhaps one of them has seen this girl you seek in Orihah. They go there much more often than I do. You could speak to them over the meal."

There was another silence. Perhaps Ammon was glancing at the sun or exchanging a look with his companion.

"I'm afraid we can't stay, but thank you. We've much ground left to cover."

Was that…Elias? I knew Elias, too. He was one of Kish's closest friends. He had been to my father's house, and he had flirted with me harmlessly many times, even in Kish's presence. Though we were never more than acquaintances, I had once liked Elias. He was young and handsome and charismatic and by far the least repugnant of Kish's friends. I had often wished Father had betrothed me to him instead.

"And we're to meet up with friends for mealtime," he continued.

"Perhaps we will see your menfolk on the road," Ammon suggested, and then I heard their feet on the gravel as they left.

I expected Naomi and Keturah to come bursting through the door as soon as the men were gone, but they didn't. The yard was quiet. I even wondered if they had escorted the men off the property or perhaps run for safety. I finally dared to pull the fabric at the door back a little to see out. Naomi was seated at her loom and weaving away as if nothing had happened. Keturah was collecting Gabriel from the grass.

He squealed in delight when she picked him up. She laughed and kissed his hands. "Are you hungry, my little warrior?"

I nearly stepped through the door, but a warning inside reminded me Keturah had not told me to come out. She had been faithful in protecting me, preventing the men from knowing of my presence here, so I would follow her one instruction. I did not go out into the yard.

Presently, Keturah walked past the door and said very softly, "Stay indoors. I think they may be watching the house." Then she took the baby out to the table and fed him. She did not come into the house until she put Gabriel down for his rest.

"They are looking for you," she said.

"Thank you for not betraying me."

She set Gabriel, already half asleep, on Shad's pallet and turned to me with compassion on her face. "Of course we won't betray you."

I looked down. "You hardly know me."

"I know Shad, and I trust him completely. If he says you need protection, you need protection. And despite those bruises, I know Shad did not forcibly take you from the city. He could not have inflicted them." She smiled. "And he would not bring you here if by some chance he had inflicted them."

"You're so sure of him."

She almost laughed but restrained it after a glance at her son. "Liam is a peaceable man, but he would surely discipline any son of his that inflicted pain upon a woman."

"Discipline? What do you mean?" His sons were all grown men now.

"Lashings most likely," she said.

No wonder she had laughed. The idea was absurd. All three of the sons I had seen were as big as their father.

"I've got to go. I don't want to leave Naomi out there alone. Stay inside. I am not sure the house is being watched, but the feeling in my heart tells me something is not right."

I felt it too. "What am I to do? Can I weave near the window?"

"Yes. Just stay indoors. I'm going to walk to my house for my weapons, and then I'm going to help Naomi prepare the midday meal for the men."

"Weapons?"

"Just a precaution. I could use Lamech's, but I prefer my own."

"You really were the girl in Helaman's army?"

She smiled. "I really was."

"You told Ammon the men would be here for the afternoon meal, but I know Naomi sent them a meal."

"Ammon?"

"I recognized his voice. One of Kish's closest friends." I paused. "And my cousin."

One pretty brow rose as she took that in. "My husband is very receptive to the Spirit. I have been praying for his presence, and I do not doubt he will show up hungry for an afternoon meal."

To my great surprise, she was right. I had not been weaving long when I heard male voices in the yard again, and before long, Liam ducked into the house.

I stood and stared expectantly at him. He looked to have worked hard. His clothing was soiled and his hair was wet with sweat.

"It seems you do bring the trouble Shad spoke of," he said.

"I'm sorry to bring danger to your family." I owed him at least an apology.

He shook his head, brushing it away. "The world is filled with dangers. We will weather whatever comes."

He passed through the main room and slipped into the bed chamber I had been using since my arrival. In a moment, he came out with a clean tunic on. "My wife will bring you in some food," he said gruffly before he left as abruptly as he had come.

I did not know what to make of his aloofness. He hadn't strung three sentences together since I had arrived, and except for just then, he had only spoken directly to me once. He wasn't angry, exactly, nor shy. I settled on uncomfortable for a description of him. Perhaps raising up a household of boys had made him uncomfortable around women, particularly my type — helpless and accustomed to wealth.

"I'm sorry to keep you locked in here," Naomi said after coming through the door. "You must be going crazy, but Keturah insists something is not right."

"I trust her," I said.

She passed me a dish filled with hearty vegetables, bread, and meat. "So do I, but I fear you may be inside for the rest of the day. Here is a book of scripture. Feel free to read it. I'm afraid there is not much else to do inside. Gid and Lamech will search the woods after the meal, and perhaps you can come back out when they return."

I didn't want them to put themselves in danger for me, but Naomi spoke so matter-of-factly that I assumed searching the woods was routine business for them. This family seemed to take many extra precautions. Even though the house was not protected in the trees, perhaps this was the perfect place for me.

Naomi stayed and talked to me while I ate but left soon after, and nobody returned.

After I became bored with the plain design of the cloth I was weaving, I fingered the book of scripture. I had been educated by the best tutors in Zarahemla. I had learned to read from the writings of this book. I had even had the fortune of reading from good copies of the official writings. I knew the words, the stories, the doctrine it contained. But my father's book of scripture had never looked like this one did.

Shad's family ate well. They were clean and comely, but they were not affluent. Though their possessions were few, they were of quality. They cared for and maintained their buildings and tools, but this book was worn, the most worn of their possessions. The fibers of the cloth were dirty where their hands had touched it. The ink of the lettering had faded. The edges were tattered, so I was careful not to pull on the fraying threads.

But it was legible, and as I began to read the teachings, I was comforted in the familiarity of the words.

"You love them as I do."

I looked up at the sound of Liam's voice. He was standing in the doorway. I could see behind him that dusk had fallen.

"You turn the pages carefully."

Because they are old. But of course I did not say that. It would have been impolite to draw attention to it. Instead, I said, "The book is well-used."

He surprised me with a laugh and let the mat fall closed behind him. He came to me and held out his hand for the book. When I passed it to him, he clutched it in his hand, reverently, but not at all gently.

"The boys have their own books, carefully copied." He frowned down at the codex in his hand. "I like this one."

I nodded slowly, though he wasn't looking at me. "Thank you for letting me borrow it." I paused. "Is it safe for me to come out now?"

He shook his head. "The boys are still searching the woods for signs of your friends."

I bristled. "They are not my friends."

"Keturah said you knew them."

"That hardly makes them my friends. They are Kishkumen's friends."

He frowned but said, "Would you like to play a game?"

I was already trying to figure out the game here, how it could be won. His laugh. His frown.

"A game of chance," he said when I did not respond. "To pass the time."

Why was he here? Why was he not searching the woods with his sons?

"I have heard games of chance are unholy."

He laughed again, and I found I liked it. His smile reminded me of Shad's.

"We won't play for money. Merely a harmless way to pass the time." He set the book of scripture down on a shelf and returned with something small in his hand. Going to his heels near me and shaking small stones across his palm, he cast me a sideways glance. "Passed many hours with this game."

"Alright," I finally agreed. "I'm weary of weaving."

"I would go crazy with boredom if weaving were one of my chores."

I couldn't help a smile.

"Tell me about this game of chance," I said, motioning to the stones in his palm.

He opened his hand, and I could see that what he held were not stones but oblong pieces of bone with intricately carved figures on them.

"All you have to do is toss them, and we score based on what is showing. Like this." He let the bones fall. "Two snakes and one man. Four points." He scooped them up and passed them to me.

I took them, glanced at him, and tossed them down.

"Two snakes and a plain. Six points."

"A plain is worth more than a man?"

The frown again. "No. You'll catch on."

It seemed to be an arbitrary point system, but as we tossed the different combinations, I did catch on.

When I reached fifty first, he smiled at me. "You're good at this."

"It's nothing but luck," I said, but I was happy to have won. I couldn't keep the smile from my face.

Liam shrugged. "I'll go see if the boys are back."

"It was…I mean, thank you for the game."

He glanced back at me over his shoulder before he passed through the door, and it was dim inside the hut, but I thought he winked at me.

When Liam did not return with news of the boys, as he called them, I straightened up inside the hut. Nothing much was out of place, or I didn't know its place, so it did not take long to put things aright. I sat on the pallet Shad had slept on, hugged my knees to my chest, leaned my head back against the wall, and let out a deep sigh. I was as much a prisoner here as I had been at my father's home, in Martha's little room near the kitchen, and in the shack where Shad had found me. Only here, I was putting these kind people in danger.

What if Ammon and Elias saw me here? What if they had already seen me? What would Kish do to these people if he found out they had harbored me?

"It's not as boring as all that, is it?" Lamech asked when he came in and saw me.

I wiped the errant tear from my cheek and straightened to look at him. "You're safe," I breathed.

He snorted as if his safety had never been in question. "You're on my bed."

I looked down at the pallet. "Oh." Did he and Shad share this one low pallet then? "Can I go out?"

"Why? Everyone's gone. It's just Mother and Father out there, and take my word, they're embarrassing."

I scrambled off his pallet. "What do you mean embarrassing?" I said as I straightened my skirt.

He wouldn't look me in the eye. "They like to talk under the stars," he said, seeming to wish he hadn't brought it up.

"Oh," I said again.

"Best to just go to sleep."

I hated to sleep with the sun. At home, at Father's house, I had lanterns filled with oil to light the dark hours. Here there was just a candle Liam had lit, and I suspected that had I not been there, no one would have bothered with the candle. It seemed they could all walk confidently, even when they could not see the way before them.

I sighed deeply. "Goodnight then."

So, I thought as I readied myself for bed, if Liam took the first watch for Shad, then Gid must take the second watch, the one that started after midnight. With only three of them home, they must divide the four watches into three, each taking a little extra time. I knew what they watched for that night, but this was a well-established routine on the farmstead. That much was clear.

I didn't have trouble falling asleep, but the problem with falling asleep early was that one tended to also wake early. I stared at the dark ceiling for as long as I could, but at last I got up and slipped outside into the cool morning.

Lamech was sitting at the fire round, though there was no fire in it.

"We have to stop meeting like this," I said in a voice that was embarrassingly still husky with sleep.

"No one gave you leave to come out."

"I have to pee," I said bluntly.

"Oh."

I barely heard the rustle of his clothing as he stood.

"I'll go with you."

"You most certainly will not."

"Livi, we found signs of your friends in places they should not have been. They might still have their eye on this place."

I wouldn't put it past Kish's men.

"It's the fourth watch!" I hissed. No one was awake. "And if they do, I will just look like your mother in the shadows. If you escort me, it will look strange."

I had a point, and he knew it.

"I can't talk about this right now," I said and ran for the small hut at the edge of the yard.

He didn't follow me, nor did he say anything when I came back and sat at the fire round across from him.

"Why did you build me that fire?" I said after a while.

"You asked me to."

"I shouldn't have asked."

Lamech didn't respond.

"Do you think they saw? Elias and Ammon?"

"No. We asked around. They were up north."

"Oh." They had asked around?

"Are you going to make a habit of waking early?"

"I am accustomed to sleeping late, but everything is different here. I'm sorry to burden you with my company."

He grunted.

"When will you bring your wife here?"

"A few months." I thought that would be all the information he would give up, but he said, "She used to live here with Keturah."

I have a place I can take you. It's with my mother.

"So, she is already well-acquainted with your family?"

He nodded and glanced to the east.

Was he impatient for the others to rise?

"Lamech, does it make you uncomfortable to be alone with me?"

He scratched his neck. A clear yes.

"When you ask questions like that, it does."

He was joking, but I had already seen the answer.

"I'll keep that in mind," I said and stood, and then I went back inside the house to leave him be.

CHAPTER 8

Gideon said people in Orihah had seen other men like Elias and Ammon out searching for me, but after they left the farmstead, we heard no more from them. I hoped they were gone for good, but I knew Kishkumen would not stop looking for me. He would tell his friends anything to keep them looking. Kidnapped, stolen from my home? How could they believe it? How could Ammon? If any one of those men would look past the façade Kish kept up, they would know I had run from him.

A week passed, and we heard nothing from Shad. A part of me was hoping he would deliver his information in Zarahemla and come back straightaway. Was it possible that I could miss someone I had only just met? I had spent much more time with Shad's family than I had with Shad himself, but I kept seeing him in Liam's smile and hearing him when his brothers joked with each other.

Naomi continued to treat me like a guest, giving me of her finest things and steering me away from the work that would hurt my hands or soil my clothing. But she had a way of teaching me the simplest domestic tasks and building upon what I already knew. Everything she taught me, she taught with love and compassion. She never made me feel I was inadequate as a girl, only patiently taught me the things I should have already known.

"Like this," she said one morning as she showed me how to knead a mound of dough for leavened bread. I watched as she folded the dough over itself and pressed it into the table, then turned it slightly. She repeated the process of folding, pressing, and turning the dough a few more times and then stepped aside so I could try.

I worked the dough for a moment as she had—it wasn't complicated—and looked up to see her pleased smile.

She moved away to pull the small cleaned and dried cloths from the line. I watched her, moving easily and comfortably about her home, and I sent up a quick prayer of thanks that God had led me to her.

"I always wished our cook would teach me to make bread," I said when Naomi returned to the table to fold the cloths. "Actually, I wished she would teach me to make anything."

Naomi glanced at me as she smoothed the folds of a cloth. "And why didn't she?"

"I think she was not very strong."

"What do you mean?"

"Father said she mustn't, and so she did not."

"Did she want to teach you?"

"I think she did."

"Then obedience to her employer was not weakness, dear."

I pressed the dough into the table again. I was starting to feel beads of perspiration at my brow. "I suppose not."

She folded the last few cloths and when she was finished,

she took them inside the house. I knew the exact shelf she would put them on, and the thought made me smile to myself.

"How long must I do this?" I asked when she returned.

"Here, I'll finish."

I nudged her away when she tried to take over. "It is time I learned to finish a task," I said quietly. "Even if it does cause me to sweat."

She laughed softly and ran a hand down my hair.

"How do you keep this so slick, dear?"

I pressed the dough down again, finding I had to push it down harder. "Father said my mother's hair was just like this."

"The luck of your birth, then."

I tried to blow a lock of hair out of my eyes.

"It's curious what things we inherit from our parents," she said.

My hair fell back into my face and clung to my moist forehead. I tried to sweep it back again with my shoulder.

"Let me at least pull your hair back off your neck," Naomi said as she whisked it up and secured it with two sticks she must have pulled from her own hair.

"Thank you," I said and pushed the dough down again.

She peered over my shoulder for a few more minutes, then she poked the dough with her finger while I took a short rest.

"If it gets too sticky, press it into the flour."

"What step comes next?"

"We let it raise until we prepare the evening meal."

"That long? No wonder you start it early in the day."

She pulled a large bowl closer and produced one of the clean cloths. "It's actually a touch late in the day to start." She glanced at the sky. "But the sun is warm and the yeast is active."

"Yeast?"

"It's the leaven we took out of the big jar."

I nodded as I watched my hands, my own hands, working the dough. It began to be soft and pliable, and I smiled when Naomi said it was ready. I placed it into the big bowl, and she placed the cloth over the top.

"To keep it clean," she told me.

"Keturah and Gabe are coming over," I said, seeing them leave their home. I smiled when Keturah set the boy down and let him walk, holding to her fingers.

When they came near, Keturah picked the boy up, passed him into Naomi's waiting arms, and stretched her back.

"For all the pain it is," she said, "I am glad that he is still holding to my fingers. I'm afraid he will take off after his father as soon as he can walk on his own."

Naomi laughed. "We'll have him for a few years yet, I think."

Keturah lifted a corner of the cloth and peered at my dough inside.

"Is this all the bread for the evening meal?" she asked.

"I thought you might mix up some more," Naomi said.

"I haven't done, but I will."

"No," I said. "I can do it." I looked between them. "If more is needed, I would like to finish the job."

"All right," Naomi said. "You remember the steps?"

I nodded.

"I'll start a venison stew," Keturah said.

My pleasure that they had allowed me to practice another mound of dough only lasted until I had to start kneading again. It was much harder than women made it look.

When the preparations for the evening meal were all

started and Gabriel had been put down for a rest, the three of us sat together and ate an afternoon meal of fruits and yogurt.

"Can you teach me to make this as well?" I asked after I drank the thick liquid in my mug.

"Of course. It is very simple."

"Can I have a look at your cuts and bruises?" Keturah asked as she set down her mug as well. "They should be mostly healed."

"They are. The scabs are itching."

She gave a nod. "That means they are healing."

While Naomi cleared away the dishes, I showed Keturah the remainder of my wounds. She inspected them all in silence, but I could tell she was pleased with the progress.

"Do you know when Shad will return?" I asked her quietly after a moment.

She leaned back, letting the last corner of my sarong flutter back down.

"I thought you would know. He didn't tell you?"

I shook my head.

She dabbed a little of her clear salve on the cut that had been the deepest as it was still weeping a little from the edge.

"It might help if I knew why he left." She paused. "Do you know?"

"Yes."

She turned her pretty eyes to mine expectantly.

I licked my lips. "I told him something. Information. He said he had to report it to his superiors."

"Information about what?"

Shad had said it was safe to tell his family everything. I took a breath. "My father." I swallowed guiltily. "I think he might have had something to do with Pahoran's death."

Keturah whistled softly through her teeth, the same way I had heard Shad do, and I wondered if she had picked it up from the brothers. "It's no wonder he left." She cast me a sly glance. "But I have a feeling he'll be back."

I shrugged. I didn't really know. I couldn't have made a good guess either way.

"Are you getting bored here?"

The look of concern on Keturah's face made me consider my actions of the past days. Had it seemed that I didn't like being here on the farm?

"Oh, no!" I assured her. "But I do feel like a burden."

"You are definitely not that. Naomi said she likes having you here."

"She said that?" I looked toward the house.

She nodded. "And there is good news. I sent for Sarai, and I've just had a letter from her. She is going to come down to stay for a few weeks."

"Lamech's Sarai?"

She nodded again. "I think you will like her very much."

But would she like me? Girls usually didn't.

"What is she like?"

"You may find her to be very quiet, but she is listening closely to everything that goes on. She is a wonderful confidant and a friend to all."

Quiet. "Do she and Lamech ever find things to say to each other?"

She laughed at that. "I adore watching the way he is with her. He tries to act tough, but he can't help himself when she is near. He's very tender to her and considerate."

I thought of the fire and the cloak he had given me. "He has shown himself that way to me, also. Considerate, I mean."

That seemed to surprise her.

"He has always disliked me," she confided.

"But that's silly. Of course he does not dislike you."

I had seen them talk to each other. Hadn't I?

She sighed. "His captain in the army was my Zeke," she said. "The boy I was supposed to marry. I hurt him, and Lamech took sides."

"Ah. Add loyal to his list of qualities," I said with a small smile.

"And unforgiving," she murmured.

Oh. I had stumbled onto a painful subject. I hesitated for a moment, but said gently, "Have you asked him for his forgiveness?"

She sat up straight, affronted. "I have not wronged him!"

I placed a finger to my lips and thought a moment. "Either he thinks you have, or you have done something entirely different to gain his offense."

She frowned, then shook her head. "He disliked me the first instant we met."

"What were the circumstances of your meeting?"

She stood and brushed off her sarong. "Gideon and I had seen him march into the city with the other recruits. We went to find him."

"You went together? Perhaps he sought his brother's attention for himself?"

"It has been an awful long time to hold a grudge over something like that," she said, exasperated. I could tell it was a situation that confused her, and she disliked it. I wondered how much tension it caused on the farmstead when they were not displaying their best manners to me, their guest.

Naomi emerged from the house with the baby in her

arms. Hardly a baby, I decided. He was nearly walking, after all.

"Would it be alright if I went for a walk in the woods?" I pointed to the thick woods at the edge of the barley fields.

Naomi and Keturah looked at each other. Naomi said, "I don't see why not. Do you think you can find your way back?"

I didn't know, but I would never know if I did not try. "I will not go far into the forest."

In truth, the forest kind of scared me, with its tall trees and dark shadows and strange sounds. But I had not had much time to myself since arriving, and Naomi and Keturah could hardly be frank and natural with one another in my presence. I thought we could all use the break.

Having lived in Zarahemla all my life, all I knew of the forest was what I had seen of it with Shad, how he had conjured fire and found things for us to eat. I had been so hungry and he had fed me so easily in the strange, beautiful place.

The trees were thick, and it was a wonder Shad's menfolk had cleared enough land to grow grains on. I put my hand on the rough bark of a tree, solid and thick. It must have indeed been very hard work for them to clear the land.

I tried to walk directly west, but there was no path to follow. Stones and trees and bushes of all kinds kept getting in my way, and I had to go around them. I felt that I was getting off course, so I found the narrow road that cut through the trees toward the farmstead and I stayed in sight of it.

As I looked at all the different plants, my curiosity got the better of me. I chose one and plucked a leaf from it. I brought it to my nose and lightly sniffed it. It smelled like a plant, nothing familiar. Tentatively, I stuck out my tongue to taste it.

"I wouldn't do that if I were you."

I jumped and dropped the leaf.

A small group of people stood on the road just a short distance away, two men and two girls.

"I didn't mean to scare you," one of the men said.

The girl next to him rolled her eyes. "Yes, you did," she said to him. Then she turned to me and stepped forward. "But he shouldn't have. Are you Olivia?"

I looked closely at the girl. I didn't think I knew her. No, to my recollection, we had never met. Should I talk to these people? No one was supposed to see me here.

She offered a friendly smile. "I'm Isabel. This is my sister, Sarai."

"Lamech's Sarai?" I asked before she could introduce the men, as she clearly intended to.

The other girl smiled and gave a little nod. "Then you are Olivia?"

"I am."

If this was Sarai, then she was Shad's family, and it was safe for these people to know I was here.

"That plant is not good for the belly," the other man said, gesturing to the bush I had pulled the leaf from, but when I met his eye to thank him, he looked quickly away.

"I didn't know," I said instead to the others. I glanced at the sky. It was probably getting to be time I returned to the farm. "Are you traveling to see Lamech?" I asked them.

Isabel giggled. "Sarai is. My husband and I have come to see you." She didn't mention the other man, who was now standing silently with his hands on his hips, letting his eyes roam over the trees that surrounded us.

"Me?"

She walked toward me, easily sidestepping the underbrush in her path. "Gid sent for us."

Isabel's husband sighed loudly. "Gid sent for *us*." He gestured to himself and the other man.

"Well of course he meant me too," she shot sharply over her shoulder, but she was smiling.

A snort. "I doubt it."

"I've just been walking. It's time I started back," I told them as I moved toward the road.

"We'll walk with you," Isabel said, and when I neared her, she linked elbows with me and turned me in the direction of the farm.

The four of them were pleasant. I even liked Isabel's husband, who Isabel introduced as Kenai. He was tall and lanky, and I could tell he loved Isabel very much by the way he smiled at the things she said and stayed near her side.

The other man walked ahead of us with Sarai. He was perhaps not as tall as Kenai, slender but not thin, and quite handsome. He had long dark hair and wore buckskin pants.

"Shad is just a few years younger than me," Isabel was saying when I tuned back in to her chatter.

"He said he was older than me." Though he had not told me how old he actually was.

"He probably enjoyed being older for once," Isabel said. "He's been the baby of his family his whole life. His brothers still treat him like a child."

"They do not," Kenai said.

"They do," Isabel insisted. "I've noticed it on more than one occasion."

"They treat him the age he is."

"Which is?" I asked.

Kenai glanced around Isabel to me. "Around twenty."

"Is that older than you?" Isabel asked.

"Oh. Yes. I'm seventeen."

Her eyes brightened. "Time to find a husband."

I could only muster a weak smile. It was time for me to find a husband, and that was the whole reason I was here in the Land of Melek—hiding from my betrothed.

"I'm afraid that's what my father thought," I said.

We had begun to cross through the fields out in the open, and they both fell silent. Maybe I shouldn't have been so frank about that.

Finally, Kenai changed the subject. "Why were you out in the forest alone."

"Keturah said it was okay."

"We've news she doesn't yet know," he said.

Isabel turned solemn. "About Zarahemla."

"What about it?" I asked.

They exchanged a glance, and Kenai broke the news. "Zarahemla has fallen."

CHAPTER 9

"But what do you mean it has fallen? To whom?"

"To the Lamanites."

It was unthinkable. The city was protected. I shook my head. "That's not possible."

Kenai was somber. "It is confirmed."

"The Lamanites are in Zarahemla?"

"They are in all the capital parts of the land. It is only a matter of time until they reach the outer lands like Melek."

"But Zeke says they will go north and try to take the passage," Isabel put in.

Kenai heaved a deep sigh and ran a hand through his hair. "Probably."

"But can they be stopped?" My head was spinning. Father was in Zarahemla. "They must be stopped."

"It's difficult to speculate," Kenai said, but he didn't seem optimistic.

"Zeke thinks so," Isabel said.

"If our armies can be amassed quickly enough."

"Who is Zeke?" I asked, trying to concentrate on something I could wrap my head around. Hadn't Keturah said something about a man with that name?

"My brother." Isabel let go of my arm and gestured to the man who was walking with Sarai.

So, this was Zeke. He and Sarai had just entered the yard near the main house, and Naomi was greeting them.

"I always hold my breath when they're together."

I looked at Isabel, but she was watching the scene before us as Keturah waited with Gabriel in her arms for her turn to greet the newcomers.

I quickly pieced together the details. "Because Keturah was betrothed to Zeke?"

"They were never betrothed." Kenai surprised me with his quick correction.

Isabel sighed. "You know they were as good as betrothed." She turned to me. "They had an understanding. Our families had an understanding."

I nodded. I was all too aware of how binding a not quite true betrothal could be.

We slowed and watched as Zeke laid a hand on Naomi's shoulder and then moved to Keturah while Naomi hugged Sarai. He laid a quick hand on her shoulder as well but didn't move on. He looked to be staring at the child, admiring maybe. Keturah looked proudly at her young son and then passed him into Zeke's hesitant arms. I laughed when Gabriel smacked Zeke in the face and then set to wailing.

Keturah laughed too and showed Zeke how to hold Gabe's fingers to let him walk.

I turned to Isabel as we entered the yard. "I think you can take a breath," I said.

She smiled and went to greet Naomi, but Kenai stayed back near me.

He folded his arms. "Have you seen the others yet?"

The others? Was he referring to Ammon and Elias?

"What do you mean?"

"Joshua. Corban. The whole crew."

I had no idea who he was talking about or why they might be coming here. "No. I'm sorry."

He glanced at the sky. "If they are coming tonight, they will be along soon."

"I didn't realize we were having a party."

He smirked. "We border the land of Zarahemla. They're not going to leave Ket out here with no protection."

"Shouldn't you greet Naomi?" I asked. But I knew that of course, he absolutely should greet his hostess.

The only reply he made was a small shrug, and he did not bid Naomi a greeting more than a slight nod I only saw because I was staring at him. His neglect was very rude, but none of the others seemed to think it strange of him. Perhaps proper manners were not as essential here as they were in the city.

"Who are Joshua and the others you mentioned?" I asked.

He looked down at me. "Ket's unit. From the army."

I bit my lip. The army? Was it as dire as that? "Do you think Lamanites will invade here?" Perhaps this was not the safe haven I had hoped it would be. But then, Zarahemla was definitely not a safe place to be in. Was Father safe? He was a high official. Would that help him? Or would that make it worse for him?

And what about Shad? Had he been inside the city when it fell? Had there been fighting? Was he wounded? Was he even alive?

"This is just a precaution," Kenai said. "You okay?"

I nodded. "Shad was there," I said after a moment.

"I know."

Somehow, that didn't surprise me.

But it did surprise me when Keturah approached us and he broke into a grin. She went straight into his arms for a quick hug.

"How've you been?" she asked him. "You're still too skinny."

He brushed her hand away from his stomach. "Sarai takes pity on us."

Zeke tried to pick Gabriel up, and Gabriel squawked.

Keturah turned. "I'll feed him," she told Zeke. Then she turned back to Kenai. "We'll talk later?" When he nodded, she went to Gabriel, lifted him from Zeke's arms, and took him inside the house.

I gave Kenai a small smile and moved to sit at the table. Everyone seemed to be staring at Zeke.

"Are you ready for one of your own?" Naomi asked him as she joined me at the table, gesturing for the others to join us as well.

The girls sat with us, but Kenai went to his heels near the fire round.

Zeke stood where he was and folded his arms. "I'm ready."

"How long now?"

"Leah says three weeks," Isabel said. "Eliza thinks tomorrow would be better."

Naomi smiled. "I recall feeling that way. I see you have all met Shad's friend, Olivia."

They all looked to me.

"We met on the road," I said. "I take it these are to be

your family. When Lamech weds his Sarai."

"They are my kinsfolk already," Naomi said. "Kenai is Keturah's elder brother."

My eyes shot to the fire round. Zeke had joined him, and they both sat on their heels. "I would not have guessed it. They don't look alike." I turned to Sarai and Isabel. "You two don't look very much alike, either."

They glanced at each other. "I look more like my father. Sarai was blessed to look like our mother."

"You are both beautiful," Naomi said diplomatically, but she did seem to mean it.

"Who do you favor, Olivia? Your mother or your father?"

I shrugged. "I never knew my mother. She died in childbirth."

They both voiced their apologies, but I just shrugged again. I hadn't even known her.

"You can call me Livi," I said, including Naomi in the invitation.

"That's pretty." Sarai had a soft, genuine voice.

"It was my mother's choice. My father honored it."

"He must have loved her very much."

"I think he did," I agreed, though I had never thought much about it. He had not remarried, and I never saw him with other women, even at parties for city officials.

"Are you going to marry Shad?"

"Isabel!" her sister scolded.

I could feel the heat rising in my cheeks, but I sat up straight. "That is not why I am here," I told them. "I was in need of protection and sustenance. Shad was kind enough to offer both. He brought me here to the safety of the farmstead."

I could see they both wanted to ask more questions, and I would have answered them honestly, but Zeke approached. As I turned to look up at him and got my first good look at his face, something about his expression seemed familiar.

"He had the foresight to get you out of Zarahemla before the invasion. It wasn't just kindness." He put an emphasis on the word kindness that I could not interpret, and the flair of familiarity made me uneasy.

I glanced between Zeke and the girls. "He didn't select me. He found me." But he *had* been looking for me, I reminded myself. "I'm nobody important."

"Shad must think you are."

I shook my head. Though Shad knew who my father was, he didn't treat me like someone special. But I looked down at my hands, recalling the way his family treated me—they had given me their only private bedroom, they had offered me their finest linens, and they had not let me complete any of the difficult chores. As much as they were able, they treated me like a princess. They must have gotten the idea from Shad.

Kenai joined us at the table and gestured toward the road.

Four men were emerging from the tree line. As they began to cross through the fields, one of them raised a hand in greeting.

More strangers. But when Kenai returned the greeting, I knew they were friends.

The others talked while the group of men approached, but I sat silently and observed them. Why did Keturah need six additional men to protect her? She was lovely and kind, but nothing more than a young mother in the country, far from cities and people of importance.

But whoever she was, these men did look like a team of bodyguards. One was dark-skinned and stocky. The other three were of medium build and coloring, and they were all carrying an assortment of weaponry. They looked comfortable, as if they had been here before—no gawking at the vastness of the field or looking as if they were trying to catch their bearing as they left the tree line.

Kenai and Zeke went out to greet them on the lane. The men slowed, and they stopped short of entering the yard.

I watched them talk to one another while I listened to the girls discuss Sarai's new house.

"We've not yet seen the house," Isabel said.

"Oh?" said Naomi. "It's quite nice. You will make it a lovely home in no time, Sarai."

"I do hope to," Sarai said.

Isabel giggled. "Somehow, Lamech doesn't strike me as the kind of man who wants a lovely home. Something rugged and serviceable, maybe."

Giving the men a last look, I turned my eyes back to the girls. "I disagree," I said. "I think Lamech is deserving of all things good and lovely."

They all glanced at each other and Isabel giggled.

"I do."

"I think so too," Naomi said, a small smile playing at her lips. "Perhaps he will show you the house while you're here," she said to Sarai.

But Sarai shook her head. "He wants to surprise me with it, to wait until we are married."

Isabel frowned. "That's ridiculous."

Sarai shrugged. "Whatever he wishes is fine with me."

Isabel folded her arms. "Well, don't let him have the only

say in everything. Your opinion matters, too."

Sarai surprised me by rolling her eyes. "I know," she told her sister.

"That's good advice," Keturah said as she came from the house with Gabriel. "But there are few things he would not do for Sarai. He's loved her since he was quite young."

They all laughed, and Sarai blushed prettily. It was true, and she obviously knew it as well as the rest of them.

"Lamech would give me anything I ask of him," Sarai said. "So I have to be careful with my requests." She looked pointedly at her sister.

They fell into a brief silence, and I filled it. "I think he would be mortified if he knew his womenfolk were talking about him like this."

They all laughed again.

"Talking about who?" Kenai asked as he came up behind his wife and put his hands on her shoulders.

Isabel ignored his question. "Will the other men need meals?"

He glanced back at them as they all ambled into the yard and began to remove scabbards and satchels.

"It's the least we can do," Naomi said. "Liam and the boys should be along soon."

There were plenty of women to prepare the food, and I felt like I was in the way. I went into the house and tried to rest, but my mind was too busy, so I set up the loom Naomi had given me and began to weave.

After a while, I recognized Liam's voice in the outside room and knew Shad's kinsmen had returned.

They were all family out there, and I felt very out of place.

When Naomi looked in to invite me outside to eat, she saw the loom and smiled.

"You do lovely work, Livi. You should bring it out and show the other girls."

I smiled sadly and set the loom aside. The other girls had been weaving all their lives. My work would not impress them.

"Perhaps tomorrow," I said.

Outside, everyone seemed to have a companion. Naomi had Liam. Keturah had Gid. Lamech had Sarai. All the others knew each other, and I knew no one.

I ate my food quietly, feeling disappointed that the bread hadn't turned out quite like Naomi's and Keturah's. It was flat and too hard. I didn't have an appetite for it, so I set the last bit of bread back on my dish and stared down at it, wishing I could get up and leave. At my father's parties, I could handle being lonely in a crowd of people. They were just people, shallow ones with whom I didn't want to be friends anyway.

I looked up from the bread. These people were loving and generous. They were faithful and had many talents and interests. Their company was rich and filled me with something I had never fully known. Meaning. Purpose. Self-respect.

But I was not a part of their circle. Not really. Not by their choosing.

"All finished?"

I looked up to see Zeke holding out his hand. For my dish?

"I...uh...yes."

He smiled warmly and took the dish from me. He turned and handed it smoothly to Sarai as she passed us.

The warmth in his smile surprised me because he hadn't spoken to me at all since his arrival. He had seemed moody, or perhaps just lost in his own thoughts. Naomi had said his wife was with child. Perhaps he was worried about becoming a father. I assumed that could weigh heavily on a man's mind.

He surprised me again when he sat beside me, and I wondered what I should say to him.

"You don't remember me," he said before I could think of anything.

I frowned. "Should I?"

"We've met. Several times."

I looked hard at his face. He did seem familiar.

"You might remember me like this."

He folded his arms across his chest, squinted his eyes, affecting a menacing glare, and scanned the yard.

I laughed when it came to me.

"On the Estate of Alma, was it not?"

He grinned. "You do remember me."

"You worked there or something, didn't you? But what are you doing here?" I glanced around at the barley farm, the humble homes, and the secluded valley in which they all sat.

He shrugged. "Gid asked me to come, so I came."

I lowered my voice. "But who is Keturah to need all these men to protect her?" I gestured to all the men who surrounded us. Several had eaten and were leaving the clearing.

He raised a brow. "Keturah is as close to a princess as our people have known in many years," he said. "Much like you."

"But I am no such thing."

"Paanchi's daughter? And what would you be if your father was made king?"

I looked down. "He is not king. He is not even Chief Judge."

"There are many who would yet see him made king."

Like Kish, who wanted to marry a royal heir.

"I am not of their political persuasions."

He folded his arms and leaned back, surveying the yard. "No?"

"I tire of my father's affiliations." I glanced over at Zeke. "He uses me in his political intrigues. It grows old."

"And heartbreaking, no doubt."

My eyes shot to his, which were warm and filled with compassion.

"I'm no expert on your life, Olivia, but I've seen him throw you to the wolves while he conducts business behind closed doors."

I felt a stone in the pit of my stomach.

"You handle yourself well," he said quietly. "Which makes me wonder why you are so quiet tonight."

I nibbled a thumbnail. "I can't be fake with these people who are so real, so genuine. I told you—that has grown old."

He nodded slowly.

"I should go inside," I said.

"Don't. Have you met the men?"

I looked across the cook fire. "No."

He rose. "I'll introduce you."

It seemed unnecessary. They would stay here for a while. I would stay here for a while. But soon, we would all go our separate ways.

I followed Zeke around the fire to meet four young men who all stood when we approached.

"Corban," Zeke said, indicating a handsome young man with a round face and big eyes.

Corban smiled at me and put a quick hand on my shoulder. He stepped back as Zeke introduced the others.

"Mathoni, Corban's kinsman."

Mathoni looked younger than Corban, but similar, with solid shoulders and the same bright eyes.

"Joshua," Zeke continued, indicating a good-looking young man who tossed his long hair out of his eyes before laying a hand on my shoulder and then stepping back and refolding his arms.

"And this stripling youth is Reb."

"Horeb," the dark-haired boy said. "After my father."

"It is my honor to meet you all," I said politely. "What are you all doing here?" I glanced around at the isolated farmstead.

"Watching the farm," Corban said.

"You can hardly protect it against an army," I pointed out.

"We're not looking for an army," Zeke said. "Not a Lamanite one, anyway."

I waited for further clarification on their presence, but none offered more information than that.

"I will wish you a good evening," I said to the men. Then I looked to Zeke. "But I do think I should go inside now."

He gave a short nod and walked with me to the house, but I paused before going through the door.

"What did you mean when you said Keturah was close to a princess?" I asked him, but my eyes followed her through the yard.

"She is the only daughter of Anti-Nephi Lehi. Have you heard of him?"

"Oh!" I had. "I have read of the Ammonites."

"Did you not know you were staying among them?" he asked when he saw my surprise.

"I thought the Ammonites had been given Jershon for an inheritance."

He shook his head. "Originally, but the armies are stationed there now." His eyes darkened. "Or, they were."

"They were unable to stop the Lamanite drive to Zarahemla?"

"Apparently. The city has assuredly been taken."

I swallowed past the lump in my throat.

Zeke put a hand on my shoulder — in farewell, in support maybe. "He'll be alright. They won't hurt him unless he resists the occupation."

I knew he spoke of my father. But I suspected my father had a hand in the Lamanite occupation. How could he not? And if he was involved, of course they would not harm him. They would set him up as a territorial king. Wouldn't they? Wasn't that the plan I had heard whispered in the closed rooms of my home?

No, the lump in my throat was not for my father. Nor was the ache in my chest. They were for the boy who had the foresight to get me out of the city before the Lamanites overthrew it. For the boy who had gone back to resist my father and the occupation he had arranged.

CHAPTER 10

I couldn't sleep that night. How could I? I didn't deserve sleep when so many of my people were prisoners inside the walls of our city and I was safe here in the land of Melek.

Why had Shad gotten me out of Zarahemla—me and no one else? He pretended it was nothing, but he had taken risks. Risks to his position in Zarahemla. Risks to his family. Was it only about the bruises? Was it only about the information I could give him? Or was there something bigger? Something so many of these men seemed to know about that I did not, though I knew more than I should and much more than I wanted to.

Sarai and Isabel slept quietly beside me, so I slipped out carefully, padded silently through the outer room and through the door into the cool outside air. Finally, I felt like I could take a breath.

I knew someone, one of the new men perhaps, would be on guard outside. He would be watching for dangers that didn't seem real to me. How could Lamanite warriors possibly be in Zarahemla? How could these men possibly protect this farm if soldiers appeared at its boundaries?

I thought perhaps I should pray, but I had never been

very sure if God heard prayers. I never doubted the existence of God, only that he would hear someone like me—a girl who was spoiled with riches, was often selfish, and could sometimes even say cruel things about others in a way I told myself was carefree but, in truth, was thoughtless. Maybe God heard other people's prayers—people like Naomi and Keturah, people who would heed His promptings. If promptings were real, then I had not been able to feel them in the cacophony of my father's home.

And if I could not hear the whisperings of God, and He would not hear me, then I had been striving to hold on to a religion that could not be true.

I groaned. I did not need to be doubting my faith just now. What I needed to do was figure out where I would go when Naomi at last suggested I leave. I couldn't stay here forever with this family. They were no kinsfolk of mine—not that any of my kinsfolk would harbor me. They would take me straight back home like a disobedient child. This was a temporary solution to my immediate problem with Father and Kishkumen.

Perhaps some of the men could tell me of other lands I might find refuge in. But then, perhaps we would all be seeking refuge soon.

I sat on a stool near the central fire, remembered how Lamech had lit it for me. I felt foolish all over again for asking him to light it but wished for the warm glow of a fire anyway.

"Olivia?"

I looked up into the dim night and recognized the man who drew near. "Gideon?"

"Couldn't sleep?"

"I am not used to retiring so early."

"Ah." He didn't remark on that further.

"Are you on watch?"

"I am." He stepped closer. "You're worried about your father."

I sighed. It was a good guess, but not the whole truth. "Father can take care of himself. I am more worried for Shad."

"Shad can take care of himself, too. And he took care of you, didn't he?"

"Indeed," I admitted. "He got me out of Zarahemla, but could he get himself safely out of an occupied city?"

Gideon absently fingered the knife at his belt as he scanned the darkness for hidden dangers. When he turned back to me, he said, "If anyone could do it, Shad could."

I worried a fingernail and wondered if Shad knew his brother had such confidence in him. "He went back because of me."

"Keturah told me." He paused. "You needn't worry. He's fine."

"How can you know that?" Would he say the holy spirit told him in his heart? Because, though I wanted to, I couldn't trust in that.

"He's the one who sent word about the takeover."

I sat up straighter. "Oh."

"Why do you think there are so many extra men on the grounds, Olivia?"

"Aren't they here for Keturah? She's some kind of princess or something."

I thought he smiled as he shook his head. "They're here for you."

"Me? But..."

"Those men who came looking for you? They're still looking, Olivia, and not just those two. Shad said to put extra men on the farm and keep you hidden, so I called in the men."

"I don't understand."

Gideon leaned forward, placing his elbows on his knees. "You're in more danger now than you ever were, even with Kishkumen." I caught a spark of the sparse moonlight in his eyes. "If Coriantumr places your father as a tribute king, he'll have every soldier in Zarahemla looking for you."

I nearly choked on my breath. "I should go," I said, my voice coming out in a hoarse whisper. "I should go. I knew I couldn't stay. I've put your whole family in danger. Keturah. Gabriel."

He surprised me with a chuckle. "We are not new to danger or hardship here. If you leave, I'll track you down and bring you back."

"Gideon." It wasn't possible for me to stay. It wasn't right of me. "Your son."

He stared hard at the ground for a moment before looking up at me the same way Shad and Liam and even Lamech did at times. "I won't raise my son to be afraid."

He was just as foolish as me.

"Fear is not tolerated on this farm," he continued.

"Fear is natural. It could save your life."

"Fear is the evidence of faithlessness."

I bristled. "Are all on this farm forced to have faith then?"

He chuckled again, the sound low and warm. "Of course not. It is only highly recommended."

A soft snort escaped, and I smothered a giggle.

"Have you not noticed this farmstead is in the middle of a very open field, Olivia?"

I thought of the long lane that led from the tree line, of how one could look down into the valley from the hills to the east and south. "I noticed."

"It is by design."

"Design?"

"So that we may know from whom our protection comes."

"It is ridiculous to tempt fate, if that is what you mean."

He snorted too, and not softly. "I have come to see some wisdom in it." He paused. "But it has taken most of my life."

The breeze rustled in the plants of the field. "I should just take a watch at night," I said when he did not say more. "I am always awake."

He made no reply. I thought he might leave and return to whatever it was he did while he was on watch. I sensed he wanted to leave, to keep his attention where it should be. But a part of me did not want him to leave me alone.

"I was afraid," I said to keep him there a little longer. "Of Kishkumen. If I hadn't been afraid, I would not have had the courage to leave."

He still made no reply, and I had to look hard to be sure he was still there across from me in the shadows.

"Fear motivates us to do things complacency keeps us from doing."

It almost surprised me when he finally said simply, "You're right." He paused another moment. "You should try to sleep, Olivia."

I stood. "I think I will." I walked toward the house but hesitated as I passed Gideon. "You said you've had a letter from Shad?"

"A short missive, yes."

"When is he coming home, please?"

I thought he smiled again.

"Soon."

I was very pleased at the news, and I fell asleep thinking of the boy who had taken me from the filthy streets of Zarahemla. The boy who had blushed when I had offered to pay for the food he had given me. The boy who had swallowed down his anger when he had seen that girl, Miriam, with another boy in the forest.

The other girls must have been very quiet when they arose, because I didn't hear either of them get up or leave the room. I slept late, and they let me. By the time I went out of doors, all of the men had eaten and gone.

Naomi passed me a dish of grain and sat by me while I ate it. I wondered if there was something she wanted to say because she never sat idle.

But she remained quiet, and eventually I licked my lips and said, "Gideon told me Shad will be home soon."

"Those boys!" she exclaimed lovingly. "I am the last to know everything."

"Honestly, I think that is for the best."

She smiled, but I could easily see it was not with happiness. "Me too," she confided.

"It is wash day," I said.

She patted my hand and smiled again, and this time she did seem to cheer up. "The boys have already hauled the water."

We each carried a large basket full of linens to the small wash hut between the homes. I didn't relish the thought of burning my hands in the hot water, and when Naomi edged me away, I gratefully let her.

"Where is Keturah?" I asked. "And Isabel and Sarai?"

Naomi shrugged. "She'll be along."

But Keturah did not come to the wash hut that day. Indeed, I did not see her until the evening when she strode into

122

the yard with Corban and Mathoni, each holding a bucket filled with arrowheads which they set in the shade of the house.

Isabel and Sarai showed up much earlier. Kenai and Lamech had taken them into town for the market. Each man carried a bundle under his arm, and Isabel and Sarai each carried a basket filled with goods.

"I've brought you a treat."

I turned to see Sarai approaching as I took the tunics from the drying line.

"I miss market days," I said as I folded the last of the tunics and placed it in the basket.

She smiled like she understood and then held out a brilliant pink fruit in her hand.

The fruit of the dragon was rare in the northern parts of the land, but I had seen many on my father's tables. They were one of my favorites, and I grinned as I accepted her gift.

"Thank you! But here, I've only one of your husband's clean tunics to give you in return."

"And one that needs mending, at that," she said as she took the topmost tunic from the basket and inspected it.

"I've no notion of how to mend it," I admitted.

"I can show you." She was both confident and sincere.

"I'll take you up on that." I lifted the heavy basket and followed her to the shade of the house where she sat, took a needle and other supplies from her satchel, and showed me how to mend.

It was not hard, but making stiches as small and precise as hers was going to be a challenge, I could see.

"Can you sew clothing, also?" I asked her after we had gone through all the tunics to see that they were intact and ready for wear.

123

"I can. And costume for dance."

"And your wedding gown?"

"Of course."

"I've some cloth, enough now I think. Might you show me how to make a lovely tunic like this?"

I fingered the sleeve of her unique and beautiful top, admiring the stitching there.

"I would like nothing so much as to sit here and sew all day," she laughed. "Bring me your cloth."

As I rose, I glanced at Naomi, hoping she did not have another chore for me to do. She was paying me no attention, so I quickly slipped inside the house and retrieved the piece of cloth I had been working on.

When I dropped the folded material into her lap, I could tell immediately that Sarai liked it.

"This is lovely," she said as she felt it. "You made this?"

"I did. Naomi showed me how."

"Did she not start you on something easy?"

I frowned at the cloth. "She started me on this."

"Well," she said. "This will be such a delight. Stand and we shall measure you."

She pulled the measuring implements from her satchel, and I presumed this was not her first request for sewn clothing.

"I almost hate to cut it," she said when she had marked out a pattern onto the cloth.

"But just think of the beautiful dress it will make."

"I'm thinking I will have to borrow it."

It felt good to laugh, to think of something besides my father trapped inside the walls of Zarahemla, besides Shad's stark little house in the city.

"This is a Lamanite style." Sarai was poised to cut the

fabric with her sharp implements, but she hesitated, waiting for me.

"I've no objection to that. The style is pretty and quite flattering on you. I only wonder where you saw it."

Carefully, her brows drawn in, she began to cut the cloth, and I understood what she meant when she said she hated to cut it. But I could see she was expert at it, her lines straight and fine.

When she was done, and not before, she said, "I spent some time in the Land of Nephi. All the women wear dresses like this. Belted." She indicated her own thick belt. "And bunched here at the waist."

That was the part that was so pretty. "I especially like that the shoulders are covered."

There were a hundred ways to tie a sarong, and I tied mine to cover as much of myself as possible. With all my father's friends gawking at me as they came through my home, it was wisdom and made me more comfortable. Kish hated it, which was another reason I tied my sarong the way I did.

It took several afternoons to sew the dress together and many more afternoons to do the embellishments that Sarai thought necessary for one of her creations. I helped with the sewing, but sat by and watched her embellish the neck and sleeves with embroidery that was exquisite, much too exquisite for what I planned to do with the dress, which was to wear it for work on the farm. But I had worked hard in Naomi's finest sarongs, and I would work hard in Sarai's beautiful dress, too.

The dress was done by the time Kenai said it was time they started for home.

"We have to make the preparations for the ceremony," Zeke said over their final meal with us. "And you have enough additional watchmen now."

125

Before they left, I took Sarai's hands in mine. "Your fingers must be bleeding by now!"

She brushed the comment aside. "It was a pleasant way to pass the time here. I will be back in a few months and we will sew another for you. And will you make me some cloth like yours? Perhaps with brown as the accent color?"

I hugged her tight. "I will."

I was wearing the dress, white shot through with the blue threads, and the longboots Shad had bought me, not many days later when I arrived for the evening meal and found Shad sitting at the table apprising his brothers of the situation in Zarahemla.

I stopped in my tracks, aware that I was staring but not able to look anywhere else.

Shad looked different. He was not shaven. His clothing was rumpled as if he had slept in it for a week or more. There was a shadow in his eyes, a hollowness, that made me wish I had told him nothing about my father and had never accepted his offer of help. He looked older than the boy who had rescued me in Zarahemla.

When he looked up, I was both gratified and surprised that he didn't seem to be able to look away from me, either. But my dress was new and clean and my hair was done neatly in one of Sarai's knots at my neck. My hands were clean, though not as smooth as the last time he had seen me, and my eyes were clear, as I was very well rested, despite my ongoing inability to sleep when it was dark.

"Has she done nothing but groom herself since I left?" he barked out.

There was silence for a moment. Then Liam stood, crossed his arms over his thick chest, and glared at his son.

Shad jumped to his feet and strode to me. He placed a quick hand on my shoulder. Well, he reached forward, but stopped short of my shoulder. He brushed his hands together and tried again. The touch was light and very brief.

"It's nice to see you again," he said. "I'm sorry." He brushed a hand over his eyes and looked back at his father. "I'm tired. I've been on the road for a few weeks."

I glanced at Liam too. He had not returned to sitting. Naomi put a hand on his forearm, and he looked down at her. Finally, he sat.

"You smell as if you've been on the road for a few weeks," I said and waved a hand in front of my nose.

Shad blanched and took a small step back.

I laughed, and when the others heard it, the tension melted away. "I'm kidding! You smell fine, but you could use a sharp blade for your face." Feeling silly, I reached out and scrubbed a few fingers over the whiskers on his cheek. "And I can launder your things. I think I owe you that at least."

"You don't owe me anything," he mumbled.

"But you are wrong," I said, stepping closer so my voice could be low. "I owe you everything."

He looked at me and winced.

I frowned. That was not the reaction I had imagined.

He rubbed the back of his neck. "We need to talk."

I stood up straighter. "We are talking."

He glanced over his shoulder at his family members who were only pretending not to listen in.

"We need to talk," he repeated.

"About what?"

"Later." He turned abruptly and went back to the table.

The others didn't seem as if they knew what Shad

wanted to talk about. If Shad was here, whole and hearty, then the news could only be about my father. But why did he not just say what it was?

It must be bad. The way he winced. The way he wouldn't look me in the eye. The way he mumbled when he spoke to me. There was something bad he didn't want to tell me.

But I could see he had no plans to tell me now, and I had no notion of how to coax the information from him.

"Livi, are you ready?"

Naomi was standing with the large pot on her hip. She had divided the food among the dishes, and everyone was either looking at me or trying not to.

I swallowed, gave a quick nod, and hurried toward the big table where the family was seated together. I closed my eyes as Liam said a prayer of thanks for Shad's safe arrival home, and I wished I could keep them closed forever against the longing I had to be part of a family like this one, and against the bad news Shad had traveled here to give me.

If my father had been captured, I didn't want to hear it. I would avoid Shad, and he would never be able to tell me. It was simple. I would stay in Naomi's company or Keturah's or Liam's. He would never catch me alone.

Until the early hours of the night when everyone else had gone to sleep.

Of course I was not asleep. But I had not anticipated Shad would take a turn at the watch this night. He had spent days traveling. Had his family no care for his wellbeing?

I sighed. I knew they did, and if he was awake, it was deliberate.

It was too late to go back into the house. He saw me immediately. He was waiting for me.

I pulled my shawl around me and straightened my shoulders.

The shadows and light played just right on his face. He was so handsome it was hard to believe what he said to me.

Without a word, I turned and walked away from him. I went toward the wash hut. It was either there or toward the forest that scared me.

"Olivia." He jogged to catch up to me. "Did you hear what I said?"

Did he think I hadn't seen him there? How could I have missed the words that tumbled out into the silence between us?

"Your father is dead, Olivia."

CHAPTER 11

I stopped and whirled to face him. I pulled my shawl even tighter around me and started to search his face in the moonlight, but there was no need to search. His words were the truth. I closed my eyes and let my head fall forward in despair.

It just wasn't possible. It was not in keeping with the plans I had overheard.

"Coriantumr. He wouldn't kill him." I looked up at him and slowly backed away from him, from what he was telling me.

"It wasn't…Olivia…"

I looked up into his face. This person who had saved me. This person who had just told me I had no family left on this earth.

"It wasn't Coriantumr. The Lamanites are the least of our worries." He scrubbed at his eyes. "They carried out your father's sentence."

"What sentence?"

"The Zarahemlans. They put him on trial."

"That was months ago. It came to nothing."

He stared into my eyes.

"It came to nothing," I repeated.

Kishkumen had seen to that.

Shad closed the distance I had created. "Those weeks you were hidden in the cook's quarters. Did you not know your father had been taken by the magistrates?"

"What?"

"How did you think Kish got in? How did you think he got the run of your father's house?"

"Father told me. The business with the courts and the trial came to nothing."

Shad slowly shook his head in the moonlight.

"They sentenced him to death, Livi. For crimes against the government." He reached up as if he would wipe the tear from my cheek. "It was carried out before—"

"You!" I slapped his hand away from me.

He pulled his hand back, startled. "Livi! What—?"

"You!" I stepped back, barely recognizing how weak my knees felt.

"Livi." Shad's voice turned low. Calming. Patronizing.

"You know exactly what!"

"Livi, keep your voice down."

"Don't call me that!"

Was that a smile hiding behind his eyes?

"*Olivia*, keep your voice down. You'll have Enos and Jared here in a matter of moments."

I had no idea who Enos and Jared were. The only thing I knew was that Shad had betrayed me. Father might have been less than righteous in the ways of the Church, but he wasn't evil. And he was all the family I had.

"You testified, didn't you? You gave them the final evidence they needed."

His jaw tightened, and his silence said more to me than his words ever could.

132

I turned on my heel. I had to get out of his presence.

Shad's hand shot out, and he grabbed my elbow. "Olivia!"

He had the nerve to be exasperated with *me*?

"I had nothing to do with your father's sentence or carrying it out. It's the biggest news in Zarahemla."

I could tell he hadn't wanted to say the horrible truth so bluntly. Still, I tried to pull my arm free from his grasp.

"That's not what I went back for," he insisted.

"I don't believe you!"

"With your father dead, there is no one to break your betrothal to Kishkumen." He paused. "There is only one way to legally break it."

I stopped struggling and glanced back at him.

"You would kill Kishkumen for me?"

His jaw tightened again, and I realized it did not mean yes. It meant no. I sighed. It was a bad idea and morally repugnant as well. Still, death was the only way out of it now.

"I asked a friend what could be done. A powerful friend."

"And what can be done?"

He looked down to where he held my elbow and slowly released it. "Nothing," he mumbled and stepped away.

But he was wrong. I could always throw myself from a very tall cliff.

"Come on, I'll walk you back," Shad said after a moment.

I hesitated, but let him follow me slowly back to the fire round. I didn't want to go into the house. I wasn't sure I could be quiet enough. I knew once I let myself cry, the sobs would not be silent.

"Are you okay?" Shad asked awkwardly.

I was biting my nail down to the quick. I didn't even try to stop doing it.

"Livi."

I wasn't sure if I turned into his chest or he pulled me there, but before I knew it, I was an uncontrollable mess against him. Even as I broke apart, I wished I could appreciate being wrapped in Shad's arms.

I couldn't say why, but I trusted his touch. I knew Keturah had been right when she said he was made to protect women, not harm them. He was, and I didn't know all the reasons why, but I did need protection. Kish was out there looking for me, and he was a bad man. If what Shad said was true, and I had no reason to believe he lied, I no longer had my father or his wealth to protect me.

I was completely alone in the world.

But I was standing in Shad's arms, and I didn't feel alone.

His hands ran over my back as I cried and down my hair. He didn't say anything—probably didn't know what to say— just let me grieve for my father while the moon worked its way through the watch.

Eventually, I sniffed. "How come I didn't know?"

He didn't answer.

"Father said everything was okay."

"He was trying to appeal the decision."

"They let him come home."

"He was still a respected man with many followers. The judges feared a revolt."

I backed away from Shad, embarrassed. I stared at the spot on his tunic where my tears had soaked it.

"If he knew this, if he knew he was condemned, why did he not make provisions for me?"

I was not really asking Shad, but he answered.

"He did. He thought Kishkumen would take care of you."

I snorted indelicately.

"He expected you would go to Kishkumen's house." He paused. "Perhaps that was why he pushed to have it done with."

I shook my head slowly. "It's nice of you to say that." We both knew it wasn't true. Father had used me as a bargaining chip and had not given any thought to my desires.

"Olivia, you can stay here. You know that, right?"

"No." I would have to run for the rest of my life, away from Kish. "I'll need to find work." Somewhere far away, somewhere he would never think to look for me.

Shad was silent again. He was probably thinking how incapable I was of obtaining any kind of employment.

"Your mother says I could sell my linens. I don't know how to do that, but I can learn."

Again, he was silent.

"Your family has been very hospitable."

"I knew they would be." He stepped away and ran a hand over his eyes. "Olivia, your father can no longer offer Kishkumen a position of power in the government. Perhaps he will no longer seek the alliance."

I remembered crawling from the hard, stone floor in my father's house. "He will claim what is his."

"But you're not his!"

The outburst made me look sharply over at him. "That makes no difference to him."

"We will figure something out."

We.

"Shad?"

"I don't know yet. We'll find some way."

"You'll still help me?"

"Well, yes, Olivia...yes. Did you think we would abandon you?"

We. He and his kinsfolk. He and his kinsfolk would figure something out. He still saw me as a charitable project. Just a girl who was helpless.

"Did you think I would take you from your home and then just leave you alone in the world?"

"Yes."

The word was heavy in the silence between us. It was a sad word. An honest word.

"I *am* alone in the world."

I heard him let out a breath. He took a slow step closer to me.

"You don't have to be."

I wasn't sure I had heard him right.

"Crying on your shoulder is not the same as belonging to your family."

"Olivia, I've been waiting out here—"

"Stop calling me Olivia! I told you in Zarahemla it's Livi."

He looked perplexed and backed away, rubbing the wet spot on his tunic. "I was waiting out here to ask you something," he tried again. "See, the only way for you to avoid marriage to Kishkumen is to break the betrothal agreement."

I frowned. "I thought the only way was to hurl myself from a tall cliff."

He chuckled.

"I wasn't joking."

"I guess there's that way too."

"There is another way? Legally?"

"How much do you know of marriage law?"

"I know I am legally bound to marry Kish."

"Unless one of you breaks the betrothal contract."

I shook my head. "I already told you. Kish will hunt me until the end of time. That is why I must leave. I'm a danger to your family. Kish won't break the contract."

"Then you must."

"Please point me to the nearest tall cliff and I shall see it done promptly."

I expected him to chuckle again, but he said, "You can marry someone else, someone who will overlook the betrothal and recognize it as false."

Another deep silence fell over us while he let me consider the idea. I heard an owl in the night, his call coming softly from the direction of the trees.

"My watch is over," Shad said.

"That would infuriate Kish. He would hunt harder if he knew I was married."

"Would you rather be married to him?"

"I told you. I would rather die than be married to him."

"So you will agree?" He glanced back toward the trees. But it was so dark, I doubted he could see anything in them.

"I will agree," I said carefully. I clenched my fists so I would not put my thumbnail between my teeth. "Who would I have to marry?"

He took a step away. His voice was hard when he said, "Someone slightly more palatable than Kishkumen. But I guarantee he won't be some fancy learned man from your father's parties, Princess."

"Sha—"

"I have to go. You should go to bed."

Why was everyone always telling me that?

I watched his shadow stalk off into the night, watched him pass a boy who had arrived for the next shift of the watch.

By the time I got up in the morning, something was different on the farmstead. Liam was more watchful of me than usual, and Naomi was extra nice to me, doing things for me she had been letting me do for weeks now. Maybe I was imagining it, but everyone seemed to be more careful with what they said. More polite. I thought we had become closer over the weeks, but they treated me like a guest again.

Had Shad told them I would be leaving? Had he and his kinsfolk found a man who would marry me? Shad was nowhere to be seen. He couldn't have possibly told them anything yet.

I watched as Liam and Lamech gathered their tools and set off toward the home they were finishing for Sarai. I glanced at all the others, busy with their morning chores, and I darted after the men.

When I caught up to them, they both gave me identical quizzical looks.

"Did you need something?" Liam asked.

Yes. To know what is going on here.

"Can I see the house?"

Liam actually smiled and nodded. "It's all but done. We could use a woman's opinion."

Lamech snorted. "Isabel said it was good. Keturah too."

"And I'm sure that it is," I said.

"It's nothing like you're used to."

I bristled. "How do you know what I'm used to?"

He glanced at me. "I don't," he admitted.

"And you certainly don't know my tastes."

138

He shrugged a shoulder and kept walking.

When we neared the house, I could see immediately that it was not like the plain house his parents lived in, nor like Gideon and Keturah's. The most noticeable difference was a high fence around a courtyard that already had ornamental plants growing in it. There were carvings on the framework of the door and windows on either side of it covered by screens that could be removed. A large stone fireplace was at the center of the courtyard. I was already impressed and felt a longing for a place like this of my own.

The inside of the home boasted four rooms and had carvings on the wood in each of them. There were tables and pallets and chairs in each of the rooms. A room at the back had barrels that would be filled with squash and corn, a cook stove, and a large basin. Dried herbs hung from the ceiling.

The other back room had only a table near the window. Liam went to it and pulled back the mat, tying it to the side. The room was filled with light from the morning sun. I stepped to the table and turned back to Lamech.

"For sewing," he said. "Sarai can keep her fabrics and supplies in here."

I ran my fingers over the smooth table. It was even polished so as not to snag any of the cloth. It was thoughtful, and exquisitely done.

"Until you have too many children to fit in the other sleeping chamber," I said lightly, but my heart was achingly full. Sarai deserved this beautiful home and this thoughtful husband.

Liam laughed. Lamech was leaning against the door frame. He looked down at the floor and smiled.

"I like it very much, Lamech. It is the loveliest home I have ever seen. Your bride is very lucky."

"I'm going to get started in the other room," Liam said and, brushing past me, he left.

"It's just a house," Lamech said, scanning the room.

"It's a home where you will raise your family," I said. "I can feel a warmth here already." I paused. "It makes me wonder what is wrong at your parents' house."

"What do you mean?"

I fingered a carving on the door. "Is there something amiss between you and Keturah?"

He sighed heavily. "There always has been."

"Do you dislike her?"

"No." He seemed surprised. "She dislikes me."

I frowned. "She told me she admires you. She adores the way you are with Sarai."

His brows shot up. "When we first met, she saw me as an intrusion. She was falling in love with Gid, and she didn't want me there."

"It is a nice thing that you both love Gideon so well, but I think you have both been mistaken."

He ran a hand through his hair and sighed again. "If you noticed it, it's a bigger problem than I've wanted to admit."

"I think perhaps one conversation could mend it," I suggested and laughed when he grimaced. "Then for Sarai's sake," I said. "To complete the atmosphere you have created here in this home before you wed and bring her to the farmstead."

He nodded slowly. "I will consider it. You're planning to attend the wedding in Melek, right?"

"Your mother invited me. I hope it's okay with you."

He seemed surprised. "Of course."

"I'm dying to get a little time away from the farm."

I blushed, suddenly realizing that sounded ungrateful.

"We all feel that way sometimes," he said graciously.

Graciousness! I could tell he was very happy about Sarai and their wedding and this home to live in with her.

"Gideon said it would be safer to take me, since everyone is going."

"He's right. We already discussed it."

I leaned against the table and folded my arms. "I admit, it sounds like all business, but to be the guest at a wedding... Well, I'm not ashamed to tell you, I'm looking forward to it."

He seemed surprised again. "It's not all business. You're part of the family now."

I shook my head. "That's kind, but I know I'm not."

Lamech had been smiling and easy since we entered the house, but his eyes sharpened. "Shad said you have agreed to marry."

"Oh, yes. He said he could find someone to marry me. Someone less despicable than Kish. To break the contract."

Lamech snorted again, and it sounded like a laugh.

Involuntarily, I smoothed down my dress and checked to see that my hair was still in place. "You think it won't work. I told him it wouldn't."

He was concentrating very hard on his sandals, not wanting to tell me how futile he thought the plan would be.

"You don't think he can? Find someone willing, I mean?"

"I'm..." He coughed. "You should ask Shad."

"He could probably use some assistance. He has his obligations in Zarahemla. I know you're busy, but maybe some of the other men could help him search for someone who would do it."

"I guess he didn't tell you he's back for good."

"No. He's not to live in Zarahemla anymore?"

His eyes were bright, almost as if he were laughing. "Olivia, what if Shad had to do it himself?"

"Do what? Marry me?"

"Would that be an acceptable solution to you?"

I frowned. "To me, of course, but I prefer not to shackle him in some farce of a marriage."

He folded his arms. "You wouldn't think of it as a real marriage?"

"Shad should marry someone he loves," I said quietly. "He deserves that. He has already done enough. I thought perhaps some very old man whose wife had died or...perhaps someone very, um...ugly."

Lamech squeezed his eyes tight, then he shook his head and said, "Come on. You've seen enough. I think I hear my mother calling you."

I rolled my eyes, but as I walked out, I said, "Truly, your home is beautiful, Lamech. Sarai will be happy here."

"Thank you," he said simply.

I didn't see Liam on my way out, so I bid Lamech farewell and set off toward the main house.

Both Shad and Lamech made it seem possible, but marriage would not set me free from Kishkumen. Even if it was legal to marry a man while I was legally betrothed to another, it could only prevent the marriage to Kish. It wouldn't prevent him from finding me and taking me back to Zarahemla.

The thought sent shivers down my arms. Despite the trouble I knew I had caused this family, I was grateful for their willingness to take me in. And though I felt vulnerable—I knew it was just a matter of time until one of Kish's men got word of my presence here—I felt safe for now, as safe as I could be, here on the farmstead with these men who had been trained as soldiers.

For all Kish's threatenings, I did not think he had ever been trained to fight. I did not think he had ever volunteered to go to a battle. His loyalties were to himself and himself only. There was some small comfort in that, and perhaps his selfishness would save me from him in the end.

It was a compelling thought, safety, but I knew I would not sleep at night until Kishkumen was no longer breathing.

Naomi was bustling about the yard as usual, and she smiled warmly at me when I lifted a stack of dishes from her hands. I wondered if she would be as warm if Shad did volunteer to marry me to keep me safe from Kish. What would she think of me stealing her youngest son's life like that?

What would I think of myself?

CHAPTER 12

Over the weeks that passed, many of Gideon's friends came to help with the constant watch over the farm and I began to recognize them, but Gideon was on guard duty the night before we left for the wedding. He sat alone at the main fire round, but of course there was no fire in it.

He looked up when I stepped from the house. He seemed to be expecting me. By now, they all expected me to be up in the night.

I sat across from him and pulled my blanket around me.

"Aren't you cold?" I asked.

"No." He paused. "And if I was, I certainly wouldn't show it."

"But there is no one here to see. Just me. And I wouldn't tell."

He cracked his neck and then folded his arms across his chest. "There are two men patrolling the perimeter of the farm."

I nodded. "And you are watching the houses."

Even after observing the men on watch nearly every night, I still did not understand how it worked or how they could see anything out here in the darkness. Knowing they were up watching did give me a measure of comfort, but mostly, it seemed like they were wasting their efforts.

"Well, they are not very good friends if you can't be cold in front of them."

I thought he might have chuckled.

"You should get some sleep before we leave tomorrow."

"I know. I haven't adjusted yet to the time kept on the farm. Sometimes I think I will always be on the time kept at my father's house." I looked up at the moon. "I do try to sleep."

He stood. "Well, hopefully once you marry, you will feel more secure. Perhaps it will help you sleep."

I couldn't think of any reply. It was a nice thought, but I doubted marrying would be the answer to all my problems. It would probably just compound them.

"Right now, Shad's acting like a martyr, but I think it will be good for him."

"I don't understand," I said, pulling my eyes back down to him.

"Mutually beneficial."

Maybe I was already asleep, because I didn't understand a word Gideon said. I yawned.

"You're tired."

Shaking my head, I just smiled wryly. "Even being tired does not make me sleep."

He was silent for a moment. Then he said, "Keturah could give you something. An herb maybe."

I yawned again. "Is there such a thing?"

"I'll ask her."

"No. I'll ask. You needn't trouble yourself."

He was silent again.

It was true, what that Miriam had said. Shad was the easiest to get along with of all the brothers, even if he had been acting strange since he arrived home. Gideon and Lamech's frequent silences made having a conversation difficult. Still, I thought they were both very kind and even friendly once you got to know them.

"Will I meet Jashon?" I asked. Hadn't Miriam said Jashon was more personable?

Gideon's eyes were scanning the darkness. "He will be in Melek."

"What's he like?"

His eyes turned back to me. "Does it matter?"

I yawned again.

"Olivia, go get in bed."

"You can call me Livi."

He grunted.

"I won't sleep. I can't."

"It's a long journey. You need to."

"Don't you?"

He sat down again. "I've been keeping watch my whole life. I'm quite used to it."

"And I'm used to being awake nights."

I heard him take a deep breath and let it out. "I think I understand," he said. "But it would be much more appropriate to speak to him when you're not in your nightclothes."

Was he laughing? And what did he mean? Speak to who?

Shad.

Obviously. Oh, I was so dumb.

"That's not why I'm up."

"I believe you."

He didn't sound like he believed me.

"I was up nights even before he came home."

147

"Sure."

"Gideon."

He *was* laughing. He was teasing me.

"I'm going in," I said and got up.

"Okay."

"You're infuriating," I said as I stomped toward the house, but his teasing made my heart light, and my heart hadn't been light in a very long time.

His low chuckle followed me into the house. When I crept silently across the floor, a skill I had perfected, I didn't let myself look at Shad's sleeping form across the room, as if that would prove to Gideon that I hadn't been waiting for him. But just before I slipped into the other room, I relented and cast a glance toward him.

He wasn't sleeping. He was leaning up on his elbow with his head resting on his hand. He was watching me, and he wasn't smiling.

The feel of eyes watching me in the dark sent my mind suddenly to a long-forgotten memory, making the shadows even darker. A memory of Kish lurking in the shadows near my chamber at Father's. The party was loud. The guests were drunken. Father had long since retreated to his office with the men of the government. Sometimes Kish went with them, but not that night. I had shut my door as quickly as possible and been thankful for my lock. And I was thankful it had been a thick wood door, nothing like the simple mat at my back now.

I stared back at Shad. Was he the reason I was up? Roaming the yard like I owned the place?

We stared at each other for so long, it seemed awkward to speak, and besides, it might wake his parents. But he finally said, "Goodnight, Olivia," and lay his head back down.

It sounded more like a command than a pleasantry, but I whispered, "Goodnight," and slipped through the mat.

Most of the preparations for travel had been made the evening before, so when dawn came, we were already gathering to leave the farmstead. Gideon and Keturah had arrived at the main house, and Shad was bent at the waist, walking with Gabriel. Lamech was pacing.

I was resigned to walk to Melek alone but consoled myself with the thought of attending a wedding with real guests and food of all kinds and laughing and dancing. For all I disliked the people at my father's parties, I had liked the parties. I liked the movement and the colors and partaking in the happiness of others. Not all the people had been bad, especially when we attended occasions on the Estate of Alma. That was where I had first seen Zeke, and probably Gideon, as well, though I didn't remember ever seeing him there.

I set out alone, but I did not walk alone for long.

"Who were you going out to see last night?"

I started at the sudden question. I hadn't realized Shad was so close behind me.

"You," I said without turning.

He came to my side.

"Why don't I believe that?"

I shrugged. "I doubt you would believe anything I said. You think I am a spoiled princess with nothing to offer the world."

It was snide, but he had been snide and prickly since making the offer to find someone to marry me and make my contract with Kishkumen void. If he hadn't wanted to help me, he shouldn't have come back for me in the dark and decrepit house in Zarahemla.

I guessed he didn't know what to say to that because he fell quiet, but he stayed by my side.

When the sun was well above the horizon, he said, "That's not what I think of you. I don't think you're spoiled."

It was a game. He thought I was a spoiled princess and also a helpless waif.

I looked around. "Why don't you walk with someone else?"

He scratched the back of his head. "I want to walk with you."

I sighed. "I don't have any more information about my father or Kishkumen and his band of thieving friends, and to be frank, I don't think I would confess to you if I did." It would place too much of a burden on him.

He winced. "I like your hair like that."

I put my hand up to the intricate bun Sarai had shown me to make. "Thank you?"

"Is that a question?"

I frowned. "I can be of no more use to you, Shad. You needn't compliment me so falsely."

"It's not false. But I liked it the way you used to do it, too. At the events in Zarahemla."

When my eyes shot to him, his cheeks colored.

I frowned again. "What do you mean?"

Shad glanced back over his shoulder. When I glanced back, too, I saw Gabriel was walking between Gideon and Keturah, holding to one of each of their hands. Gideon was smirking at his brother and Keturah reached over to smack him in the chest, as if to tell him to quit it. When Gideon caught my eye, he tried to wipe the smile from his face with the palm of his hand, but his eyes were filled with humor.

150

I looked to Shad again, the red making its way to the tips of his ears, and I wondered if there was any truth in what he was saying.

I don't want that.

I remembered him flushing red in his neat little house in the city that first morning.

Or rather, it is not mine to take.

I did not know what to make of him. Either he was using me to further his career, or he wasn't. Either he was trying to get more information out of me, or he wasn't. Either he wanted to help me be free from a marriage to the horrid Kish, or he didn't.

"I was glad when you came back to the farm," I said tentatively. It wasn't like me to be shy, but I sensed he was being genuine — and that changed the rules of the game.

He looked at the ground in front of us. "I'm sorry it took so long. I hurried."

"Because of me?"

He snorted softly. "I didn't come home to see Gid."

A slow smile spread over my face. I couldn't help it and I glanced back at Gideon again, but he was busy with his son, who was fussing and ready to be carried.

"Are you saying if I wasn't here, you wouldn't have come?"

"Definitely not."

"Not even for the wedding?"

"I would have met them in Melek."

"Shad?"

"Hmm?"

"Did we ever meet in the city?"

"No."

"You're so sure?"

"Yes. I was to make it a point that we never meet."

"What do you mean?"

He sighed, a heavy and regretful sigh. "Olivia—"

"I told you to stop calling me that."

He laughed. "You also told me to stop calling you Livi. So, which is it to be?"

I laughed too. "Whatever you like best, I suppose."

He cleared his throat. "I'll think on it. Your father referred to you as Olivia, and that was the name I knew you by."

"What do you mean?"

He rubbed the back of his neck, a gesture I was starting to realize meant he wasn't comfortable with what we were talking about. "Did you think your father let you out into the city alone?"

"Of course." But with all my father's secret plans coming to light, I wasn't sure what to believe about him. He was a good father to me. I loved him. I knew he loved me. But I knew he wasn't a completely honorable man. I turned to look up into Shad's face. "Didn't he?"

He slowly shook his head. "He didn't."

The truth of it slowly began to dawn on me. It all made sense, and it wasn't the shock it would have been two moons ago. "That's why all of Kish's reprehensible friends were always around, wasn't it?"

He stared into my eyes for a moment, then winced and looked away. "What would you say if I told you I was one of Kish's reprehensible friends?"

He couldn't possibly like Kish, even if he associated with him—*especially* if he associated with him. Shad wasn't like Kish. It wasn't something I merely knew, it was something I felt in the deepest part of my heart. He had handled me like a wounded animal, had picked out simple but pretty clothes for me in the market. He had brought me to a haven far from Zarahemla and told his family I was something special, something I really wasn't. He had called for the extra men to guard the grounds where I stayed.

I thought of the men who had come looking for me and what it would mean for Shad to betray Kishkumen and whoever he worked for. Perhaps this was all some elaborate trap, but it didn't feel like a trap.

Was he their friend? Or was he mine?

"I would say it was not even possible." I looked around at all the people traveling with us—his kinsmen and women, his friends. "Your loyalties lie with your true friends." I worried a lip. "I envy you your friends, Shad. I have never had a true friend."

"I know," he said quietly.

Gabriel was still fussing behind us. He didn't want to be carried, but he had already walked a long way for a child who couldn't yet walk on his own. Keturah offered him a bit of corn cake, but he shrieked, and I presumed he did not want that either.

Shad glanced back. "Maybe I should walk him again."

But when I turned to see him, Gideon whisked his son up and plopped him onto his shoulders, and Gabriel squealed in delight.

It was Shad's turn to smirk. "It's weird to see him being a father."

I gave Gideon one last look. "What do you see him as instead?"

Shad frowned. "A fighter. A warrior."

"Perhaps he has changed."

153

He looked surprised. "Why would he want to?"

I shrugged. "Necessity? There is a little boy who needs a father, but there are no enemies on the farm."

"But there could be at any time."

"Why must you all be so watchful?"

"Because things can change forever in the blink of an eye, Olivia. You, of all people, should know that. One minute you were home and safe, and the next, you were scrounging for bits of wasted food."

"Thanks for bringing it up," I said bitterly.

"I'm only pointing out why we must be watchful. Evil can enter when we are complacent."

"What does evil have to do with it?"

"If you don't follow Christ..." He leaned toward me, intent to make me understand. "If you are not for God, you are against Him. You must choose a side."

"What makes you think I haven't?"

"What makes you think you have?"

I ground my teeth. Of course I wanted to follow Christ. I could easily see that his family lived happily in their beliefs. I wanted to be happy, too.

"If you associate with Kish, but come here to the farm and put on your Christian face, then you have not decided either."

"You don't know anything about that."

"Because you haven't told me."

"Because it is not mine to tell."

I scoffed, almost laughed. "You are as infuriating as your brother!"

His eyes went to Lamech, then back to me in question. "What has he been saying?"

I discreetly pointed behind us toward Gideon. "He was teasing me last night, I think."

He looked doubtful. "Gid doesn't tease. He commands, and everything is seriously life or death to him."

I shook my head. Lowering my voice, I said, "He *was* teasing me. I was unsure at first, too. He was teasing me about waiting up for you to come on the watch." I tried not to blush but was probably unsuccessful.

Shad looked doubtful again. "Last night?"

I nodded.

"*During* the time he was supposed to be watching for danger?"

I laughed.

"I would have to say that's not possible."

"Well, apparently, it is. I dare say you don't know your brother as well as you think you do."

He took a deep breath. "Perhaps not, but I don't like the idea of you knowing him so well."

"You were gone for a long time, and you've been brooding since you came home. I know all your kinsmen better than I know you."

"I don't like the idea of that either."

My heart was beating fast, and not from the exertion of the trail, though I was not accustomed to the walking. I looked up at him. "So change it."

He smiled at the ground in front of us. "What do you think I'm trying to do?"

Well, that was the question, wasn't it? Was he trying to get more information out of me, or was he trying to be my friend?

I went with my gut.

"Miriam was right. You are the best one of all your brothers."

"I heard that," Gideon called from behind us.

Shad and I looked at each other and laughed.

"And I wholeheartedly agree," Gideon finished.

Shad's expression changed, darkened, and I watched him curiously. Either he didn't think Gideon could believe it, or he didn't think it could be true at all.

CHAPTER 13

Shad's dark mood lasted the rest of the journey. He lost the playfulness in his voice and his replies to my questions became brusque enough that his mother and Keturah and even Liam threw him many reprimanding glances.

"This is Melek?" I asked him as we entered a small clearing in the trees that could barely be called a village. From what I could see, it was no more than fifteen or twenty families with small huts on both sides of a single lane.

"No. This is Sarai's village."

"Oh."

"Melek is another half an hour's walk to the north."

"Oh."

"Sorry it's so distasteful," he said.

"No! It's not that."

"Sure sounds like it is."

I took a breath, trying not to become brusque and irritable myself. "I had it in my head this was to be a large party."

He shrugged out of his travel pack and set it at our feet. "Oh, it will be large. But it's a celebration for Sarai and Lamech, not for you."

"You needn't be rude. I didn't know what to expect, that's all. This village is charming, and I am sure Sarai has had many happy times here."

"That's not always going to work, you know."

"What?"

"You won't always be able to say something polite to cover your mistakes."

"I don't know what you mean. And anyway, I don't make mistakes."

He looked at my straight face and laughed. I gave up and burst into a smile too, and with that simple shared laughter, his dark mood started to lift.

"My father used to place me by his side at parties so I could learn what to say. He would tell me, 'Pay special attention to the pretty women and do as they do.'"

He nodded, searching the small village for something.

"I'm sorry if my politeness offends."

He looked suddenly back to me. "It doesn't."

Lamech came over. "There are many people for you to meet," he said with a grimace. "We should get started so we can get it over with."

"I thought it was better for me not to meet anyone."

"It is safe to meet everyone here. They can be trusted with your identity."

"You're not going to tell them who I am, are you?" My eyes shot to Shad, who shook his head.

"Of course we won't."

Lamech said, "You are simply a friend Sarai met in Orihah during her stay. You are shy and uncomfortable in crowds. Come on. I will begin introductions."

"But I want to enjoy the party."

"I told you. The party is not for you," Shad said. "You are here for your own safety because you can't stay at the farm alone."

I folded my arms and pouted. "How am I supposed to pretend to be shy?"

Lamech almost smiled. "Just pretend everyone you meet is Shad."

My cheeks got hot. Now Lamech was teasing me?

"See. It's already working."

I couldn't look at Shad. It would complicate finding me a husband if he knew I liked him. I had been trying my utmost to hide it for months.

"I don't know what you mean."

Lamech scoffed. "You know exactly what I mean." He jogged a fist into Shad's shoulder. "You blush every time he gets near you."

I raised my chin. "Well, honestly, I should be surprised if any girl could help that."

Lamech whistled.

"And I think maybe you're jealous that Shad is so much better looking than you."

He snorted, and I grinned. But a quick glance showed Shad looked uncomfortable. It was a discomfort I had caused, so I quickly said, "Would it not be more proper for Naomi to introduce me? Or perhaps Sarai, if she is not too busy, as I am to be her friend from Orihah?"

The two looked at each other and must have agreed silently because Shad led me to his mother.

It was almost as if she had heard our conversation, because she said, "Oh, Livi. I have many friends to introduce you to."

And with that, Shad disappeared, but not before he had squeezed my arm.

I stared after him, trying to decide if it had been more like a caress.

When I looked back to Naomi, her eyes were gleaming.

"I wish I could introduce you as my daughter, but Liam says the time is not yet." She sighed. "And besides, such good news would detract from Lamech's happy day."

I didn't see how anyone would believe I was her daughter. I was seventeen. Surely, I would have met these people before now, and they all knew she had only sons.

Fearing she had not been informed of the plan, I said, "But I am to be introduced as Sarai's friend."

She nodded and lifted my hand in one of hers, patting it with the other.

From the corner of my eye, I thought I saw Ammon. Across the small clearing, he was talking to a man who was tall and handsome. The man was young, but definitely older than me—Ammon's age, I guessed. But why would Ammon be here in this tiny place?

Naomi followed my gaze.

"What is it?"

I pulled my eyes back to her. "Nothing." When I looked across the clearing again, he was gone. I swallowed. Maybe it was my imagination. "So many people," I said.

"Well don't be nervous. I'll introduce you to them all."

I swallowed again. "Who is that man talking to Sarai and Lamech now?"

"Darius." She smiled. "Keturah's younger brother."

Keturah's younger brother and Gideon's younger brother. It didn't take a genius to figure they were in something together, maybe something bad. But I looked at Naomi again, her beautiful countenance, and I found her handsome son talking to some men not far from us. His countenance was good too. Bright and good. I couldn't believe he would be into something bad. If he was an associate of Kishkumen, it wasn't because he wanted to be.

But if he was, and if Ammon was here, he would surely be recognized.

I let Naomi introduce me to a few people—Keturah's mother, a pretty girl named Melia, and some others—and I pretended to be shy. But before too long, I said, "I would really like to just sit over there with Shad."

Naomi beamed and sent me off.

"What are you doing?" Shad asked when I sat demurely next to him near someone's outdoor fire round.

"I'm being shy."

When he snickered, I leaned closer.

"I thought I saw Ammon, Kish's friend. The one who came to the barley farm."

Shad stilled, but his eyes began scanning the village.

"Where."

"He was talking to Darius."

"How do you know Darius?"

Was that a bit of jealousy?

"I asked your mother his name. Obviously. What are you two in on? Tell me and don't lie about it. I already know Kish is up to no good. There is nothing you can tell me that would shock me."

"Did he see you?"

"I don't think so. His back was to me. I'm not even sure it was him."

161

Shad glanced around and then got to his feet, pulling me up with him. "Come on. Let's get into the trees."

We walked casually out of the village together, but when we were in the trees, Shad sped up, hustling me along in front of him.

"You don't need to herd me."

"I'm not sure you understand the urgency of not being seen."

"Believe me, I do. I will run back to the farm without stopping if you ask it of me."

He chuckled. "Okay. I guess you understand better than anyone. Here." He pulled me to a stop. "This is far enough.

I whirled on him. "Now tell me what you are into."

His eyes sought mine, and I thought he wouldn't tell me. He would say it was a secret. He would say it was dangerous or it was none of my business.

"Darius and I are spies for a man high in the government." He paused and added reluctantly, "My cousin, Jared, too. We have infiltrated the Order of the Nehors in Zarahemla, and Darius has just obtained a foothold in a secret group known among the Nephite governors as the Gadianton robbers. He spies for all three groups, and they all think he is loyal to them."

I could tell he was not lying to me. His voice was steady, and there was not a hint of dishonesty in it.

"Our mutual employer chose Darius to infiltrate the Gadiantons. He has experience in battle that I don't." He seemed almost angry about that.

"I believe you. But what does it have to do with Ammon?"

"Ammon and Kish and all their friends are among the

members. To be initiated in, they must kill someone in cold blood. For this, they receive a bracelet of black onyx that allows them admittance into all meetings and any of the group's secret strongholds."

I had no words to reply to what he was telling me, but the information did not come as a complete surprise.

"Your father employed the group for some of his less desirable tasks—to do his dirty work, so to speak."

I nodded. This did not surprise me either, for I had heard bits and pieces of their planning meetings and my father's instructions to Kish.

"Your marriage came up for barter when Kish began to require more than monetary payment from your father. As I understand it, your father has always had you followed when you've gone out into the city alone. For your own protection, and because you are the beautiful daughter of a powerful political leader, I applaud him in this action."

His words were straightforward and informative only. He was not complimenting me.

"When your father promised you to Kish, it was conditional. Kish and his followers would get him placed on the judgment seat, with the ultimate goal being to place him as king. He already had the support of many people, and in truth, I believe they targeted Paanchi for that reason. They made him promises that were too alluring to resist."

He paused while I digested this, but he seemed determined to get through it all.

"When it became apparent your father could not gain the judgment seat by the voice of the people, Kish had the betrothal document altered and withdrew the protections he had in place for your father. He has corrupt friends in all levels of the government, and he used these connections to see your father's sentence made sure. Likewise, his betrothal to you is real only in his head."

"Well, that's a relief," I said weakly.

He started to pace. "But it's as you said. It is made to look real and binding. You could be imprisoned for refusing it."

My eyes dropped to the ground.

"I could be imprisoned for harboring you. Any employer you had could be imprisoned for paying you."

I worried a nail as I thought about the implications of that. I had put his whole family in harm's way, and for what? A few more months of freedom?

Shad tentatively took my hand in his, and I looked up into his face.

"All you have to do is break the contract. It's a kind of loophole."

I bit my lip. "It is a loophole because no man will want a dishonored woman." Shad and Liam would have to beg someone to marry me. Maybe pay someone.

"Kish will have no legal recourse," he persisted.

I dropped his hand and turned away. "The law means nothing to Kish. He will find me, and it will not matter that I am married to some stranger. No one can keep me safe from him."

I heard him shift. "I can."

He was so confident, but Kish had so many men. An army of men.

Looking over my shoulder, I saw him standing there with his shoulders square, ready to take on all my problems, to fight all my fights for me.

What if Shad had to do it himself? Would that be an acceptable solution to you?

It was ever so much more pleasant of a thought than marrying some extremely old man from Orihah, which was what I thought he had intended for me.

"Even if you could, I wouldn't let you," I said.

His face fell, and his eyes clouded over.

"I mean, I couldn't let you sacrifice your life like that. It is too much to ask. Too big of a commitment."

His frown eased, but he shook his head.

"Marriages in your family, Shad, they're real." I gestured back toward the village, toward his brother's wedding. "They have real commitment. They have love in them."

There was hurt in his eyes when he said, "You don't think you could love me?"

I stared at him, and then I laughed.

He took a step back, but I reached for his hand.

"I've loved you almost from the moment I saw the moonlight on your face in that wretched old building in Zarahemla."

His eyes narrowed.

Suddenly, there was a high shriek in the forest near us. Shad didn't seem to hear it, but I jumped and skittered into his arms. I had heard the animals of the wilderness could be dangerous.

"Be still," he said, but his hands pulled me closer. "There is no danger." Then, as Kenai materialized from the shaded woods, Shad put his lips next to my ear and whispered, "There are no lizards in the forest."

I wriggled away from him, but his words warmed my heart even as they sent a shiver down my neck.

Kenai was brief. "Darius says there is trouble."

Shad stepped around me. "Livi saw a man from the

Gadiantons with Dare. What's he thinking bringing him here?"

Kenai rubbed his arm, casually as if this were not terrible news. "I'm sure he had little choice in the matter. He doesn't like to mix his real life with his false one."

"Like to? It's not safe, and now Olivia can't show her face in the village."

"I've already talked to Zeke. Take Livi to Eliza's. No one will think it odd if Eliza is not at the celebration, being big with child. Zeke will stay with them, and you can be present for the ceremony."

"You think I care about the ceremony?" Shad paced back, clearly annoyed.

Kenai stayed calm. "I think your mother and family care about the ceremony, and if Ammon remains, I think he will expect to see you at the ceremony. It may even be why he's here. He couldn't give Dare a good reason for his presence."

Shad let out a breath. "Fine. Where does Zeke live?"

Kenai grinned. "I'll show you a back way."

Eliza was nice. She was expecting her first child, but she was up and doing for me what I should be doing for myself.

"No," she said, when I offered to cook over the fire for her. "I enjoy it."

Reluctantly, I sat down. I fingered the beautiful carvings on the chairs and felt like a burden.

"Kenai carves those," she said. "He and Zeke have been friends since they were infants."

I laughed. "How can infants be friends?"

She laughed too. "If anyone could manage it, it would be those two. Come now, don't be glum. Are you very sad to miss the celebration?"

"I was very much looking forward to it, but I am not so

166

sad to miss it. I am sad that the beautiful idea of it is gone."

She smiled as if she understood. "I am sorry for that, but Zeke says it can't be helped."

Zeke looked up from a scroll he was reading by candlelight at the table.

"What are you reading?" I asked him.

"The words of the prophets, no doubt," his wife said with a smile.

He returned her smile, but made no reply himself.

They were both abed when Shad returned for me. I wasn't sure if he would. I thought he might stay at Keturah's parents' where all the other men were staying.

I saw a beam of light fall across the rug when he pulled back the mat at the door.

"Livi? I know you're awake in there."

"Shad?"

"Were you expecting someone else?"

I nearly giggled. "No," I said as I ducked out the door.

"Come on," he said as he turned toward the lane.

"Where are we going?" I asked, but I didn't really care.

"I thought you might have trouble sleeping."

A moment of panic hit me when he didn't answer my question. Was this when he would take me to Ammon? Or worse, to Kishkumen? Was it part of some scheme?

I shook my head. I knew Shad to be an honorable man. I knew him to be good, but the conflicting ideas warred inside my head, and my imagination won out.

"Shad, where are you taking me?"

He turned back when I stopped walking.

"There's a cove near a pool of water." He hesitated. "Would you rather not go?"

167

"It will just be us?"

He flashed a smile. "Gid would be cranky if I got him out of bed to sit in the moonlight."

I nearly choked on my relief. Would I ever trust anyone again?

"Is it far?"

"Not very."

I took the steps toward him.

"Are you okay?" he asked. "Is it the darkness?"

I smiled. "I am not afraid of the dark. You know I like it."

"You seem nervous."

"I can handle myself with a boy in the moonlight."

"You won't need to. It is dark and we are alone. I kind of hoped that would work to our advantage, but I will treat you like the lady you are."

"I am not rich. My father is gone, and I have nothing."

"I am not talking about your worldly wealth. That is not what makes you a woman of worth."

"Maybe not to you."

He scoffed. "True, but Kish doesn't count."

I giggled, but Kish was still a looming worry.

"I'm sorry about your father," he said awkwardly. "About what happened."

I took a deep breath and blew it out. "He made his choices."

"And you are suffering the consequences."

His voice was soft in the night, perhaps angry on my behalf, but I was here with Shad because of the choices my father had made. Thinking of what Shad had revealed about Father's intentions made my heart ache for us both, but walking next to Shad reached a piece of it that I had not dared open up before.

The softness of his voice, deep from his chest, made me feel very much alone in the woods with him, and as he spoke simple instructions, and guided me along the dark path with gentle hands, I knew that he did intend to marry me himself.

It wasn't long until we came to the cove he had spoken of, and as far as I could see into the shadows, there were no men waiting to haul me back to Zarahemla, just an empty cutback in the bank that was lined with large stones and slick with moss.

We came to the water's edge, and Shad invited me to sit. He sat close to me and stretched his legs out in front of him, the water lapping at his heels.

"I brought you here for a reason," he said. I nearly panicked, but he turned to me and continued. "I've already told my family I intend to marry you to keep you safe from Kish."

"And I've already told you it won't make me safe."

"They are already planning it."

"Well, it would be nice if you sought my consent."

"You said you would agree to the scheme."

"When I thought it was to be to some very old man from your town, perhaps with a burn or a scar, who could get a wife no other way."

An owl howled in the night. "You would prefer that?"

"Of course not! You're exasperating! I know that I am helpless and you must feel very noble in your endeavor, but a lady like myself would still like to give her consent."

"I've been asking for it!"

"No, you haven't!"

He lowered his voice. "I am now. Will you agree to marry me?"

"Was that so hard?"

He growled.

169

I laughed and leaned forward to kiss him.

He was surprised, I could tell, but he liked the kiss. I could tell that, too. I wanted to linger, perhaps indulge again, but Shad pulled away and slid back.

"You shouldn't be so bold," he said.

I studied him in the moonlight. "Well, didn't Miriam ever kiss you?"

He was quiet for a moment. Finally, he said, "I kissed her."

Oh. It was a power thing. He wanted it all.

I started to ease away, but he reached out and pulled me back. The bite of his fingers triggered something in me, some fight or flight instinct, and I shrugged him off and skittered away. When I finally stilled, my back was up against the rocks and my knees were tucked up to my chest, my arms wrapped around them. I wasn't sure how I had gotten there.

"Livi!"

I had stunned him. I had confused him. I had hurt his feelings. I didn't care. He did not get to be the one to say when I would kiss a boy and when I would not. I would be the only one with a say for myself.

He moved closer, and I squeezed my eyes shut tight. Where could I run to? It didn't even matter. I couldn't get up. I was paralyzed where I was.

"Livi."

By the tone of his voice, I knew he had thought it through, and Livi was the name he had chosen to call me. The sound of it cut through my fear and spread like warmth through my heart.

"You don't need to be afraid of me," he soothed. I felt his hand touch my arm, and I shook my head vigorously, but he didn't move it. He held on more firmly, caressing it like he had done earlier in the day.

"I am not the man who hurt you. I never will be."

I felt tears leaking out of my eyes, though I squeezed my lids shut as tight as I could and tried to hold them back.

"I was wrong. You can be the one to kiss me." I could hear a smile in his voice. "I don't mind at all."

I sniffed and peeked up at him. It was stupid, cowering from him as I had. "Perhaps we could just kiss each other."

He moved closer and wiped the tears from my face with his fingers. He shook his head, but then his eyes dropped to my lips. His gaze returned to meet mine, and I knew he was asking if it was okay.

I gave him the barest of nods and let my eyes drop closed as he leaned forward and kissed me in a way that made me believe he could protect me and maybe love me.

CHAPTER 14

Zeke was sitting outside when Shad returned me to the house.

"Are we in trouble?" I asked Shad, unable to hide my smile.

Shad shrugged. "He probably can't sleep."

Shad brought me to the gate and opened it for me. He raised a hand to Zeke, but leaned down to say, "Goodnight," into my ear. Then he turned and walked away into the night.

I went directly to sit across from Zeke. There was no point in pretending I hadn't been out after dark with a boy.

"I hear you are to be married," Zeke said. There was no censure in his voice, and perhaps it was just as Shad had said and Zeke, in fact, could not sleep.

"Word certainly travels quickly. I have only just given my consent."

"Then let me be the first to congratulate you."

"I take your congratulations with much thanks."

"Your father would have liked to see it. I often heard him speaking highly of you to some dignitary or other. He was proud of you."

I smoothed my skirt down. "He often told me that himself."

"A good father."

I peered at him and wondered how much he knew. Probably all of it.

"Are you prepared to be a father?"

"I believe so."

"What are you doing up?"

"Practicing, I suppose."

He meant it. He had risen from bed to wait up for me.

"Thank—" I had to swallow hard. "Thank you."

"I know you must feel alone, Livi, but you don't need to. You've friends and soon you will have family, a family I would let a loved one marry into."

I nodded.

"Now. It is time for you to be in for the night."

I was feeling delightfully sleepy. "I think you're right. Goodnight."

I wanted to think about Shad. I closed my eyes and imagined him walking alone through the dark to come to me. He knew I would be awake. He knew I would be willing to go with him. It didn't matter if it was wise to let him know. I had kissed him! My feelings weren't secret anymore.

I wanted to think only of him, to search out in my mind if I could trust in his plan to save me from a life with Kishkumen. I only wanted to think of his eyes, the way they had asked if he could kiss me.

But I kept thinking about my father.

Was Shad right? Had he been taken while I had been in hiding, before I had even left the city? Why had Martha not told me? If I had been out and about, I would have known it. If what

174

Shad said was true and everyone knew about Father and his sentence being carried out, it couldn't have been kept from me.

But his sentence! What had he done to warrant such a thing? If the judges had found him guilty, they must have had evidence.

And now I was alone because of what he had done, because he had craved power, because he had tried to take it for himself when the people did not give it to him.

But I thought of Zeke sitting in the darkness waiting for me to return. He was hardly old enough to be my father — the idea was laughable — but perhaps like an older brother, and the idea of that was welcome and comfortable.

I thought of Gid and of Lamech and how they teased their younger brother, how they now teased me. It was like being part of a family, I thought, though I had certainly never experienced anything like it. I thought of Keturah's easy laugh and her helpful hands, her healing balms, the beautiful weapon she had given me to help me feel safe. I wore it often, and it did. I thought of Naomi's gentle instruction and even Liam's stern frown, so much in contrast to the way he had taught me his game of chance to help me pass the time, to take my mind off my troubles and the dangers that lurked outside.

They all had much more practice being in a family than I did.

I finally fell asleep wishing I knew how to reciprocate the care they all took of me. Shad was right. Saying something polite or diplomatic wasn't going to keep working. It kept me a step removed.

I made an effort not to sleep late the next morning, but still, Eliza had already fed her husband and was cleaning up the meal by the time I ducked through the mat at her door.

"Zeke says you're to stay here this morning," Eliza said as she passed some flat cakes into my hands. "He says the village is not safe for you."

I nodded. "Must I sit indoors?"

She glanced toward the brook. "He didn't say."

I nodded again, grateful. But I would gladly sit inside if the men determined it was safer.

Eliza brushed off the cooking stone and rubbed her mixing bowl with ashes, but I could see she kept sneaking glances at me from the side of her eye.

"Have I embarrassed myself by sleeping too late?" I asked, unable to resist a nibble at the cake in my hand.

She colored prettily. "Not at all," she assured me. "I've been fighting the feeling, but I feel like we should know each other, like we have met." Eliza finally sat down and looked at me, her morning chores complete.

I looked up at her, too. Her face did seem familiar.

"I'm not sure," I said, taking a bite of the cake. "I am the daughter of Paanchi."

Her eyes lit, and she rose up, straightening her shoulders. Dipping her head, she reached back and removed the clasp that held her hair at the nape of her neck.

"I lived on the Estate of Alma!" she said.

But she needn't have said it. Her hair. Her pretty face and rosy cheeks. I knew exactly who she was.

And exactly how I had treated her.

"Swallow or you will choke," Eliza laughed.

I swallowed, but the cake seemed dry. "Is that where you met your Zeke?"

She nodded vigorously. "Poor, sorry soldier that he was."

I smiled at that. "I didn't recognize him until he enacted his vicious frown for me, and then I knew him immediately! He stood watchful along the walls many a time when I visited the Estate with my father."

"His is not an easy face to forget. But they have put it out that you are from Orihah."

"It is not safe to be the daughter of Paanchi just now," I said quietly. "It is not even safe for you to be harboring me here."

"Don't worry about that," she said. "I'm sorry I didn't realize before where we must have crossed paths."

"You were expecting a stranger from Orihah, and I don't mean to give offense, but I don't think we ran in the same circles."

She gave me an understanding smile. "I didn't grow up in Zarahemla, and Helaman's wealth, though it was my family's also, created a lifestyle I was not comfortable in. I didn't care for Uncle's parties with the men of the government and the dignitaries from other lands, though I was often invited to attend them. All the rich foods and the glamorous ladies — I was not comfortable there. Indeed, after my father went to the war, I scraped up food from the forest wherever I could, and I was much more accustomed to that."

Scraped up food? Perhaps we had more in common than I thought.

But I thought of myself and my friends giggling about the country girl with the wild hair, and I looked down. "Was I perhaps part of the reason you didn't care for your uncle's parties?"

She smiled again. "Perhaps." She waved it away. "But how fortunate that we have a second chance to be friends."

"My home," I confided to her. "It became unsafe for me

to be there. I had to leave, and I was without food for a time because I didn't know how to procure it in the city without funds. Shad found me hiding in the shadows and took me home to his mother."

"You're lucky. I know Naomi to be kind, and she has suffered much for her faith."

Suffered?

"What do you mean?"

She shifted on her seat. "It is hers to tell. You should ask her."

It was kind of a secretive comment, and I wondered why she wouldn't tell me.

"Zeke said you went out last night," she said instead. Was she changing the subject?

If she was, I was willing.

"Shad came to ask me to walk with him."

She grinned. "A moonlit walk? How lovely."

"It was, but I..." Could I tell her? "I did something strange. Offensive."

She frowned. "What do you mean offensive?"

"Not offensive. Just, confusing."

She waited for me to go on.

"I, well, I kissed him."

Her eyes gleamed. "That offended him?"

I shook my head, unable to hide my smile. "No. Well, yes. He said I shouldn't be so bold."

She nodded slowly. "Perhaps not. But sometimes men are not bold enough."

"When he said that, I got mad. I mean, it hurt my pride. And I tried to move away but he grabbed my arm."

The sky was light and I was clearly the last person in the

village to be eating my morning meal. It seemed strange to see the women at the other houses going about their normal day, calling to their children, starting the bread for the evening meal, hauling buckets and dishes and linens around their homes, because I was thinking of a life from long ago.

"I crawled away. I couldn't get away fast enough."

Eliza was studying my face with curious eyes.

I licked my lips. "I've been treated with force before, and I just reacted."

Understanding lit in her eyes and she reached over to squeeze my hand. "Go on. What did Shad do?"

I shook my head. "He was kind."

"I'm not surprised at that."

"But I think he was mad at himself for forgetting not to touch me."

"If he intends to court you, you will have to touch sometimes."

I almost laughed. She was silly and kind, and I wished I had gotten to know her at those stupid parties. "I know. It doesn't happen often, but I don't want him to think I don't want him to touch me at all."

Her smile was sweet and knowing. "Just tell him that, and then he will know."

"But how?"

"Just walk up to him and tell him what happened might happen again, but you don't want that to stop him from courting you."

Courting. It sounded so silly when he was only marrying me to protect me. He needn't even court me. I would do anything to keep away from Kish, and that made courting seem very unnecessary.

"He might think that was too bold, too."

She leaned back and looked me over. "I'm thinking that boldness is something he will just have to get used to."

I laughed again. She was right. "He will have to take me, flaws and all."

"Boldness is not a flaw," she said, her voice taking a more serious tone.

I sighed. "I have many other scars to bring to the table."

"And so does he. No one is without them."

"I never thought of him having problems. He seems so sure of himself."

"Not sure enough of himself to kiss you."

I blushed deeply.

Eliza laughed and touched my hand again. "You should find out what kinds of scars he has, because once you are married, they will be yours, too."

"Who said anything about marriage?"

"Livi, that's what courting leads to." She paused. "And Zeke might have mentioned something about congratulations being in order." Her grin was cute and mischievous.

I looked over at her. "Did Zeke have scars?"

"Why do you think he wore the vicious frown all the time?"

I guessed he did have scars and they were none of my business. I guessed Shad probably had them too, but what were they? What could possibly be in his past that had hurt him?

Miriam.

My stomach roiled slowly. She had just seemed like a girl, not a ghost from Shad's past I would have to deal with.

His brothers.

I loved their teasing, drank it in like water, but I tried to think of it from his perspective. It was true that Shad was the best looking of them, but the others weren't ugly. They were all talented and smart and strong. Perhaps he felt less than them. Perhaps he didn't feel he measured up.

I thought of his discomfort when I had been bantering with Lamech. Lamech had been in the war with the others, and I suspected he had all but run away to do it. Shad hadn't. Had he not been allowed to go? Had he been too afraid to go? Had he been too obedient?

He has experience in battle that I don't.

Scars.

Scars were things that had healed over. Perhaps neither of us had scars, but open wounds instead.

But when I saw Shad coming up the path later in the morning, grinning and handsome, he didn't look wounded.

"Did the celebrations go as planned last evening?" I asked when he sat before us.

He shrugged.

"The marriage is to be finalized tonight?"

"It is."

I bit my lip.

"You still can't go," he said, but there was a smile in his eyes.

I folded my arms and pretended to pout.

"But would you like to meet my eldest brother today?"

"Yes, of course!"

"Come on then," he said as he stood.

We bid Eliza goodbye and he led me down the lane toward the main road of the village, but before we reached it, he turned off into the trees.

"Better to be safe," he said with a note of apology.

"No. Thank you for your vigilance. I do not want to be discovered."

I caught a smirk on his face as he said, "You can't help being polite, can you?"

"What do you mean?"

"Thank you for your vigilance?"

"What's so wrong with being polite?"

He shook his head. "Nothing."

"Obviously something. Enough to make you smirk."

"I wasn't smirking."

I laughed. "Perhaps the politeness is more noticeable because you grew up with only brothers."

He shrugged. "Perhaps, though my mother would be sorry to hear you say that."

"For all her efforts," I laughed. "Then perhaps it is more noticeable because you spend your time with unsavory men in Zarahemla."

"More likely." His lips still smiled, but the light in his eyes had dimmed.

We traveled much longer than it should have taken to get to the small village, but when we emerged from the trees into a meadow that was bordered on one side by a small river and a cascading waterfall, I figured Shad did not intend to take me into the village.

"It's so pretty!" I said. "I've never seen a waterfall before. Well, I've seen the ones in the city, but they are manmade and nothing like this."

"Kenai's directions were good, then. I've never seen this either."

As we drew nearer, a figure stood up at the top of the falls.

"It's Jashon," Shad said when he heard my soft intake of air. "It's safe. No cause to worry."

A second figure stood, and I could see they had been sitting on a log that spanned the river at the top of the falls.

Shad raised a hand in greeting, which Jashon returned, and then he turned and offered his hand to the woman who was with him.

When they had descended into the meadow, Shad introduced me first to Jashon and then to his wife, Salome.

"I hear you are to be my sister," Jashon said with a smile.

"It seems I cannot get Shad to reconsider," I said, my heart thudding at the thought that so many people already knew this detail of my private life.

Jashon's eyes took me in, but he was looking at his brother when he said, "I should think not."

I glanced between Jashon and Salome. They were both much older than us, ten years perhaps. Perhaps more. Jashon looked very much like Gideon. His eyes were dark with wrinkles beginning to form at the corners, but his face was alight with good humor. Salome was slender, had hair a shade lighter than her husband's, and though she was not smiling now, had seemed quite pleasant upon our introduction.

"Jashon," she said, a note of reprimand in her voice, and I realized what he had meant.

Blushing slightly, I looked at Shad. The look on his face was unreadable, but the look in his eyes was fierce.

If Gideon had said that, I would have thought he was teasing Shad, but Jashon… Something about the way he had looked at me and was now returning the look in Shad's eyes made me think he did not wholly approve of me as a sister, as a member of his family, as his youngest brother's wife.

Which gave us something in common.

"Do you know why it has to be?" I asked him quietly.

Jashon turned back to me.

"Yes, my father has apprised me with the details. But I am not so sure that is how it has to be. There must be other ways to deal with your predicament. We can find them."

"Did it not occur to you I might just want to marry her?" Shad shot out. He glanced at me, but turned back to his brother.

Jashon was quiet for a moment. He scrubbed at his jaw. "That is the only thing that occurred to me."

"Jashon!" Salome said again.

"You should give your brother more credit than that," I said. "If he thinks I have beauty and charms, he has resisted them quite well up to now."

Salome burst into a sweet laugh. "Come, Livi, I have much to tell you about Liam's sons."

CHAPTER 15

Salome took me by the arm and we strode along the bank of the river, leaving the two brothers standing together at the base of the waterfall.

"Jashon thinks Shad only wants to wed me because I am pretty, doesn't he?"

Salome squeezed my arm. "I think he suspects Shad may be overlooking other options because of your pretty face."

"That is what I think as well."

But I didn't think it was his only motive. He wanted to save and to protect like his brothers had done. He wanted to be something for me that I had never had, and I did think that came from a place of love, even if he was not exactly in love with me.

Salome nodded slowly.

"Naomi and Liam seem to be pleased," I said. "I wonder that they do not see it as Jashon does."

"I'm sure it crossed their minds, but how much the better for Shad if his heart can be engaged."

"While he offers himself up as a sacrifice?"

She laughed. "It's hardly that. Shad is of an age to marry, and by all accounts, he's taken with you."

"He might have to face down my betrothed."

How awful it was to call Kishkumen my betrothed.

"And he will have his family behind him," she said confidently.

Perhaps in spirit, but I knew Kish would pick a moment when Shad was not surrounded by big and strong men. I wished I didn't know Kish well enough to know that.

After a pause, Salome asked, "And you, Olivia? Would you find it a sacrifice to marry Shad?"

I glanced over my shoulder to see that Shad and Jashon hadn't moved. They stood stationary in the meadow while Salome and I wandered through it. They wouldn't overhear us.

"I would find it the highest of honors."

I felt her eyes on my face and knew my cheeks were turning pink, and I thought of Zarahemla, how I had flirted with many boys and even men and never blushed.

"I've never seen this flower before," I said, to change the subject. "Not in the city." I fingered an airy, yellow bloom. "It's pretty."

"And nourishing. You can eat the whole plant."

"Truly?" I asked, considering it again.

She nodded. "And that one." She gave me kind of a strange look. "I guess there aren't many wild plants in the city."

I shook my head. "Keturah has been showing me some useful plants."

Salome smiled. "A great skill of hers. She studied much with her mother and the healers of the army."

"She says all plants are here for our use." I paused, looking around at the lush meadow, letting my eyes rest for a moment on Shad and Jashon, who looked very much like the brothers they were.

I quickly drew my eyes back to Salome. "I'm afraid I have not spent much time in the study of anything." I felt useless all of a sudden.

"Naomi says you weave a fine cloth."

"She said such a thing?" But I shook my head. I had spent much of my life failing to develop any talents. "Naomi is generous with her compliments," I said.

"I know Naomi to be honest and forthright. I'm sure she meant it if she said it."

Salome's sincerity made me feel warm and comfortable.

I fingered a scar on a tree where someone had cut it.

"It looks like target practice," Salome said.

"Or someone with some frustration to vent."

She touched the scar with a finger.

"Better on a tree," I said, kicking myself for the hurt in my voice. I cleared the lump from my throat. "How did you find this place?"

"Keturah told us with so many people in the village, it would be a good, private place to meet you."

I wondered exactly how much she knew of my situation, if she knew why I had to hide.

"It is beautiful. That waterfall is divine."

"It is. It's hard to imagine Keturah training here to be a warrior."

"Did she?" That might explain the tree that had been used for target practice.

"So I hear."

"I've never wanted to be a warrior," I said.

"Nor have I, but Jashon taught me to fight, to aim a bow, and there have been times I have been glad of it."

I thought of the barley farm, of Naomi's gentle

instruction. "Knowledge is never a bad thing to have," I said. But then I thought of my father and how I had looked away from his dealings. How I wished I had not come to the knowledge of those things—things I could not forget. I thought of that terrible day in Martha's kitchen and wished I could expunge some knowledge from my mind—the sound of fists on flesh, the feel of bones cracking, what it felt like to have no control over my life, what Kishkumen's kiss felt like.

"Can I ask you something?" I said after a moment.

"Sure."

"Would you marry Shad if you were in my situation?"

"I would marry Shad in any situation. Men are not made better than Liam's sons."

"Even if you thought he might be hurt by doing so?"

She turned to me with concerned eyes, but the concern was warm and personal. It was for me, not for Shad.

"It is my understanding," she said slowly, "that Shad has been trained to take care of himself."

"This whole family is in danger because of me, because they harbor me."

"Livi, they know that, and they have all made their choices. They do not, any of them, fear death. They only fear God and His wrath if they do not serve His children."

"I can see none of you will hear reason," I said.

She laughed. "The ways of God are not the ways of man. Try to see it from an eternal perspective."

"I see Kish dispatching us all to our eternal rest."

She laughed again. "He is just a man, Livi."

"He has influence."

She put a small hand on my arm. "So does Shad. Now, look there. It must be time to start back."

She indicated the men, who were walking toward us through the long grasses of the meadow.

We parted from Jashon and Salome near the village when they turned off the path to attend the celebration, and I realized she hadn't told me anything about Liam's sons I hadn't already seen for myself. Shad escorted me on to Eliza's home.

I wore one of Naomi's nicest sarongs with the longboots Shad had bought me in Zarahemla. The boots looked plain, but they were comfortable. I felt like I could walk through anything in them.

I was admiring the boots when Shad said, "Livi, it's all going to be okay. I will make it safe for you."

"You are overconfident." I paused. "Jashon thinks I will hurt you."

He snorted. "He thinks I will hurt you."

"Will you?"

"I'm not planning to."

"I'm actually starting to believe that." I paused again. "Look, about last night, when I scrambled away from you."

He stayed silent, listening, and let me take the time to form my thoughts.

"I panicked. But it wasn't about you."

"I know," he said quietly.

"It might happen again. I can't control it."

"I know," he said again.

But when the moments went on and he didn't say any more, didn't say things to make me feel better, I thought that it hadn't gone as smoothly as Eliza had said it would.

We made it through a forest full of trees and all the way back to Zeke and Eliza's gate before he said, "The wedding is tonight, and you have to stay here."

189

"I know. I don't want to go to your little village party anyway. It will be such a bore."

He laughed, correctly assuming I was not serious.

I did want to go to the party.

And later, after Eliza had fallen asleep — quite early, if you asked me — and Zeke had gone to see some old friends who had come for the celebration, I slipped away and thought I would just have a peek at it from the trees and see what a little village party looked like.

It wasn't right to disobey. I was the one they were all trying to protect, after all. They were putting their safety on the line for me. But how dangerous could it really be? Who would see me in the trees beyond the fire's light?

Even though I was unfamiliar with the village and the forest, and though it was heavy twilight, I had no trouble finding the celebration because of the noise. I had only to set out, and the beat of drums beckoned me on.

The elders chatted with each other, and the youth laughed. Even the youngsters had been allowed to stay up, and they squealed as they ran, unchecked, through the village paths. An area had been set aside for a drum circle and for dancing, and dancers in colorful costumes performed the traditional marriage dances in whirling circles.

It was a little like the parties at my father's, but different, too. I remembered how superficial the people could be at my father's receptions. He would want me to impress this dignitary or entertain that soldier or political ally's lascivious son, to make someone's homely daughter feel welcome.

I thought, too, of the things my friends and I had said about Eliza, the poor girl from some poor country village somewhere, there to beg riches from her uncle. We talked of her plain clothes and her wild hair. Nothing had been off limits. None of it had been kind, and we hadn't ever cared if we were out of earshot.

Where were those friends now? When I had left my father's home, I had chosen a filthy, decrepit, infested building to hide in rather than trust any of them to give me aid and not turn me over to my father or Kish. They weren't very good friends, as it turned out.

My thoughts turned to the generous girl who had opened her home to me, humble as it was, as if it were my own. I thought of her there now, sleeping peacefully in her bed because I had promised I would stay there during the celebration.

I looked back out at the revelers, and getting a peek didn't seem so fun anymore.

I was sliding into the thick shadows of the trees, ready to turn and go back to where I was supposed to be, when something didn't feel right.

I stilled and scanned the village, picking out the few people I knew—the happy bride and groom, Kenai, Liam, Salome, and him.

Kishkumen.

He was looking right at me. He held a dish of food, forgotten, and was staring hard at the place I had been standing moments before.

Run.

I should have waited to move until he turned away. He wasn't sure he had seen me. I could see it in the confusion on his face. But the moment I moved, he knew. Maybe it was the glint of light on my skin or hair, maybe the flash of my bracelet or Keturah's beaded barrette. Maybe the fear in my eyes.

But I was running before I even knew it. My feet moved on their own. I had always been comfortable in the darkness, and I was grateful for it now. I wanted it to swallow me whole and make me invisible. My eyes were good in the dark, but not good enough. Branches snagged my clothing and scratched my arms and legs as I ran straight through bushes and undergrowth in my panic to flee. The ground was uneven, and I slipped to my knees. Despite the sharp pain, I scrambled up and kept running.

At length, I had to stop to catch my breath. The forest was quiet, but not still. I tried to see the stars through the trees, or find the moon at least, but the high branches of the Iaca trees were too dense.

Going to Eliza's was absolutely out of the question. What if I should lead him there? But I was so turned around in the woods, I couldn't have gotten there if I had tried.

There would be no slipping back into my bed where I belonged, no pretending I hadn't left, and there would be no sleeping tonight.

Was that a step? The brush of leaves? Could he have found me in the dark? When nothing happened and no one came crashing through the trees, doubts started to fill my mind. Had it even been Kishkumen? He wouldn't be here in Sarai's tiny village. It was preposterous.

But it wasn't preposterous. He was here. I had seen him, and he had seen me.

I kept moving, picking my way through the underbrush. Something was wrong with my knee, and I felt the sticky blood when I reached down to probe around the wound, but I couldn't stop. I kept moving as carefully and quietly as I could. I had to get away from the village. I had to lead Kishkumen away from those lovely, innocent people.

I became aware of trickling water, and nearly splashed into a stream before I looked around and realized where I must be.

I stilled and stared into the dark cove. The squeezing in my heart eased a little when the surroundings began to look familiar.

There was the stream, lit by moonlight coming through a break in the trees, and the little cutback in the bank where I had retreated from Shad after I had kissed him.

Had it just been the night before? Was it just that morning I had been lightheaded and giddy thinking Shad could really manage to give me a future? Had I really believed in his strong kinsmen and his vigilant kinswomen?

Oh, I was so naïve!

Kish would find me here and he would drag me back to Zarahemla—by my hair if he had to. Or if he felt like it.

I shuddered.

The moonlight had let me see my surroundings and given me a measure of peace, a measure of sanity, but standing there in the open in the soft glow of it was unwise.

I hurried to the cutback and crawled up into it, feeling embarrassed at the panic that had drawn me there the first time, and feeling bone-deep fear of the man who had forced me into it again.

But one thing I was not afraid of was the dark. Though my father could afford many candles and torches to light our evenings, I had spent many nights awake, even after the parties had ended and the household was at last asleep, and many nights drifting through the dark streets of Zarahemla searching for something I could not even define, for whatever was missing in my life with Father.

I squeezed my eyes shut at the thought of my father. *What have you done? What have you done?* I wanted to scream at him. And I wanted him to laugh and show me off to his friends again, to put his arm around me and grin when I had pleased the dignitaries he wished to impress.

But the tears found their way out.

There.

Near the stream.

There was a definite footfall, and my eyes shot open.

Had I gasped?

I slowly moved my hand to cover my lips to prevent another one, but I should have just held my breath — held it until I passed out — because the movement drew the attention of the man who was standing at the stream, scanning the darkness.

Looking for me.

"Olivia?"

CHAPTER 16

Fear roiled up in my stomach and chest. I went utterly still, but I couldn't have moved a muscle if I had wanted to. My ears buzzed, and I thought I might pass out. Was I holding my breath?

"Olivia!"

He was still scanning. Had he not seen me?

The man was tall and dark like Kishkumen, but...

His feet were silent on the forest floor as he moved off in the other direction, and as I watched his slender form disappear, I realized it was not Kishkumen, but Darius.

There was no reason for anyone from the village to be searching for me. Nobody knew I was gone.

What was Darius doing? Hunting for me at the behest of Kishkumen? I knew Kish had influence, but here in this tiny village? Were there others besides Darius? If he could get the men of this village to do his bidding, I was done for. I might as well get up and walk into the firelight of the village and give myself over to him.

But I couldn't do that. I still had one hope left.

God?

I began to pray in my heart.

I let the familiar darkness comfort me, even as I heard more footfalls come and go around me.

"Livi?"

I didn't know how long the shadow had been standing at the stream before I noticed it.

"Are you okay?"

The shadow came silently toward me. He knelt so we were at eye level with each other. I had seen those eyes before. I had seen them here, in this place.

A wild cat called from a distance, and I flinched. He heard it, too, but gave it no notice or response.

"Come here," he said and stretched out a hand to me.

I shook my head but realized he couldn't see me well in the shadow of the earth and rocks. He sensed me there in the dark night more than he saw me, and I was grateful his senses were so honed.

He was silent for a moment. "Are you hungry?"

A slow smile started to overtake my lips.

"You don't need to stay here with the lizards."

Ignoring his outstretched hand, I fell forward into him, throwing my arms around him and nearly knocking him off balance. But he was steady enough to hold the trembling girl in his arms.

I kissed his neck and his ear and his jaw. It might have been an accident.

"I saw him," I whispered into his neck.

"I know, and we have to be quick. He has men searching this whole area."

"I know. I've heard them." I kissed his neck again. Accidentally.

He was here! He was warm and solid, and I was not alone anymore.

"Are you ready to travel?"

"I will run back to the farm if you ask it of me."

"I'm afraid we will have to go farther than that."

Shad helped me from the cutback in the bank and led me into the water. When he didn't lead me out of it, I realized he was hiding our tracks. He was taking extreme caution, and my heart squeezed. Could we really get away? Could he really keep me safe from Kishkumen like he had boasted, like he had promised?

We traveled a long way through the water. My feet were numb and my boots had worn blisters on my heels and toes, but I would not complain. I would not stop until Shad said it was safe. Still, I hated to think how the blisters would feel when my feet warmed up.

It must have been a mile or more before Shad carefully stepped from the water.

He turned to me. "Here." He was pointing to the ground. "Step on these stones so your feet won't leave a mark in the mud."

I swiftly did what he said and waited for more instructions.

"Get behind me and follow where I lead."

Didn't he know I would follow him anywhere?

He moved steadily through the forest, but slowly, as if it was not urgent to get as far away as possible. The moon moved through the sky, and still he moved silently through the shadows. Finally, he drew to a stop and turned.

"You couldn't just stay with Eliza?"

I drew back at the censure in his voice.

"I didn't think it would do any harm to look at the party through the trees."

"I told you that party was not for you."

I folded my arms. "You did."

He backed up and started to pace, agitated.

"Keturah's brother ran for someone who can take you farther. I have to return to the celebration. I will be missed."

"Surely Naomi would understand just this once..."

"Not by my mother, Livi."

"Oh," I said dumbly.

"Any odd behavior from me or my family will be noticed."

"Do you think Kish knows I'm staying with them?"

"No." He shook his head. "But he wouldn't deign to come to this village if he did not suspect something."

I knew that as well as he did. This village was beneath Kishkumen's notice. He knew something.

"I'm scared, Shad."

He stopped pacing and touched my arm awkwardly, grasping it like he would grasp a piece of wood he meant to chop with his axe. "My friend will see you to safety."

Was there any place that was safe for me?

"I meant I was scared for you."

"I can take care of myself," he bit out, but then he sighed and said, "As long as I get back, he will see nothing amiss, but it won't be long before he realizes he can't find you and goes back to the party." He groaned. "Do you know how lucky you are that it was me who found you?"

Before I could answer, I heard a scuff in the gravel path and cowered behind Shad's back when he turned toward the sound.

"Onah."

"At your service," came the hushed but cheerful reply.

I peered around Shad and saw two men approaching. The taller one was Keturah's brother, Kenai. I didn't think I had ever seen the other one. How had they found us in the dark when all of Kish's men couldn't?

Shad stepped back and offered a curt introduction. "Livi, this is Gidgidonah. Onah. He will take you to safety."

"Hello," I said.

Despite the dark forest and clandestine nature of our introduction, he actually stepped forward and put a formal hand on my shoulder, so there was nothing for it but to return the gesture.

"I have to return," Shad said, his eyes shooting between me and the other boys. "Take her to Jashon's. Anais will be welcoming. You know the place?"

Onah seemed to hesitate. "I've been there."

"I guess I don't have to tell you the level of secrecy this requires."

"Kenai told me. No one will be able to follow her."

Onah was confident in that, and Shad seemed to sense it too. He gave a simple nod and turned to me.

"I'll come for you when I can," he said as he was backing away. "Or Jashon will take you home. Try to stay out of trouble."

I sniffed, and he came back. My hair had come loose in my flight from Kishkumen, and he took a moment to brush the stray wisps away from my face. He looked deep into my eyes as if he were willing my tears not to fall.

"You are strong," he said. I started to shake my head, but he repeated, "You are strong, Olivia. You crawled from that kitchen and you left Kishkumen in your past. I will keep him there." He took my face gently in his hands, his thumbs brushing my cheeks. "Do you trust me to do this for you?"

I stared back into his eyes and nodded, aware that neither of the other men had spoken or moved.

I saw approval come into his eyes, and he put a brief kiss on my forehead. He looked down and the moonlight caught the tips of his long eyelashes. He looked back up, a smile touching his lips, and then he turned and jogged into the night with Kenai.

"You ready?" Onah asked after a moment of awkward silence.

I searched the darkness to the north, but I could no longer see Shad and Kenai.

"Yes."

He turned back the way he had come, and I followed him into the night.

Onah was obviously comfortable traveling in the dark forest, but I found the going difficult. My knee was caked in dried blood and it still hurt. I was afraid the travel had done more damage to it. My feet had warmed up, and the blisters made every step painful.

We hadn't traveled too far before Onah said, "So, what kind of trouble are you in?"

"Trouble?"

"Why did Kenai run four miles in the middle of the night to find me?"

"Four miles?"

I sensed a shrug.

"Give or take."

"Kenai didn't tell you?"

"Just that you needed to be to Jashon's before morning."

"Oh." It was considerate of Kenai to preserve my

privacy. Or perhaps it hadn't been about that at all. Perhaps Kenai didn't even know what we were all doing out here in the night.

Onah was patiently waiting for the answer to his question.

"I'm sorry to involve you in my problems," I said. "It would have been simpler if Shad had just taken me himself. Or even simpler if I had just stayed hidden like I was supposed to." The guilt and fear clawed up my throat.

"Hidden?" He stopped walking and turned to me.

From what I could see in the moonlight, Onah was around Shad's age, handsome enough, and very used to navigating among the trees at night. He had no idea why he was here, but Kenai had only to ask for his help and he came.

"Livi, what kind of trouble are you in?"

I worried a nail, trying to decide how much to tell him, how much he needed to know.

"An unwanted marriage."

Perhaps Kenai had told him something of it, because he didn't look surprised, just raised one eyebrow and frowned. Or perhaps he didn't think a girl running from an arranged marriage was all that uncommon.

"I saw the man at the wedding celebration. Or, more to the point, he saw me."

I could feel Onah's eyes in the dark as he looked me over. I could almost read his thoughts. He thought I was a spoiled girl who wanted to choose her own husband and was putting up a fit to get her way. He was wondering why he had bothered to come out here during the second watch.

"He is evil, Onah." I remembered Kish's fists. I remembered the fear in Martha's eyes. "He plots against the government and the Church of God. He removes men from power. Men who are in his way — they disappear." I swallowed. "If he does not do the killing himself, he surely orders it done."

"Livi, I don't think —"

"My father was in his way," I said before he could call me a liar straight to my face.

Why did it matter so much that he understand?

"We'd better get moving," was all he said. "It's a bit of a walk."

By a bit of a walk, he meant it would take us the rest of the night to get there. And even though I had told Shad I would run all the way to the farm if necessary, I was realizing I was not capable of it.

"Onah," I said, stopping to catch my breath and stretch my back.

I could see in the rising light that he was even more handsome than I had thought all those miles ago in the dark. But I could see now that his clothing was homespun, not fine like one would purchase at the market. He was poor, or perhaps humble was a better word, like the rest of the Ammonites, but he was happy and comfortable here in the woods. He could survive here.

As I had been stopping periodically all night, he was used to it and stopped to wait for me. It hadn't seemed to bother him overmuch, though he had stressed several times that we still had a long way to go, but this time he seemed impatient, glancing ahead of us and giving a more devoted searching to the trail we had just come over.

"Is something wrong?" I asked, straightening up.

He shook his head. "I'll be glad when you are well and hidden at Jashon's."

I grimaced. It wasn't just me. There was an eerie feeling in the woods.

"I'm ready," I said.

"You sure?" His eyes showed concern, but whether it was for me or for our travels, I didn't know.

"Very sure." I winced as I took the first steps toward him. "How much farther?"

"Just down in that valley," he said, and I could see that his concern was for me. "It's been a bit arduous, through the dark."

"A bit?" I said under my breath, and he chuckled.

"How do you know the way to Jashon's?" I asked as we began the descent into the green valley that boasted many large fields of crops and several distinct settlements.

"I apprentice with Leah. I've taken medical supplies here a few times. Apparently, their methods of healing are quite rudimentary."

I looked around the pretty, dawn-lit valley. It seemed so charming. What did he mean by rudimentary?

"The Mulekites live here. Many of their people mingled with the Nephites at the time of Mosiah, but Anais's clan was proud of their royal heritage. They came out from Zarahemla and have kept their blood lines very pure."

I had read about Mosiah and the people of Mulek, prince of Judah, but what good were bloodlines when anyone who wanted power bad enough could just wrest it away?

"Has their pure blood kept them healthy?" I asked, impertinence creeping into my tired voice.

Onah's dark brows rose and he grinned at me.

"I take that as a no."

"Take it how you will, but I am still bringing them Leah's

medicines—for which they are always grateful and for which they always pay me."

"Are you a healer then, too?"

"I've much yet to learn."

"Have you always sought to heal others?"

Somehow, with the light, it felt more natural to make conversation.

"Once, I had to run four miles to fetch a midwife for my mother. The birth was complicated and dangerous." He had a great, humble grin. "I told myself that would never happen again."

I giggled. "You're not a midwife, are you?"

He outright laughed. "Of course not. I stick to the poultices and tinctures and broken bones."

"What would you do for this?" I stopped and held out my leg, tugging up the hem of my skirts a bit so he could see the wound there.

He sucked air through his teeth. "You've got quite the gash there." He went to his haunches to inspect it. "The cut is small and straight. It looks worse than it is."

"If only it was. I'm afraid I twisted it also."

He noted the bruising and fingered it gently. He looked up at me, squinting into the sun.

"You've been walking on it?"

I laughed. "Only a bit."

"Imagine if we hadn't taken my shortcut." He flashed his great smile again. "Come on. Let's get down there so we can clean it."

Leah was apparently a careful teacher of healing, for Onah's hands were quick and gentle as he tended to my wound. It was clear he was knowledgeable and confident. After I had shown him my knee, he had started pulling up roots, taking a few leaves from this plant or that, scraping bark from trees or plucking berries from bushes, and by the time I was seated in the shade of Jashon's house, he had poultices ready and herbs to make teas for me to drink.

"Feel better?" he asked, looking up?

"I think I will, thank you." I looked around. "Is Jashon coming back?"

"As soon as he can leave unnoticed, I imagine."

I wondered how long that would be. If Kish was already gone scouring the land of Melek for me, surely he wouldn't notice Shad's family had left the village.

"Will you stay?"

He stood, backing away. "Not here. I'll tell Anais you're here, but it's probably best if you're not seen in the villages."

I sighed. It seemed we were so far away from Kish and Zarahemla and even Melek, but I knew Kish's influence was far reaching and it wasn't impossible that he had followers here. I would stay hidden this time.

"Anais is Salome's father?"

"Her father-in-law. He is the chief ruler here. Salome's son is the next in line to rule."

Her father-in-law. Did that mean she had been married before her marriage to Jashon?

Anais showed up before Onah could go to him.

"There is a man approaching," I said as we ate the simple meal we had prepared together.

Onah looked up. "Anais," he said, and stood.

The man was around my father's age, perhaps a bit older. His skin was darkened by the sun, but fair like a Nephite. I was glad to see curiosity in his eyes and not anger.

"Young Onah."

It was a welcome of sorts, but it was all he said. He expected Onah to tell him what we were doing at this house that did not belong to us.

"Anais, meet Livi, Shad's bride. She needs a place to hide."

I stood as Anais turned his curious eyes to me.

"There is a man who wishes her harm," Onah said, and I wondered why he didn't add that I was legally betrothed to that man.

Anais's brow rose, but he just nodded sagely. "You are welcome in the Valley of the Little King, Livi, and the home of Jashon." He turned back to Onah. "Have you any herbs with you?"

"No. I'm sorry. I left in a bit of a rush." His glance at me almost made me smile. "Are you out of anything you can't gather in the valley?"

Anais shrugged and said simply, "Neel."

"I'll ask him before I leave." Onah paused and then answered the question in Anais' eyes. "I can stay the night." He glanced at me again. "But not here."

CHAPTER 17

After Anais left, I slept through the morning. When afternoon came, it was quiet, and for a moment, as I lay in the strange, soft bed, I didn't remember where I was. I might have been home with my father, sleeping in after a late party, but when I thought of my father, all the worry, fear, and disappointment flooded back into my chest.

When I heard the knock on the door of the comfortable home in the trees, I knew where I was and the beautiful dream of my father fell away.

"Livi?"

"I'm here," I called, recognizing Onah's voice.

"It's late. You haven't come out yet, and I thought maybe something was wrong," he said, but as I swept the door open, his voice trailed off.

I had helped myself to some of Salome's nightwear, as I had nothing with me but the longboots Shad had given me and the clip Keturah had snapped into my hair. Onah's eyes dropped as he inspected me, and then they rose back to mine.

"It's late. I thought maybe something was wrong," he said again, as if I hadn't just heard him.

I put a hand up to my hair. I hoped it didn't look tousled.

"Well, of course you're not shy, Onah," I said. "We spent the greater portion of the night together."

Red crept into his cheeks. "No! No, of course not. It's just..." He swallowed hard. "Your, uh..." He gestured to my clothing. "Last night you were..."

I rolled my eyes. I was perfectly modest. And he was the one who had awakened me.

But Onah was sweet. I could see I was making him uncomfortable. I should let the mat fall between us and go change. That would be the decent thing to do. But though it might have been unkind of me, I enjoyed his stammer and the red in his cheeks because they were pure and they were honest.

The boys I had known in Zarahemla, the men at my father's receptions and meetings—they were all worldly. They thought it was their right to look at me, to make advances toward me. At first, I had thought their admiration was real, but I had learned it wasn't admiration. It never was. It was lust and entitlement in their eyes and in their intentions.

Zeke had been right. I had learned to handle myself well. I had learned to dodge and to coyly play their game, to politely and effectively excuse myself from situations I didn't want to be in.

Onah took a step back and rubbed the back of his neck.

I was about to let the mat between us drop when someone called out, "Hallo!"

I looked over Onah's shoulder to see a woman coming up the path with two young boys at her heels.

Her quick glance at my clothing was informative and nonjudgmental, not at all stunned like Onah's gaze had been.

She said, "I'm Bethany, kinswoman to Salome."

My inclination was to tell her Anais said I could stay here, but her welcoming smile suggested she had already talked to him. He had probably sent her.

"I'm Olivia. My friends call me Livi."

"Then Livi it will be." She turned to Onah. "You might take the boys out to gather medicines and herbs while I see to Livi."

"Of course," he said, and jolted back another step. He shot us a crooked smile and turned away. He gathered the boys with a whistle and jogged into the trees with the two boys running after him. It was clear they had an acquaintance. It did not surprise me that the boys followed him eagerly.

"Well, now," Bethany said, rubbing her hands together. "Get changed into something of Salome's, and we'll wash your travel things."

I nodded. "She won't mind?"

"Would you? Of course not."

She all but shooed me back into the house, and I went to the closet where I had found the night clothes. Salome had good taste. She was not extravagant, as I had been at my father's house, but her choices of colors and fabrics were just the things I would have chosen myself—serviceable but pretty and feminine.

As I fingered the cloth of the dress I put on, I wondered if I would ever have pretty things again. I did not have money, nor a viable way to earn any. Even if I married Shad for his protection, he was not rich either. But I supposed Jashon to be a man of modest means, and his wife had lovely things.

I thought of the night Shad had found me, holed up with the lizards and starving, and it felt very silly to be thinking about fine clothing.

209

"Have you eaten?" Bethany asked when I returned to her, my arms laden with my soiled clothing.

"I just woke."

She nodded and continued to prepare a dish of food from the items she had brought with her.

"I can help," I said, setting the clothing down.

"Not necessary. I'm done. Here." She pressed a dish into my hands.

The food was plain but hearty and welcome—cheeses, breads, fruits, and meats.

She watched me eat for a moment.

"Am I doing it wrong?" I asked through a bite of meat.

"Your appetite is healthier than I thought it would be."

"The journey through the night was long."

"Anais said your presence here is not to be shared with others."

"I'd be grateful if you didn't shout it from the rooftops."

She smiled but her eyes narrowed. "Are you in danger?"

I swallowed. "I hope I have come far enough away that I am not."

"Far from your home?"

"Not exactly."

She was quiet for a moment.

"I don't mean to seem secretive, but I'm not sure if it is safer for you to know all, or safer for you to know nothing."

She smiled again. "Then I shall take no offense in whatever you decide is best."

Bethany was direct in her words and her actions. She set immediately to work laundering my clothing, and unlike Naomi, she just scrubbed it in the stream.

"Do I look too incompetent to launder clothing?" I asked

as I watched her squeeze soap through the garments.

She glanced up at me. She was small, even petite, but I could tell she was accustomed to working hard. Her hands were strong and deliberate. A lock of hair fell in her eyes and she brushed it aside with a slender arm.

"Not at all."

I frowned.

"Did someone tell you that?" she asked. "That you're incompetent?"

"No." I bit my thumbnail. I should stop trying to break the habit. It was a part of me.

"I didn't mean to offend. I meant only to help," she said as she straightened and began to wring the water from my dress. "I guess you just have that look about you."

"I look incompetent?"

She gave me a toothy grin. Her cheeks were a pleasant pink and her eyes shone. "You look like a princess."

"A princess?"

She took a long look at me, a long slow look like Onah had. "It's that shine in your hair, the straightness in your shoulders, the way you carry yourself. Your diction."

"Diction?"

She laughed. "The way you talk. It's like you're ordering about servants."

I frowned again. If only she knew. My first words had probably been directed to a servant.

Had I made her feel like a servant? Had she made me feel like a princess?

"I'm sorry if I ordered you about," I said slowly.

She laughed boisterously, quite boisterously for the petite little thing she was.

"Not at all. I'm blessed in service." She watched me for a moment. "My husband is the son of our chief ruler. I have my own servants, to be sure."

"You have?"

She waved her hand. "Anais insists. He thinks it helps people remember who is in charge. But I grew up doing for myself, and I'll continue to do for myself."

I watched her as she folded my clothing over her arm and came out of the stream, grateful that I hadn't had to step into the cold water again.

"You are all the goodness in the world," I said. Then, impulsively, I embraced her and squealed when my wet dress slapped me in the back as she returned the gesture.

We giggled all the way back to the house, and when we arrived, Onah was sitting in the yard playing some kind of game with the little boys.

Bethany hung my clothes on the line and said she would see me again in the morning.

"There's enough food in there for another meal," she said, glancing at Onah. "You could do worse than this one," she said, patting Onah's shoulder as she passed him and called for her sons.

Onah flushed, and I realized what she thought.

"You didn't tell her why you're here?" he asked me when she was gone.

My eyes met his. I shook my head. "I didn't know if I should."

He nodded. "It's probably better if she doesn't know you're fleeing a betrothal."

I sighed and turned to get the food Bethany had left for us.

Onah was quiet as we ate, and finally, I said, "It might be safer for you if you don't know either, but I'm going to tell you."

Onah ate quietly as I told him about my father, his public aspirations to be the Chief Judge, his secret aspirations to be king. I told him about the men who supported him and did his bidding, making those who opposed him disappear or change their minds. I told him about Kish, how he was one of those men, and how my father had offered me to him in exchange for some political foothold. I told him of the day in the kitchen, of my time hiding in the streets of Zarahemla, of Shad finding me, and the kindness his family had shown me. Finally, long after he had finished eating his portion, I told him of the wedding and of Kishkumen seeing me there because I was not obedient enough to stay where I was told.

"I knew the dangers, and still I strayed. I let my curiosity get the better of me, and I placed everyone in danger because of it. So many people have gone out of their way for me, yourself included."

His brow raised.

"And I'm so unworthy of it."

He pushed my dish toward me. "Eat," he said, and after I picked up a piece of bread, he said, "What does your worthiness have to do with it?"

I frowned. "Everything."

He leaned back and folded his arms. "We are not kind to people because they are worthy of our kindness."

"Everyone I knew in the city would disagree with you." I smiled wanly. "There are some who are not kind at all."

"It sounds like you didn't know very many nice people."

He had no idea.

"Everyone was kind to my face." It was awkward. I

shouldn't have said it. "When are you leaving?" I asked him quickly.

He leaned back and took a breath. "I was thinking I might stay a bit longer," he said, and it sounded like an admission. He glanced away. "Salome has kinsmen here. Men that could protect you from whatever danger you are facing, warriors who have braved many battles, but I feel the fewer people that know you're here, the better."

"You're right. Shad would agree."

His eyes narrowed when I mentioned Shad, and he said, "I don't think the men here would protect you from an unwanted betrothal. They might even be of a mind to take you back."

I met his eye. "Would they take me back to a man who hits me with his fists?"

His eyes went soft, but he shrugged. "They respect contracts." He paused. "And so do I."

"Illegal ones?"

"Probably not." He paused again. "But I don't know them very well. I've been here a few times with medicines. That's all."

"Bethany's boys seemed to know you."

A ghost of a smile touched his lips. "I do most of my dealings with Neel, their father. I know him to be good and fair. Anais was right to send Bethany to you. She can be discreet."

"It's getting late," I said.

Onah glanced around. "So it is." He stretched. "I'm going to stay here tonight."

I eyed him. Not that I minded, but did he sense a need? I stood and gathered the dishes. "Goodnight, Onah."

"Sleep in peace," he said.

That would have been nice, but it wasn't to be. It was hours before I would feel sleepy, and my heart was troubled. I had too much time to wonder what was happening in Melek and in Zarahemla. When I went out to look at the stars, Onah was asleep on a bedroll in the yard. I stepped silently past him and let him sleep. He looked boyish laying there, long and lean, his hair tousled, his mouth slightly open.

Jashon and Salome's home was peaceful. The house was tucked back into the woods, not far from a large open field that separated it from the rest of the village. I wondered if Jashon had deliberately built it there, so opposite from the location of his childhood home in the middle of the barley field. The house was sturdy and filled with possessions of quality, not opulence. It was apparent they were people of importance here. The moonlight that illuminated the field was tempting, but I couldn't go there. To come all this way and then go stand in some open field alone? I might be young. I might be a bit naïve about some things, but I wasn't—

"Going somewhere?"

I nearly jumped out of my skin. I whirled but didn't see anyone in the shadows that surrounded the house. My eyes found Onah on the ground, quiet and still.

A man stepped from the shadows and said, "Be at peace. I am Neel. I came so Gidgidonah could sleep. He seems to think you're in some trouble."

My eyes went again to Onah.

"He told me enough," Neel said. "Though I suspect he's keeping plenty aback yet."

"Then I thank you for coming."

He let the silence drag out, just the soft rustle of leaves between us. Was he angry? Suspicious? Shy?

"Is there a reason you're out tonight?"

Curious then.

I bit my lip. "I don't sleep well, not at night. I thought the cool air might help."

He shifted his weight. "Best to stay inside. This valley has seen its share of trouble."

I didn't know what trouble he spoke of. Something grave, by the sound of his voice. Neel was a complete stranger to me. Onah, too, and being alone with them, especially here in the dark, should make me nervous. I should go into that house and bar the door. But Shad had said these men were trustworthy. And Shad had proven himself trustworthy.

I felt suddenly very alone in the world. I had no home and no family.

And what is so wrong with that? I thought in the next instant. I remembered Shad's words. I was strong. I had crawled out of that kitchen and away from my home. I had left everything I knew, trading my dignity for my honor. I had learned to heed the feelings of my heart, and my faith had increased. I had learned to trust in good men and to believe in the opinions of honest women.

I had lost all but gained so much.

"You're right, Neel. I bid you goodnight."

CHAPTER 18

Before the sun rose, when the light was soft, I stepped silently through the house. I had felt empowered when I retired to bed, but I felt melancholy in the stillness of the morning. I missed my father. He could be loving, funny, even warm at times. I longed for my familiar home, and I even longed for the life I had led in which I was never required to think of anything of importance, certainly not of how I would eat, how I would survive, who I would marry and whether it was right or wrong to let him go through with it.

I pulled Salome's wrap more tightly around my shoulders, letting myself wish for a moment that it was very fine silk and I was a very fine lady. How could I miss such a shallow life?

I had not known there were boys like Shad. Like his brothers, like Onah. Honorable boys who would protect me, instead of boys who leered at me and tried to trap me in dark hallways.

I don't want that. Or rather, it is not mine to take.

In the corner of the main room, I found a dusty loom and next to it a basket filled with fragments of thread. The fragments were subtle, earthy colors that reminded me of Salome. Several unfinished attempts at cloth lay folded at the bottom of the basket, and I smiled, thinking perhaps she would not mind if I made use of her scraps.

I had a very fine start on a piece of fabric, a simple but pretty pattern emerging, when I heard a call outside the home. I thought it would be Onah, but when I rose and went to the door, I saw that it was Jashon and Salome, and with them were two boys. Both were taller than me, and the one with the crook in his nose reminded me of someone, perhaps putting me in mind of the Ammonite warriors I had heard tale of.

Salome smiled when she saw me, and Jashon lifted a hand in a wave. The boys were involved in a conversation, but they fell silent and halted when they noticed me standing in the doorway.

Jashon gave one of the boys a push on his back to get him moving and exchanged a look with his wife.

I went forward to greet them. I felt a little silly welcoming them to their own home, but I said, "Hello! Good afternoon. I'm afraid I have made myself at home, but I have nothing prepared for your refreshment."

Salome reached out for my hand and gave it a warm squeeze. "Nonsense. Of course you didn't know we would arrive today."

I shook my head, then glanced around. "Kenai's friend, Onah, is around somewhere."

Jashon gestured to the trees. "He's on guard in the trees where he is supposed to be." He gave me a curt nod, brushed past me, and went into the house.

Salome gestured to the boys. "Did you meet my son at the wedding?" she asked me.

I turned my eyes to her son, the one who looked like

Jashon. He had chestnut brown hair, a shade darker than his mother's, but green eyes that were a perfect match for hers. He was taller than she was, but perhaps not quite as tall as his father.

"No," he answered for me, stepping forward to place an eager hand on my shoulder. His smile was wide and friendly, and I immediately liked him. Something about his confidence was very attractive and put me at ease.

"I'm Ardon," he said. "And this is my friend, Nephi," he added, indicating the other boy and offering me a wide smile.

I smiled back. "I'm Livi." I turned to his friend, and that twinge of familiarity turned into an uncomfortable coil of recognition. For just a second, I wanted to hide from him, but I lifted my chin and said, "I believe we have already met."

His eyes narrowed as if he could not quite place me in his memory, but he would.

"In Zarahemla," I said to the others when they shot questioning looks toward Nephi and he just shrugged.

Bethany arrived with food and stayed to help us prepare more when she saw that her kinsfolk had arrived.

I found a bowl and some meal and began to mix dough for the flat bread that Naomi and Keturah called corn cakes. Salome dropped in some butter and smiled at me, and no one seemed to know this was not a chore I had done every day of my life. I found immense satisfaction in that and thought perhaps I was not a hopeless case and could someday be as proficient as Naomi at taking care of a family.

I tried to imagine what my life would be like if Kish succeeded in taking me to wife. Would we have a family? Would I spend my life protecting my children from him? Would I spend my life with foul-smelling kisses and hidden bruises?

"Everything all right?"

I looked up at Salome. She was wondering why I had stilled, why I was staring into space. Bethany was watching me, too.

"For now."

As we were setting out the meal, warm and aromatic, Onah and Neel walked into the clearing. Neel went to his wife and nodded to the rest of us. Onah stood awkwardly at the edge of the yard and sent me a small smile. Jashon gave a shrill whistle, and Ardon and Nephi came from behind the house where they had been chopping wood.

I helped serve the food and then sat between Salome and her son, but when Salome rose to tend to the others, I was left sitting with Ardon, Nephi, and Onah.

They were involved in a conversation they were all enjoying, but I caught Nephi's eye as I swallowed a bite of food. "Was it very bad?"

His smile dimmed.

"Zarahemla," I said. "When it fell."

Recognition dawned on his face, and though we had never been formally introduced, I knew he remembered taking my hand and running together through the city. He blew out a breath. "My family left before it happened. My mother and us kids, my younger cousins…"

"You helped them," I said. "To safety."

He shrugged.

"Your father stayed?"

He nodded. "He said the people would need his leadership."

"He was brave," I said, but I could tell it was the wrong thing to say because his face went red.

Was he afraid for his father? Was he angry that he had been sent away from the action? Had I implied that he had showed cowardice in leaving the city?

"You look different," he said after a moment.

I wanted to laugh. I was sure I looked very different without the jangling bangles encircling my wrists and the delicate henna designs around my eyes, without the intricately laced sandals and the artistic hairstyles that took two maids hours to fashion.

"Your eyes," he continued. "There is a light in them."

"What do you mean?" I asked, but of course I knew the mask he referred to, the one I had affected at my father's parties and campaigns, the polite distance I kept between myself and others.

"It wasn't there in Pahoran's courtyard party or the House of Paanchi. Your eyes were not as bright on the steps of the Grand Plaza or in the Zarahemlan markets. They definitely weren't as bright that night on my grandfather's estate when you were with Elias."

My eyes shot to his, and in them I found complete understanding of who I was and exactly where he knew me from. He remembered every detail. I could see it so clearly in his eyes, I knew he had been affecting his own mask with Ardon and his family, and I knew where he had learned to do it.

Ardon slid forward on his seat. "Your grandfather's estate?" He looked between us, disappointed to be left out of the secret we shared. "Who is Elias?"

I glanced at the older couples who were laughing together over some amusement and paying us no mind. Leaning closer to the boys, I said, "Nephi and I attended some of the same political functions in Zarahemla."

Ardon took that information in, and for some reason—perhaps his slight frown or the astute narrowing of his eyes—I sensed that he knew the value information could carry.

I licked my lips. "Elias is a mutual acquaintance."

Nephi scoffed and crossed his arms over his chest. "He is not nearly so dear to me, but I thought…" He squinted at me. "I thought he was a bit more dear to you."

It was a question of sorts. He was just curious, but I felt fire in my eyes when I looked at him. "You know he wasn't."

Nephi held my gaze a moment and then grimaced and look away.

I licked my lips again and glanced at the others. The light was soft and the rustle of the leaves and stalks of grain around us made our conversation seem private. I looked at Ardon.

"Your friend helped me once, though I don't know if he knew at the time just how much."

Nephi's frown was deep, and I thought perhaps he had known exactly how precarious my situation had been.

"It was an event at the Estate of Alma. My father asked me to entertain the son of his friend while they discussed business. I often did that. It was our routine. My father had many friends of significance, and it was important to keep his supporters happy." I started to nibble a nail but clasped my hands together in my lap. I had never told this story to anyone, never said these things about my father.

"He seemed nice at first, even polite. People liked him. He was charismatic. I thought he was handsome. It was hard to look away from him, and I found myself enjoying his company, but as he became more and more inebriated with drink, his words and his demeanor became lewd and suggestive. He said strange things, too, things that made me uneasy."

I took a moment to breathe, to think of my next words, and Ardon glanced at Nephi, who was staring at the ground as if he was trying to remember the night I spoke of, though I suspected he remembered it very well.

"Elias wanted to leave the party. He wanted to find a place in the dark, a place to be alone. I tried all my tricks to dissuade him." I couldn't help a small, wry smile. "I had many tricks, ways to evade and avoid and redirect advances I did not welcome, but this time, this time I was afraid. I realized I would not be able to get away, and just when I thought I would have to offend Elias and displease my father, Nephi approached us."

Salome and the others had gone quiet, and I knew they were listening to me, but it was well they knew what kind of life they were protecting me from.

"He drew up at my side as if...as if..." My eyes sought his. "As if he had been watching us and waiting for the right moment to intercede, though he made it seem like chance."

Nephi straightened and met my gaze.

"You remember," I said.

His eyes were shadowed and filled with emotions I could not name. "I remember."

I glanced around at the others. "He told Elias his friends were looking for him. He said there was a wager to join."

Nephi shrugged. "I knew Elias to have a weakness for wagering."

"Did you know of his intentions that night? Toward me?"

He met my eyes again. "I knew more than I wanted to and more than you did."

The yard fell quiet.

After a moment, I continued. "Nephi showed me the

family's private entrance to the estate and escorted me home through the dark streets. He helped me climb in through my window to keep my presence there unknown. I barred myself in my room till morning." I looked at Nephi. "And that has been the extent of our acquaintance."

Ardon raked a hand through his hair and blew out a breath. "I can see there will be many nuances of politics to learn when I take my grandfather's place in meetings of state."

"I do not relish the idea of you going there," Salome said.

Jashon put a hand on her shoulder.

"We've talked of this, Mother," Ardon said, his tone kind but hinting they had spoken of his responsibilities to his tribe many times. "We must have contacts outside our tribe, especially if we intend to increase our trade. Do you think me incapable of learning to move within the circles of those in positions of power?"

"Well of course you are capable."

"And I have Nephi to instruct me."

Nephi scoffed. "My father hardly lets me experience anything. He shelters me."

"My father did not shelter me," I said, thinking that perhaps he should have. "I can tell you information about many of the leaders you will find yourself dealing with."

Ardon couldn't conceal his grin. "I'll take that as an invitation to appear on your doorstep."

"Should I ever have a doorstep," I laughed, "you would be most welcome on it."

Jashon cleared his throat. "Are you and Shad planning to stay in the city?"

"We aren't planning anything."

Jashon's eyes narrowed.

"Or rather, we have not planned anything together. There has been no time for that, but I'm sure he thinks he has it all worked out to his best advantage."

Jashon dropped his chin, a small smile touching his lips.

"But of course we could not return to Zarahemla, even if Moronihah and our armies somehow take it back. Kishkumen is there, and if he ever finds me, the consequence will be severe."

I felt Nephi straighten next to me. "Kishkumen?"

"You know him?"

His lips went tight. "One of Elias's friends."

"Well, yes, but…"

Nephi turned dark, knowing eyes to mine.

"But Elias is not a friend of mine," I finished.

"And clearly not a very loyal friend to Kish. They're not exactly the kind of people you want to be friends with," he said, looking at me but speaking to everyone.

I glanced at Ardon. "And not exactly the kind of people you want as enemies."

Ardon exchanged a look with his kinsman, Neel.

"There is rumored to be a faction in the government," Nephi said slowly, as if he were trying to decide whether or not he should tell us. "One that plans a takeover. They are crafty and, though the courts have tried, nothing has been proven."

"What kind of faction?" Neel asked.

"My father says they want to instate a king."

"Kingmen," Jashon supplied.

"But what is wrong with having a king?" Salome asked. "We have a chief ruler like unto a king, and it has worked for hundreds of years, since our forefathers came out of Jerusalem with Muloki, Son of Zedekiah. We have peace and safety here in the valley."

"Nothing is wrong with having a king," her husband told her, shaking his head slowly. "Not if he is righteous."

"But we are not as safe as you think," Neel added. "And Ardon is right to seek alliances among other tribes and peoples."

"It is a new time, Mother."

Jashon sighed. "And there is much unrest. So much that my people are talking of sailing to the lands north. My family is talking of it."

Salome frowned down at her hands.

"Would you go?" I asked Ardon. "Would you take your people?"

He shook his head. "These are the lands of my people. We will live on our lands as we have done for generations. My people wouldn't leave, even if Grandfather considered it."

I looked at the lines around Jashon's eyes, the strain in his wife's. His family was thinking of leaving the Land of Melek, but his wife could not leave her son.

Was Shad thinking of leaving? Did Jashon think he wouldn't? Did he think I would tie Shad to Zarahemla as his wife tied him here? There was unrest in the government, but surely the daily lives of the people would not change overmuch, even if the kingmen did succeed.

Neel looked pleased at his nephew's pronouncement, but everyone else seemed troubled. I wished I could say something that would ease their minds.

"My father is a kingman," I said into the silence. "He was. He was the man they meant to place on the throne. He and several of his cohorts were apprehended, sentenced to die, or so Shad says. Perhaps the government will stop a rebellion before one occurs."

I looked up into Salome's kind eyes.

"We will pray for peace," she said after a moment. "But for now, we should all get some rest."

Jashon stood abruptly and motioned to the boys next to me. "I'll take the first watch. Onah, you sleep."

I had felt it almost silly that the men kept such a vigilant watch on the barley farm, tucked into Orihah among their friends and kinsmen, but ever since I had caught a glimpse of Kishkumen's calculating eyes at the wedding, I didn't think there were enough men in all of Melek to keep watch.

I stood, too. "Thank you all for what you have done for me. I am in your debt."

Salome came to me. "You are family," she said simply. "Come into the house now. The boys will sleep outside."

But of course I could not sleep. I tried, but long after I could hear Salome's breath become slow and deep, I stared at the sliver of moonlight that slipped through the small window. After failing at a valiant effort to close my eyes, I rose and crept from the house.

I wandered to the edge of the tree line. My feet were bare, and I felt the coolness of the fine dirt as I stepped over it.

A shadow parted from a dark tree.

"Gid said you do this a lot."

"Gideon didn't have a problem with it."

"My brother is a little too indulgent."

My foot brushed over a stone, but it was smooth as if it had been worn down. I smiled and tucked a bit of hair behind my ear.

"I'll go back in," I said. "If it's distracting you from your watch."

He paused, not giving answer to that. Or perhaps the pause was his answer. After a moment, he said, "Gid told me what happened to you. He told me why Shad got you out of Zarahemla."

I stood before him in the silent woods.

"I think he did the right thing," he said. "And you are welcome here for as long as necessary, but I don't think the problem will go away by hiding from it here."

He paused again, this time waiting for a response.

I had suspected Jashon would be here in the dark. I had suspected his opinion differed from his brothers' opinions.

I took a breath. "I agree."

He shifted.

"I have always disagreed with Shad. He has this notion that a marriage would save me from the threat of Kishkumen, but it will not. In Kish's mind, I already belong to him, and he will not stop until…until…"

"Until he is stopped."

Jashon's voice was quiet in the still night. Calm. Sure.

I rubbed a rough fingernail over my thumb. "Yes, I suppose that is the right of it," I said after a moment.

"Then let us go stop him, Livi."

CHAPTER 19

Stop Kishkumen.

Was it possible?

I watched Jashon through the morning. It was like we had not shared a midnight conversation about traveling to Zarahemla, about entering an enemy-occupied city and making my illegal betrothal go away.

He took all three boys fishing, and they came back mid-morning with fish for the afternoon meal and fish to dry. The next day, they brought back a small deer and Salome and Bethany showed me how to make venison and prepare the meat for travel.

"I'll take these things to the stream and clean them," I offered when we finished hanging the last strips of meat.

They both thanked me for my help, but it was I who owed gratitude to them, I thought as I rinsed the dishes and set them out on a large, flat stone to dry.

"He looks like Shad."

I turned when Onah approached. I offered him a smile but turned back to the setting sun. "There is a family resemblance, I suppose."

Jashon and Salome were silhouetted against the evening

sky, walking arm in arm through the stalks of grain. With all the guests at their small home, it was no wonder they sought a place to be alone.

"You have hardly taken your eyes from him these past days."

I glanced at Onah again. "Is that jealousy?" I teased.

He scratched the back of his head. "I don't know."

"Surely you have a girl at home, some sweet girl you are missing."

He shrugged.

"I hadn't thought myself to be staring, but it is not, perhaps, for the reason you imagine."

"No?"

I smiled. "I feel safe with him." I turned to look at Onah. "I always felt confident in my home. My father allowed me many freedoms, and I went about my days with an air of independence." I paused and turned back to see Jashon and his wife disappear into the woods.

Did you think your father let you out into the city alone?

I took a deep breath. "But my father created a false sense of safety for me. I had unseen guards, and my independence was a lie."

Onah's profile was strong, and his calm silence invited me to confide in him further.

"I have become suddenly very aware of my frailties, Onah. I have neither the skill nor experience to protect and provide for myself. I cannot save myself from the dangers of this world."

"Your heart is not engaged then?"

"With Jashon?" I laughed. "Not even a little."

"With his brother."

I sighed. "I hate to confuse them."

He turned toward me.

"Gratitude," I said. "And love. They feel very much the same."

He nodded slowly and let the subject drop. "How is your knee? Ready to travel?"

I grinned and held it out for his inspection. "Your remedies worked wonders."

He stooped to inspect it, ran a brief knuckle over the area that had been bruised, then straightened. "I'm traveling with you as far north as my village."

"I think you've stayed a bit longer than you planned. You must be anxious to get home."

Onah's eyes were dark, but he smiled. "My presence seemed more appropriate with the family home."

"And so it was," I agreed. "Thank you for bringing me here," I said more softly.

He flashed his great smile. "It was no trouble, Livi."

"You are good," I said. I heard the word — good — and it sounded silly. It sounded trite, like a description that was not strong enough for this loyal, helpful, and intelligent boy. But it was the exact right word. "I feel safe with you, too," I added.

He glanced toward the place Jashon had disappeared. "I'll take that as a high compliment. Now, come on." He bent and picked up the dishes I had set to dry. "We've a long journey tomorrow."

He was already moving toward the house, and I followed him toward all the things that would bring me peace, and somehow, when I lay down on my pallet, I slept.

It was still dark when Salome woke me with a soft hand on my shoulder.

"Little Sister, it is time to go."

I opened my eyes to see her shadowed silhouette above me, but I thought of her kind face and the concern I knew would be in her eyes, and I wished I truly were her sister.

Ardon was outside with his father when we emerged from the house. They were conversing quietly in the predawn light but stopped when they saw us. Salome pressed some bread and cheese into my hands.

"Eat," she encouraged.

Before I had finished the food, Nephi came up from the stream, beads of water dripping from the tips of his hair onto his clean tunic, and Onah and Neel stepped from the trees into the firelight.

"This is from Bethany," Neel said as he stepped forward and set a bundle on the table next to me. When my eyes found his, he said, "Clothing, I think."

I let my fingers touch the cloth. She had sent me clothing?

"Thank you," I said after a pause that was too long. "You must tell her thank you."

He nodded and helped himself to food.

Jashon was giving last minute instructions to his son. I watched them together, so obviously similar in almost every way. Was Ardon not to accompany us into the city? He had spoken with anticipation of going to the city, but when I saw him move to stand protectively near Salome, I understood why this would not be the time for him to go there.

Though Ardon stood back and accepted food from his mother, Nephi was tightening the straps on his traveling gear. Onah was doing likewise, and just before the sun began to rise over the distant hills, Jashon looked to the horizon and said, "It is time."

If Onah and I had traveled the path Jashon led us on, I didn't recognize it, and anyway, Jashon did not seem to be following established roads.

My longboots had only required a little kneading after their trip through the river with Shad to return to their previous softness, and though Onah had supplied me with healing salve for my blisters and cuts, I was careful to check often for tender spots in order to prevent more wounds. I did not know what would come in the days ahead. I only knew I would need to be at my best and strongest to get through it.

After several days, it was time for Onah to turn off toward his home. Jashon's farewell was not lengthy, not much more than a thank you and a nod, and though I had begun to suspect it was a mark of honor to have earned a nod from Jashon, it did make the goodbye too brief.

"Will I see you again?" I asked Onah as the others moved away.

His eyes were dark like obsidian as he glanced beyond me to Jashon and Nephi. He gestured me on with a nod in their direction, and his lips turned up at one corner as if he could not quite help smiling. "I'm sure our paths will cross again, Livi."

I nodded, though I knew my nod did not carry the weight Jashon's did, and then I turned and hurried after the others.

We didn't travel as quickly as Onah and I had, and we camped for several nights. On the fourth day, when the light became soft in the evening, Jashon stopped in a sheltered grove of trees. While Nephi built a fire, I rummaged in my pack for food. Most of our preserved foods were used up, and I was eyeing the birds tied to Jashon's pack, which he had shot with his sling during the long hours of the day.

He treated me to a rare grin when he saw me staring at the limp birds. But his voice was gentle when he said, "I will show you how to prepare them."

I didn't enjoy the task, not even a little, but I managed to do as he instructed.

I glanced at the falling sun as I slowly plucked out the feathers. "It would go faster if you did it," I said, biting my lip as I pulled on another feather.

"You're doing fine," he said. "Remember to use both hands, like I showed you."

I repositioned two fingers of my left hand on the bird's thin skin and plucked as quickly as I could with my right hand.

Nephi had the fire going strong, and he sat down to watch. "I've never plucked a bird, either," he said, gesturing to the bird at Jashon's feet. "Might I try as well?"

Jashon raised a brow but tossed him the bird without comment.

"We had a cook," Nephi said, then he snorted. "I speak six languages and know enough mathematics to design a night sky, but I fear my education is severely lacking."

Jashon stared at him silently for a moment. "Nothing that can't be remedied," he said at last, and he set about constructing a spit on which we could roast the birds. Finally, he gave Nephi a long look and glanced over to include me when he said, "As long as you know how to learn, you know enough."

It was a generous thing to say to a boy who didn't feel as if he knew anything and a girl who truly didn't.

"How close are we?" I asked.

"This is Amnihu," Jashon said simply.

My stomach flipped. We would be there tomorrow if we were on the hill Amnihu.

"Are you anxious to get home?" I asked Nephi as Jashon took the bird from me, skewered it, and set it on the spit.

In the moment Nephi seemed to hesitate, Jashon donned his sword and wandered off into the forest.

My eyes shot to Nephi's. Even I knew that a man didn't take his sword when he only meant to hunt wild game.

"A precaution," Nephi said, reading the alarm in my eyes. "We're within a day of an occupied city."

I pressed my lips together and nodded, though it did feel as though Jashon knew something he was not sharing, and perhaps Nephi as well.

What might they be keeping from me?

"To answer your question," Nephi continued, interrupting my thoughts. "I am anxious. My father will not be pleased that I left my mother and siblings."

"Are they safe?"

His eyes flicked to the west. "As safe as they can be."

"Well then. What more could your father want of you?"

He finished with his bird and knelt to affix it to the spit as we had seen Jashon do. "My safety," he said.

I knelt next to him. "Surely your father can't think to keep you far from harm all the days of your life. You are practically grown."

He laughed. "Surely not. It is likely my obedience that interests him more than my safety."

I touched his arm and waited slow moments for his eyes to meet mine. "I wish my father had taken a care for my safety. I wish he had taken a thought to his own." I thought of his secret meetings and quiet dealings and supposed he had thought he was providing protection.

"And now you must marry Shad to ensure your safety."

I sensed Jashon in the trees beyond our camp and met his eyes as he stepped into the firelight.

"Shad thinks so."

Jashon watched me closely as he knelt to check the doneness of the birds, but his eyes didn't narrow like they had the first time we met.

I studied the sky as Jashon and Nephi talked over our plans. The fire burned low, and I wondered if we would be successful.

"We'll go in tomorrow morning," Jashon said.

"In broad daylight?"

I straightened, drawing Nephi's attention. Jashon and I had already planned this part out, but how could I explain it?

"Kishkumen hides among his friends," I said. "Or rather, his friends hide him from the officials. The only way to get to him will be to let him find us first."

Nephi's head whipped back around to Jashon. "You don't mean to use her as bait!"

Jashon shook his head. "Not exactly. We will let it be known that Olivia is inside the city. That's all."

Nephi gave Jashon a long look. Finally, he said simply, "In what way can I be of help?"

"It's not—"

"You forget," Nephi cut in. "I'm acquainted with Kish and his friends."

"I doubt your acquaintance will be of help," Jashon said, shaking his head.

"I doubt it as well. They would neither know me nor trust me. I only meant, I know of the importance of putting a stop to this sham of a betrothal and a stop to Kishkumen's band of Gadiantons, as well."

Jashon's eyes changed in the low light. They glinted as he watched Nephi. "Where did you hear that name—Gadianton?"

Nephi leaned forward, placed his elbows on his knees and studied his hands. The fire crackled and the wind rustled the leaves around us. Even in the circle of heat from the fire, I shivered.

I had heard the name also, and as my mind sorted through the faces that had passed through my father's house, I felt sure I had even seen the man called Gadianton.

"Gadianton is not his true name," I said.

Jashon and Nephi turned to look at me.

"At first, I thought Shad was using me for information." I couldn't stop a rueful smile. "But I slowly realized that if he even suspected what I knew, he'd have pressured me for more information." I kept my eyes focused on the fire.

"What are you talking about? What kind of information?"

I licked my lips. "There are many pretty girls in Zarahemla. Do you think Kishkumen persists in tracking me across the countryside because he wants a pretty wife? One who is the daughter of a man who no longer has political sway? He's tracking me because of what I know."

"Olivia, what aren't you saying? What do you know?"

I looked up into Jashon's eyes, so like his brother's. "I know all of it."

I wasn't trying to be deliberately vague, but how could I condense years of overheard conversations and how I had ignored them, denied it all and pretended not to know.

Jashon's eyes were bright. Where I might have seen confusion, I saw clear comprehension.

237

"We know that Gadianton has planned strategic assassinations. We have a list of possible targets and a fair idea of the timeframe, but we don't know who the next target is."

"After Pahoran?" I glanced at Nephi. "The next Chief Judge."

The fire crackled between us, but there was an eerie stillness in the forest around us.

"I mean, that was one plan I overheard, but I don't know if they will go forward with it during the occupation. It can do no good to them since the judges do not control the city."

I had barely registered the absence of animal sounds in the forest, but when I heard the high-pitched cry of the margay, I knew the reason why the forest had fallen still.

Jashon made the low call of an owl, and in a few moments, seven men appeared in the firelight, each one from a different direction.

"You're late," Jashon said as he leaned forward and tossed a very small log onto the fire. It was a moment until it caught, and when it did, the clearing lit enough to see the men.

Zeke was there in the flicker and shadows, and his burning gaze made me drop my eyes in shame. I had crept from his house during the night when I had promised I wouldn't.

I grimaced and inspected the other men. I recognized Kenai, the man who had run to find Onah and who had returned to Melek with Shad. There were three others I didn't recognize, but when I turned to get a better look at who had come in behind me, I saw that it was Gideon and his father, Liam.

As the men got settled and Jashon offered them food, I realized that he had not been completely forthright with me about coming here. This had been planned. This was about more than my betrothal, about more than Kishkumen.

Gideon went to his heels next to me, and to my surprise, Liam knelt on my other side. They surrounded me with a feeling of protection I hardly deserved.

"Do Naomi and Keturah know you are not on watch tonight?" I asked them.

There was a gleam of laughter in Gideon's eyes, but it was Liam who said, "You would think we had given her a gift of fine jewelry when we told her she could take a watch."

Gideon shook his head. "She wouldn't have been nearly as excited about jewelry."

I smiled at that, thinking of the pretty barrette she had given me, and searched the edges of the firelight. "Is Lamech in the trees?"

"At home with his wife, though he wished to be in both places."

"But why are you here? What is happening? I fear I am wholly uninformed."

"Uninformed?" Jashon broke in from the far side of the fire. "Olivia seems to be the only one who knows anything."

All eyes turned to me.

"The target is Nephi's father," Jashon continued.

"A small bit of information you might have mentioned sooner," Nephi added.

I gave him an apologetic smile and looked around at the others. "I heard my father say many times that information itself is of no value until it is."

"That's the truth," Kenai said. "Olivia, have you met my brother, Micah?" He gestured to the man sitting next to him, lanky like Kenai but with darker hair and an endearingly boyish smile that didn't match the worry in his eyes. "And my father, Kalem."

I shook my head, though I did remember seeing Kalem at the wedding in the village.

Kalem gave me a small nod, but I could see worry in his eyes, too, and knew that he had things other than introductions on his mind.

Zeke studied Kalem an extra moment, but turned to me and said, "Livi, this is my brother, Jarom."

"I would never have guessed," I teased, for they looked very much alike. They both rolled their eyes at that, but they seemed to draw closer to each other. I could see it was a topic that made them both uncomfortable. "But though your features are the same," I added, "it is your unity that makes you look like brothers."

They glanced at each other, their lips twisting in the same way to prevent what I suspected would be the same smiles.

"You know everyone?" Jashon said to Nephi.

Nephi glanced around and nodded.

Jashon sat straighter and did not waste more words. "We'll go into the city tomorrow. I think it best if we get an early start. Once Kishkumen gets word that Olivia has been seen in Zarahemla, he will find us. That will be the easy part. It may take a bit more finesse to get him to sign a decree of divorce, but Olivia says she has information he will not want revealed. A simple threat should be all it takes. Then, we will see that Darius and Shad complete their mission in safety."

"How are we to enter the occupied city?" Zeke asked.

"Olivia says there is a place that is unguarded where the wall simply does not exist."

"I said it is unguarded by the Lamanites. Kishkumen's men will be watching it, and who knows who else will have their eyes on it."

Jashon looked to Kenai.

Kenai leaned back and folded his arms. He looked at me. "Any idea how many men?"

"I'm sorry, no."

He smirked and turned back to Jashon. "The guards will not be a problem."

Jashon gave a curt nod. "And persuading Olivia's bridegroom that Olivia is not the girl for him?"

Liam put a hand on my shoulder, and that seemed to be the only answer Jashon needed.

A sudden sting hit my eyes.

"How do we know the way in is not guarded by a thousand men now?" Jarom asked. "And what could Livi possibly know about Kish that would persuade him to end the marriage contract?"

"There were no men watching the wall when Shad took me over it before. No soldiers and definitely none of Kish's men, though he said they regularly watched it. And as to what I know..."

I looked to Jashon to see if I should answer the other question. His slight nod indicated I could tell them.

"Kishkumen is the man who assassinated Pahoran on the judgment seat."

I heard murmurs and the rustling of clothing as the men straightened and leaned toward me.

"Each of his men made an oath of silence in exchange for a position of power in the new government, but of course, I would make no such oath, and I have the scars to prove it."

CHAPTER 20

It was no secret I didn't always love mornings after a wakeful night and, knowing what this day would require of me, I expected to hate this one, to be groggy and moody and have trouble opening my eyes. But the light was soft and pink through my lids, and when I eased my eyes open, Shad's kinsmen were near.

I knew it was by design, and I felt safe. I felt wanted, and I knew that even though I was, strictly speaking, bait for a trap, each one of these men would absolutely give his life before he let Kishkumen hurt me.

For that, I would be as brave as was needed.

I sat up and gave Gideon a tired smile. He nodded, but before either of us could speak, there was a commotion at the edge of the trees.

Zeke and Micah were hurrying into camp.

Liam looked up. Gideon got to his feet, but Zeke passed him and went to Jashon.

"There is an army outside the walls of Zarahemla."

Everyone started talking at once, but Jashon raised a hand, and Zeke continued.

"We think it is Nephite. It must be. Kenai and Jarom

went on to get a closer look."

Jashon's brows rose.

Nephi was on his feet. "Do they intend to take the city back? Can it be done?"

Gideon folded his arms. "If the bulk of the Lamanite army has moved on, it could be done."

"Moved on? Moved on to where? Zarahemla is the capital city!"

"Moved on toward the isthmus."

"Oh." Nephi scratched his head and paced. "Well, what do we do now?"

Several of the men looked at me, but Jashon said, "We wait."

But he obviously didn't intend to wait where we were, because we packed up quickly and left the clearing before the sun topped the hills to our east. The morning was cool and dewy, and I was grateful for the longboots Shad had given me as I walked through the tall, wet grasses.

We descended as we walked, and I realized we must have met the others at the top of Amnihu. It was difficult to get a view of the larger terrain, as we were walking amongst many trees and foliage, and I was grateful also that I had these men and their knowledge to rely on.

It was still early morning when the trees thinned and Zarahemla came into view. We drew to a stop near a ledge on the trail and watched. Men were already through the west gates of the city, and a large host of soldiers sat waiting on the plains of Zarahemla.

"Aw, we missed it," Nephi said, disappointed.

Gideon shrugged and replied matter-of-factly. "Not all of it."

Jashon made no move to lead us farther. I watched for a while longer, but eventually sat on the soft ground and leaned back against a fallen log. I stretched my legs out into the sunlight so my boots would dry.

Gideon had his arms crossed over his chest, but he pointed at something and spoke to his father. "Look there."

"Can you actually see them fighting?" I asked.

Gideon and Liam turned to look at me over their shoulders. Liam shook his head, and Gideon broke away from the others. He sat near me on the log and leaned forward, his elbows on his knees, so he could talk to me.

"There was likely only resistance at the gate. Coriantumr didn't leave enough men here to defend it against an army."

"How do you know? Can you tell?"

His eyes narrowed a little as he looked toward Zarahemla. "I've seen many takeovers, Livi."

I could see the army outside the gates, and I could see that the gates had been breached, but I didn't know how he even knew this army was a Nephite one. We weren't close enough. He seemed so sure, though, and I decided to keep my trust in him.

"What of our plans, then?" I asked. "To help Shad and to dissolve my betrothal."

"We'll wait and see what Kenai recommends for gaining entrance into the city. Kishkumen and his men might lay low for a while, postpone their own plans. And it's entirely possible that with the army here now, the gates will open again." His voice softened. "Our plans might change, Livi, but we won't stop until we have accomplished what we came here to do."

We were supposed to be have been inside the city by now. Kishkumen was supposed to hear that I had been seen.

The men were moving, coming back toward me, and I could see Kenai and Jarom were in their midst. Some of the men went to their heels. Some of them sat or stood, but they all gave their full attention to Kenai.

"Moronihah," he said.

Nephite.

A sense of relief went through the small group, or perhaps reassurance of what they all seemed to already know.

Kenai turned to Zeke. "Seth is here."

"You went all the way into the ranks?"

Kenai shrugged, and Jarom smirked.

"He will meet us when the takeover is complete. Coriantumr is dead. A great battle happened to the north, toward Bountiful. Many were killed. Seth says they will fight those who oppose them here, but it is to be a peaceful takeover of the government. Moronihah will return it to the Judges and most likely let the Lamanite soldiers return to their homes."

"Let them go?" Nephi exclaimed.

Jashon turned to explain, his voice patient and informative. "We haven't prisons to hold them all, nor food enough to feed them."

"Who is Seth?" I asked.

Gideon leaned down to me again. "Seth fought with the two thousand sons of Helaman. He is descended of Zoram, but has long since been adopted into the Ammonite clans. He is a great warrior." He turned to Kenai. "Was Eli with him?"

Kenai shook his head, and I didn't miss an amused smile he shared with Jarom. Then he pointed to the south. "We'll wait it out at the top."

I turned and looked back up the hill. I had hardly noticed the incline when we ascended it, as it was more gently sloped on the south side, being in the foothills of mountains we had already traversed, but the way back to the top was steep.

Gideon laughed when he saw my face. "We can't stay here. We'd all roll down the hill in our sleep."

"We'll have to stay on the hill another night?" I asked as I got to my feet.

"Maybe a few. It depends."

"Depends on what?"

He eyed me a moment before he replied. "Lots of things."

I looked at my boots. I knew the plans Jashon and I had discussed had been complicated by the army and the takeover, but I was afraid I would lose my nerve if this dragged on.

Liam edged closer, and I sensed he wanted to say something, so I looked up into his brown eyes.

And he didn't need to say anything.

I knew he would free me from my betrothal to the horrible Kishkumen, and he would see that I was safe and provided for as long as I needed it, whether I married his son or not.

I thought of all the words that had come from my own father's mouth, saying this to that man and that to another, making deals, making promises, making wagers and bargains.

But one look from this honest man said more than my father ever had or ever could have.

I did something silly and placed my hand on his shoulder.

A softness came into his eyes and he said, "Come on. Let's get you back up to camp."

When we were back to the place we had camped, Gideon untied my bedroll from his pack, and Zeke uncovered the fire that had been buried that morning. I glanced around at the others, most of whom were busy in some way, cutting more wood or arranging gear. I was disappointed that there would be an indefinite wait. Thinking of encountering Kishkumen again made me breathless for a moment, and my hand went to my chest.

Liam might have sensed my nervousness because he drew a small bag from his satchel and poured several small sticks into his hand. He opened it for me to see, but he needn't have. I knew what would be inside. I took the sticks from him, knelt, and tossed them.

The others watched us play, and soon, many of them had joined in. As the circle became more crowded, Liam stood and edged away. He offered me a small, endearing smile, and went to sit under a tree with Kalem, who was sharpening his knife with a whetstone.

A few of the men started to toss in wagers, but I thought in the end, they all took back their own money. I had already seen by their regard for each other that none of them would want to get gain from his brother's loss. It made my heart warm.

"You have the magic touch," Micah said.

His words were kind, but his voice was steely, and a glance at Gideon advised me not to make mention of his tone.

"Did Micah bet against me?" I asked Gideon later when I found him sitting at the edge of camp alone, dressing out a pile of rabbits. "Did he lose money?"

"He fears for his brother." He paused. "Darius is in some trouble."

"With Shad," I said.

He sighed heavily. "With Shad."

"Will you and your kinsmen be able to right all the

248

wrongs of the world?" I asked and sat next to him, eyeing the rabbits warily.

"I only wish we could."

"But there must be an opposition in all things."

Gideon turned and studied me for a minute.

I remembered that first day when Shad had been so surprised that I knew of the teachings of the prophets.

"I must really look like a spoiled princess," I said.

He raised a brow.

"I have read from the original books of the prophets, you know. My father indulged many of my whims."

He considered that as he peeled back the skin from the meat of the animal he was dressing out. "It's not a whim to learn of the Christ," he said at last.

I shrugged and turned my gaze toward camp where the other men were moving about, stoking up the fire, inspecting their weapons. "My father thought it was. Nevertheless, he procured opportunities for me. For that, I will always be grateful."

"He loved you, Livi."

"I know," I said simply. "But I think in the end, it did not matter. I think in the end, he loved himself more."

"Would you wish for a different ending? Do you wish to be back in the city, attending extravagant parties and shopping in the Grand Plaza?"

His tone was light, but I got the impression he was not talking of parties and shopping. I chose my words carefully.

"For myself, I am not displeased with the turn my life has taken, though I will not lie and say I haven't been homesick for my father and yes, even for the market. But for your brother, I still feel he is making a sacrifice he may regret."

Again, he took a moment to study me, his hands stilled over the rabbit. It seemed that Gideon would not talk unless and until he had something of worth to say.

Finally, he asked, "Livi, do you believe you are a child of God?"

"I was taught to believe that, yes."

"Then you understand that your worth does not come from being Paanchi's daughter. It does not come from the status he could gain through your marriage. It never came from wearing bangles and henna decorations on your skin. Your worth will not come from being Shad's wife, or even from your skill at the domestic arts you have been learning."

I looked up at him.

"And your worth would not be diminished even if your father had succeeded in giving you to Kishkumen."

I held his gaze for a moment. "Keturah is a lucky wife," I said.

A side of his mouth tipped up and he turned back to the rabbit.

"Livi, Salome was married to the son of the Chief Ruler of the Mulekites before she was married to Jashon. Keturah's father was a tributary Lamanite king before he died in battle."

"I have heard Lamech call Sarai Princess many times," I said slowly.

"Because he knows who she is. He knows her worth."

I bit my lip.

"Is it any wonder Shad wants a princess of his own?"

"I told you, my father was not made king."

"And I told you, your worth is not determined by what he is or is not."

He was saying that my worth was not determined by my

earthly father—or any earthly thing—but by my heavenly one.

I suddenly sensed a presence next to me and turned to see Liam had gone to his heels there. He reached out for one of the limp rabbits.

I thought the conversation was over when Liam softly cleared his throat. "My boys all know that what happens to a girl without her consent has no bearing on her worth or worthiness."

He didn't say any more, and neither did Gideon. I let his words roll through my mind as the evening went on, as we cooked and ate the rabbits, as we prepared for sleep and others prepared to take a watch through the night.

Without her consent.

A man who spoke so little as Liam spoke did not say empty words. So, what could he have meant? Being wed to Kishkumen against my will?

I thought of what Gideon had said about Salome and Keturah, and Sarai.

Because he knows who she is.

Lamech.

My stomach knotted up.

Without her consent.

I thought of the boy who had given me his cloak when it was cold and made me a fire when it was dark.

He was not Liam's son.

Had I ever doubted Naomi's worth or importance on the farmstead? Never! I had envied her and followed her and clung to her instruction. She was the mother I had never had, and she was beautiful and strong and worthy in every way of a kingdom that would surely be hers after the time the Christ should come for the second time.

When would I see myself in the same way? When would

251

I see my worth existed beyond the walls of my father's house?

I didn't get up to wander the camp that night, but I should have.

"Shad was here?"

Jashon and Gideon turned from their conversation.

"Only for a few minutes. He had to hurry back to the gates of the city."

I wanted to stomp my foot. How could he come and not wake me?

Jashon and Gideon both chuckled. "Don't pout, Princess. You'll have too much of him soon enough."

It was several days before Jashon judged it safe to enter the city. Though the gates weren't open to travelers yet, he thought the guards could be persuaded to let us pass, but I was confused when the gates came into view.

I was walking with Nephi, and I turned to ask him, "Why are there Lamanites guarding the gate?"

He shrugged, his eyes dark and his frown deep as he studied the gates.

Jashon drew up beside us. "It is how it is done. See? There are Nephite guards as well."

"For what purpose?" Nephi asked.

"Until all the soldiers of the Lamanite army have made an oath to stop fighting and have departed for their homeland, there will be Lamanite guardsmen here at the gate. It is a courtesy we allow, and it does take some time."

"Is it a courtesy they extend as well?"

I heard Gideon snort from behind us.

"No," Jashon clarified.

"Will they let us through?"

"We will soon find out." I couldn't place the note of

emotion in Nephi's voice. Was it trepidation? Excitement? Homesickness?

We weren't the only people outside the gates, but as we drew closer, the other people seemed to drift away and open a passage for us.

I saw Shad.

He had gone to his heels near the wall and appeared to be playing his father's game of chance or perhaps something similar. He glanced up when we approached, but he didn't seem to recognize us at all and our arrival didn't even cause a hesitation in his play. He must have won the toss because he grinned and the other men there groaned and cursed.

There was only one guard who seemed to be attending to his guard duty. He was a man, young but older than me. Dark, but not so dark as the near naked Lamanite men who lounged against the wall and sat in the grass cleaning their nails with their long daggers. He leaned against the gates where they met in the middle.

Jashon stepped forward to address him, but Zeke laid a hand on his shoulder and stepped past him.

"Kimner!" he called, and the man's eyes lit with recognition. "I see you survived the skirmish."

At that, Kimner cracked a smile. "Barely a skirmish at all." He came off the gate in one swift movement. "More like a scuffle."

Nephi left my side and surprised me when he walked up to Kimner and said, "Is my father all right?"

Kimner adjusted his stance and ducked his head, but it was a nod.

"Can we gain entrance to the city?"

Kimner reached out and ruffled Nephi's hair. They were

253

of the same height and stature, and his silliness made me smile.

"These people might revolt if I open the gates for you and not them." He gestured to the people that were scattered through the outer fields and camped on the plains of Zarahemla.

"Is there—"

Kimner reached out for Nephi's hair again, but Nephi ducked away.

"Is there no way in, then?"

"For you?" Kimner smirked. He glanced at the other members of our traveling party, and his eyes landed on me. I saw recognition in them, though I was nearly sure we had never met. He turned them suddenly back to Nephi and said, "For you, of course there is a way."

"Who is in charge here?" Zeke asked, eyeing the men near the gate warily.

Kimner snorted. "No one." But he seemed to draw himself up and said, "I am the senior Nephite guard."

Zeke leaned toward him and lowered his voice. "A fact we mean to exploit."

Kimner laughed. "If you say you have a need to enter the city, what can I say against you? But beware. The takeover is not yet completed, and it is dangerous beyond these walls."

Zeke glanced pointedly at the Lamanite soldiers outside the walls.

Kimner scoffed. "Lazy turtles." He turned and moved toward the gate, and because I was curious about him and watching him closely, I didn't miss the slight beckon of two fingers low at his side.

Gideon didn't miss it either, and his hand was at the small of my back urging me forward before another word could be spoken.

"Quickly," he whispered.

And with no more fuss, Kimner, Zeke, and Micah hefted the gate slightly open and we all stepped through it one by one. As I slipped from the cool shade of the morning, Kimner caught my eyes and murmured, "Good luck."

CHAPTER 21

"Do you know him?" I asked Nephi as we hurried through the streets of Zarahemla.

The morning sun shone on his hair as he glanced at me sideways and let out a long breath. "He was a guard at the Estate when I was a child."

"I gather he still treats you like one" I said, thinking that if Kimner had worked on the Estate of Alma, perhaps that would explain how he seemed to know me.

"He thinks he's hilarious."

"I think it's nice," I said. "To be known by friends."

He let out another sigh and squinted down the road that led to the Estate of Alma. "I suppose," he allowed.

"Are all these men going to stay on the Estate?"

"Did you want to take them to your father's house?"

"Perhaps I could pack some of my things," I said wistfully, certainly not serious but wishing I could be. "I had to leave them all."

He looked at me curiously. "This is quite fine," he said, gesturing to the adornment Keturah had given me for my hair. "I've not seen its equal in Zarahemla."

"Then you don't know where to look," I laughed. I had

many similar adornments, and many finer, though none with a secret weapon inside.

He laughed, too. "I confess, I don't look for jewelry much when I'm in the markets."

I was aware of the sound of quick footsteps around us, crunching through the gravel and creating soft puffs of dust where the gravel had worn into dirt. Some of the men talked quietly, maybe adjusting our plans for later, but most of the men were quiet.

"Look there," I said after a few moments. "There is another guard detail at your gate."

Nephi's eyes turned toward the entrance to his home. "Nephite," he told me. "That is my father's guard."

I had been to the Estate of Alma on many occasions, but only in the evening and only down lit pathways that led to the large house. I had assumed the guards at the gate had only been stationed there for temporary security during the events, but the tone of Nephi's voice made me think that perhaps a guard was something Helaman, like Liam and his sons, employed at all times.

Once Nephi and some of the others had greeted the two guards, we passed through the gates and were immediately in a blooming garden where flowers adorned hedges and the air smelled of blossoms and pine.

"Did it always smell like this?" I asked Nephi.

He frowned and looked around. "Like what?"

"Like a peaceful day."

He shrugged.

Gideon drew up next to us. "You go with Zeke to find your father," he told Nephi. "I will take the others to Eliza's house."

Nephi immediately veered away, taking his leave with a jerk of his chin that passed for a nod. I watched him join Zeke, and then I turned to Gideon.

"How long will we stay here?" I asked him.

He adjusted the strap of his travel pack. "As long as it takes."

Something in his hesitation made me think he had a departure date in mind. I thought of Shad and Kishkumen and of Kimner at the gate, and I decided not to question him further.

Eliza's house turned out to be a spacious guest house on the property with large rooms and a common area where we could all meet together. Most of the men dropped their gear near the entrance, but when I slipped my pack off, Jashon took it from me and carried it through the door. I followed him to a room in the back where he set the pack against the wall and turned to go.

"Thank you, Jashon," I said as I sat on one of the beds, lovely and plush like my bed at home had been. I was already anticipating the feel of the fine linens.

He gave a quick nod. "Rest up. I imagine we'll have food in the common room in an hour or two."

I stood up. "I could help cook—"

He raised his hand. "Helaman will want to send something from the kitchens."

"Oh," I said, and sat down again.

"The cooks here are good."

"So much like home," I said, a touch of melancholy slipping into my tone that I knew I couldn't hide.

He frowned. "Would you rather cook your own meal? There's a stream full of fish, and I could go for some grain."

I shook my head and tried a smile. I couldn't tell him about Martha, how I worried for her and hoped she was well.

How I appreciated her ever so much more now that I knew of the work it took to make a nice meal without ruining the food and had experienced the chapped hands and aching back for myself. How she had mothered me the best she could in my father's house. How doing the work made me think of her and feel close to her.

He lingered for a moment but then left without another word. I sighed deeply, curled down into the bed, and fell immediately to sleep.

A loud commotion in the common room woke me, and though there was no window in my room, I sensed it had grown dark. I lay in the stillness for a moment, listening to the low murmur outside my door. Another burst of boisterous laughter drew me from the bed and out into the hall. As I entered the room, the laughter died down and Zeke got up and came to greet me.

"We woke you. I'm sorry."

"Don't be," I said. "It is nice to hear laughter."

He folded his arms and gestured behind him with a small turn of his torso. "There is food. Come and eat."

A woman was clearing away dishes from a long table that hadn't been there when we had come in. I smiled at her and she gave me a dish to hold while she filled it with breads, meats, fruits, and cheeses.

I sniffed at one of the meats. "Is this achiotl?" I asked, tasting a bit with my finger.

"It is. A specialty of our new —"

"Martha!"

I dropped my dish on the table and flew into the arms of the woman coming through the door, pausing only long enough for her to set down the large pot she was carrying.

"Livi!" she cried, then "Olivia," was muffled into my hair and she squeezed me tight in a fierce embrace. "Olivia, Olivia!"

I drew back to look into her face. She was grinning, but there was fear in her eyes.

"Where have you been?"

"There is so much to tell," I told her.

The room had gone silent and many curious eyes were on us. I turned to the men and caught Liam's eye. Gesturing to Martha, I said, "The best cook in Zarahemla." Then I turned to Martha and hesitated but said, "My kinsmen."

Her eyes grew round. "There is indeed much to tell," she said.

I glanced at the other woman. "Do you have time to talk?"

The other woman wore a smile as big as Martha's and generously waved Martha away. "No pack of wild boys is too much for me to handle. Go on with ye. Catch up with your girl."

I started to draw Martha toward the door, but she said, "Now don't go running off so reckless." She went to a sconce on the wall and took down a small torch to light our way. As she did so, I saw that Liam, Jashon, Gideon, and Zeke were all watching me, but none of them made a move to follow. I gave them a little wave, one that only Zeke returned, and grabbed some bread and cheese from my plate before heading out into the courtyard with Martha.

It wasn't full dark, but the light at the edges of the sky was soft. Twilight would soon ease into night, and I was glad Martha had thought to retrieve the torch.

"There is a path that meanders down to the stream," she said, gesturing. "Just here. You eat and then you can tell me where you have been."

"But what happened? What happened with Kishkumen? Where did you go? How long have you been here at the Estate of Alma? Were you hurt?"

She chuckled. "Slow down. I'll talk, but you must eat."

I bit into a piece of the cheese.

She gave a curt nod and began. "You had many hiding places in your father's house when you were a little girl. That day..." She hesitated. "After that horrible man left, when I couldn't find you in the kitchen, I thought perhaps you had hidden yourself under the back staircase or in the storage area with the festive decorations. You weren't in your rooms, and you didn't come to mine. With your father gone and Kishkumen presuming to be master of the house, I knew I couldn't stay. Many of the other servants had already fled. I chanced to see Deborah in the market square and knew her to work here, so I inquired of work on the Estate. She said several of the kitchen servants had left because of the rumors of the Lamanite forces to the south. She plucked my bag off my shoulder and led me here straightaway. I owe her much."

"It is she who is lucky. You're the best cook in all of Zarahemla."

We had come upon a bench in the path, and I could hear the trickling of the stream around us. Martha pulled me to sit next to her and ran a hand down my hair.

"Now, you tell me how those boys came to be your kinsmen."

I looked down at my hands, reveling in the feel of Martha's loving hand on my head. "There is nothing official about it...yet," I began, "but certainly as official as anything Kishkumen cooked up."

She clucked. "That horrible betrothal."

"Shad says there is a loophole, a legal one. He says that if I were married to someone else, the betrothal would lose its validity."

"And who is Shad?" she asked gently.

I licked my lips. "I was hiding in the city. In a falling down building in the northeastern region. I was hungry and exhausted. Shad found me there and offered refuge at his parents' home in—" I bit off my words and glanced around at the dark shadows that surrounded us. "Outside the city," I continued. "I have been under their protection these many months."

The torch hissed and dropped an ember onto Martha's hand. She quickly brushed it away and scrubbed it into the dirt at our feet with her sandaled foot.

"That hardly makes them your kinsmen," she prodded.

I licked my lips again. "Shad has offered to break the betrothal for me. To become my husband."

The torchlight flickered between us. "I see," she said after a moment. "But is he like unto that Kishkumen?"

His name was a sneer on her lips.

"Oh no! If I could dream up a man to marry, I couldn't dream of someone better."

Her brow rose and she sat up straighter. "You do fall into some of the loveliest mishaps," she said with a knowing smile, but when I met her eye, she grimaced and amended. "And some of the worst."

"Well. Shad's kinsmen are here to dissolve Kish's claim to me."

"So many just for that?"

I shook my head. "No. They've some other purpose here, something to do with one of their brothers, I think."

"It's a dangerous time to be conducting business in the city," she said, getting to her feet.

I stood, too, and hugged her tight. "They are wise and brave enough to do what must be done."

She drew back and looked into my eyes. "Then they are worthy of you. Come now. Let's get you back."

Martha bustled about helping Deborah clear away the food. When they were done and she had extracted my promise to visit her when I was able, they left and some of the men moved the table to the side of the room. Someone produced a small ball and began bouncing it on his ankle. Soon many of the men were playing, even some of the older men.

Liam did not get up, just folded his arms tightly across his chest and watched the others.

"Are games of chance more your style?" I asked as I lowered myself down to the floor next to him.

He tilted his head and nearly smiled but offered me an answer that was not quite an answer. "It is good for their coordination." He said it as if his sons were young and he had to justify letting them play games.

"Are you worried about Shad?"

"He has been in contact."

Another answer that wasn't an answer.

"Have you been to Zarahemla before?"

He sighed. "I seldom leave Orihah.

Again, it wasn't an answer to my question, but I didn't want to ask more—I thought perhaps I was annoying him—so I just sat next to him and watched the men play ball with skillful knees and elbows, ankles, hips and even their heads.

"I have three daughters already," he said in the low voice I had become accustomed to hearing from him—so unlike my own father's booming one. "And the fourth is the only one who needs me in Zarahemla."

Liam was a quiet man, and I had long since known that his sons were much the same. But none of them had ever needed words to draw upon the holy spirit. If his arms hadn't been folded so tightly against his chest, I would have taken his hand in mine, for I knew how to talk without words, too. Instead, I put my arms around him, folded arms and all, and lay my head on his shoulder. And even though I was not yet sure of Shad's love for me, nor mine for him, I was sure of Liam's.

Having slept through the afternoon, I lay wide awake in the night. There was a dim light in the common room as I passed through, and I said, "Good evening," as I swept past Kenai at the door. I had been with these people long enough to suspect there was probably at least one other guard roaming about, notwithstanding the guards that Helaman employed, and I reasoned that was why Kenai only murmured a soft greeting and didn't follow me outside.

I wandered through the gardens, the smooth stones of the pathways cool on my bare feet. The paths were not lit bright, like they were during the grand events and parties, but sconces were set into the walls at intervals that made it possible to follow the paths. The soft breeze rustled the leaves, and the luminescent moonlight was so enchanting it put the cozy torch light to shame. Eventually I came full circle and heard the stream. I spied the bench Martha had shown me in the distance and determined to sit there for a while, but as I made my way toward it, I heard low murmured voices approaching from the direction of the main gate.

Unsure who the people were—two of them, perhaps, or three—I hid myself in the dark shadows of a large hedge.

I caught sight of them in the light of a sconce as they approached the entrance to Eliza's house. It was a man and a woman, both tall, and they halted when they saw all the travel gear at the threshold. The woman gestured to it and the man took her hand and drew her toward the stream.

As they made their way toward me, I shrank back even farther into the darkness. I didn't fear them, for surely the guards had known them and let them pass through the gates, but it was not precisely proper for me to be out wandering alone after dark in my night clothes. Likewise, it might not have been precisely proper for them to be out together at night, either, and I thought perhaps a meeting on the path would be somewhat awkward.

I was still as they passed me. They seemed to be my age. The man was young and familiar.

Darius?

It *was* Darius, Keturah's brother. The man Kishkumen had followed to Melek, to Lamech's wedding in the little village. Did he know his brother was just beyond the door he had passed by?

The couple walked swiftly past the stream and turned onto a path I hadn't noticed.

Darius and the girl were swift and quiet, but something about their presence made me uneasy. The men had been stalling for days, and I realized now what they had been waiting for. Darius was the final player in this exploit his kinsmen had been preparing for, and he had just arrived in Zarahemla.

The soft breeze in the leaves sounded ominous now and the moonlight didn't seem enchanting anymore, so I skirted along the shadows toward Eliza's house and the safety of my kinsmen.

"...Not in her bed."

"Why didn't you stop her? Why didn't you keep her here?"

"She wanders at night."

Two men were standing where the path split into two. One path continued on to Eliza's house and the other led to the main gate. One of the men was Liam, and the other might have been Gideon but for his darker hair. It was Shad, and he was not pleased that I was not in my bed. He backed up to pace and pushed a hand through his hair.

"She's safe here on the estate," Liam said easily.

Shad just grunted in annoyance, as if he could not quite bring himself to agree. He leaned back and looked up at the night sky. Finally, he let out a deep sigh.

"Why did you bring her here?"

I bit my lip in the darkness.

"To break the betrothal."

Shad shook his head forcefully. "That's taken care of. Her presence is not necessary."

Liam folded his arms and nearly smiled. "Maybe she wants to see her betrothed before she is married to him."

"I told you. Kishkumen has been —"

"I meant you."

Shad opened his mouth to speak, but no sound came out.

"Did it never occur to you that she might have a desire to marry you?"

Shad stepped back. "She wants out of her betrothal."

"All the silver in my pocket, she wants a real marriage to the boy she loves."

Shad rubbed a hand around the back of his neck. "She agreed to marry because it will break her betrothal."

Liam stepped closer to his son and studied him for a long moment. He placed a hand on Shad's shoulder and waited until Shad met his eye, man to man.

"You have three older brothers. All war heroes. God's warriors."

Shad tried to look away, but Liam gave his shoulder a shake.

"Livi needs a hero, to be sure, and you are completely capable of being that for her."

Shad straightened, even under Liam's heavy hand.

"But she needs more than your strong arm. She needs your strong heart."

Shad's chin dropped.

"Falling in love does not mean you are weak." Liam looked down, taking a moment to think, and then he looked back up at his son. His voice was low when he said, "Livi is a pretty girl."

Shad snorted. I guessed it was in agreement.

Another small shake of the shoulder. "I raised boys that can look past the outer appearance."

Shad didn't say anything to that.

Liam stepped even closer. "You are so focused on her beauty that you have failed to look upon her heart."

Shad was frowning, but I couldn't stop a small smile from spreading over my lips.

"Have you not taken the time to notice what she cares about? Do you not know that this—" Liam gestured to the dark night around them, "that these nighttime strolls are the time she uses to commune with God?"

Shad remained silent.

"It is the time she looks into the heavens and thanks God

for the boy who rescued her from the worst situation of her life."

"She would have accepted the help of anyone. If you could have seen…If you had been there…

"*You* saw, Shad. *You* were there. God sent *you* to be her protection."

"She's in danger here."

Liam was shaking his head. "No danger you cannot protect her from. Danger must be faced. It cannot be side-stepped."

I had thought to step into the light, to reveal myself to them, but I couldn't now.

"Sometimes the ones we love get hurt. Sometimes we can only pick them up when they are broken. We cannot control the depravity of others, but you are protection enough for that girl and man enough to hold her heart."

Shad was very still as he looked back into his father's eyes. "I have to go," he said at last. "The meeting will begin soon."

Liam nodded but surprised me by clasping Shad into a fierce, quick embrace. "Go with God," he said.

I watched as Shad trotted silently off toward the main gate. When I turned back, Liam had covered half the distance between us. He held out my longboots and nodded in the direction Shad had gone.

I grabbed the boots from Liam and hugged him as fiercely as he had hugged his son.

"What do I do?" I asked as I donned the boots.

"You have faith."

I looked into his eyes. "I do."

He nodded once. "Follow him."

And with no more direction than that, I did.

I ran toward the big house, my nightclothes swirling around my boots. I tread through the kitchen gardens and trailed my fingers along the estate wall until I found the family entrance. I opened it and left the safety of the Estate of Alma.

CHAPTER 22

The lane was dark. Small torches lit the main gate, but I was able to stay in the shadows enough to evade the guards' notice.

There was something in the air, something dark and heavy. Perhaps it was in my heart and the Spirit warned me of dangers to come. But Liam had instructed me to follow Shad, and I thought he somehow knew it would be all right.

I turned onto the lane that led into the heart of the city. I hadn't been here in months, but it was my home and I knew many pathways that others probably didn't. Shad had spoken of a meeting and, remembering all I had overheard in the past, I had an idea where it might be taking place.

I took a deep, silent breath and slipped quickly though the side streets and narrow alleys until I stood in the shadows before my father's house.

It was quiet and still, but it wasn't dark. Light glowed through the window coverings and the house appeared to be very much occupied. For a moment I had hope that my father was here, sitting in his office with his feet up on a pillow. Perhaps they had forgiven his so-called crimes of conspiracy and rescinded the order for his death. He was the son of Pahoran!

Surely, they would not take his life.

I swallowed. Martha would have told me if this was so. She would have told me if he had returned to his house, and she had very much avoided the topic altogether.

No. It was not my father who occupied this house.

I heard a low murmuring from down the street and the scuff of boots on the stone roadway. Three men approached, and I stayed very still to watch them.

Two of them were involved in a conversation, but the third was watchful of their surroundings. He looked furtively about them as they walked. I studied them as best I could in the dark street. I did not know any of them, but I watched them obtain entry to my home with little more than a light tap on the door. It was opened swiftly, as if someone were waiting just on the other side to open it for them.

I did not wait long before I heard and saw similar figures approach the house, and I knew that I had found the meeting. Shad was supposedly in attendance, but I didn't see him approach the door.

I did, however, see Darius. He was alone and stalked through the street briskly. He looked neither right nor left, just walked past me and up the few steps to the door. He raised his hand to knock but didn't. His hand hovered there a moment before he dropped it, spun on his heel, and disappeared back into the night.

I should turn around, too. I should go back to the Estate of Alma as quickly as possible—run there and open the family entrance, hurry across the gardens to the guest house, put my head back on my pillow where it belonged, and let Shad's kinsmen do what they were so well-equipped to do.

Follow him.

I didn't know why Liam had said that, and I didn't know why, when men stopped arriving at the door, I moved silently toward the back of the house and let myself in through the kitchens, the same door I had let myself out of so many months ago.

I stood still in a walkthrough pantry and listened.

The kitchen was dark and still, but I could smell food had been cooked there during the evening. Embers still glowed in the cook fire under the stove. Were the attendees dining in my father's house?

I could hear the rumble of voices as I moved through the pantry into the kitchen.

Was there a new cook here? Did she sleep in Martha's little room? What would I do if she caught me here? I couldn't help the small scuffs my feet made on the floor or the brushing of my nightclothes—my nightclothes!—against the tables and baskets as I moved. I stopped to listen again, but I heard no movement from within the kitchen or servants' rooms.

I stared up the staircase that led to the dining hall and other public areas of the house. Or rather, I stared into the blackness that hid it. I didn't think the muffled voices were coming from the dining hall, but it was not the way to go. I didn't know if it was just my own fear, but something warned me not to go up those stairs.

Instead, I moved toward a back hallway. It was dark, too, but lighter due to a small window up above, and I was able to move quickly through it to the stairs at the other end. The noises above me had grown quieter, and I knew that I must be getting farther away from the meeting.

I wanted to listen to it, to hear what had Shad and Darius so secretive and so tied up. I wanted to know the reason Shad could not stay with me at his home in Orihah, but I was afraid I did know. I was afraid he was trying to stop the assassination of the Chief Judge, and I was afraid he would be found out.

Follow him.

Liam had faith in Shad, in his abilities to move within this circle of conspiring men and in his ability to keep me safe from them. I trusted Liam, and despite the scarcity of his presence in Orihah and his brooding after he returned, I trusted Shad as well.

Trusting Shad had not brought me to him, had not put me into loving arms with a worry-free future, but to a place where I could be of use. If I could hear the words of that meeting, I could testify against Kishkumen and all the others, and I would see the true villains condemned to death just as they had seen my father was.

Was that why I was here? To take vengeance for my father? He was ambitious. He was a trifle conniving. But he was not evil.

And evil was what I felt here tonight—in each man that passed me on the road, in the darkness of the staircase that led to their meeting, and in the heaviness of the air that portended something terrible.

I came to the family portion of the house. My own room was just down the hall. It was dark and the door was slightly ajar, but I resisted the temptation to go there and gather up all my beautiful dresses and perfumes and bangles. I moved in the opposite direction, toward the public areas—the dangerous areas. The men would be in the large hall or the formal dining room, my father's receiving room, perhaps—one of the areas large enough to fit the twenty men I had seen go through the door.

I came to my father's room and lingered a moment. I let my eyes adjust to the moonlight coming through the window. It was not how he had left it. Someone had used the room. I could sense it even more than I could see the clothing strewn about, the chair moved, the covers about the bed moved aside. Even the smell was wrong.

I wrinkled my nose and moved on through the hall. The voices were becoming louder, and soon I was outside the receiving room. I didn't risk looking in, but it must have just barely held all the men who had come that night.

Light spilled out into the hallway, and I was careful not to step into it. There was an alcove in the wall, and I stepped into that instead.

"...Are finding greater success with the young crowd, boys who do not want to fight their fathers' battles."

That was Kishkumen.

"Good. It's as we expected."

That voice was familiar as well, but I couldn't place it.

There was some movement, then the same voice said, "Tonight, we welcome our brothers from the south. Josiah is of the Order of Nehor, and he comes to consider an alliance."

I didn't know any Josiah, but I had heard of the Nehors. From what I knew, they were not entirely bad, not like the whisperings I had heard of the Band of Gadianton, but they could be swayed toward bad causes if there was something to gain.

Another voice spoke, one that I was sure I was not familiar with because his accent was very thick.

"I am Josiah of Ani-Anti. I represent Zaaron, chief ruler of the Order, and I bring Caleb, his kinsman, whom he has appointed to speak for him."

275

A low murmur went through the men in the room.

"But he's just a boy," someone said.

The murmurs slowly quieted until finally Josiah said, "Caleb has been trained in all aspects of the Order, and it is he who speaks for Zaaron, not I."

Josiah sounded older than a mere boy, but his endorsement of Caleb was genuine and very firm.

"We arrived with Coriantumr but have no real interest in his objectives. He's a fool with foolish interests."

Another murmur went through the room, but quieted quickly again when a younger voice said, "Our Order applies its power where it can be of most use. So, tell us how we can feature in your plans, and don't leave out the part about how it benefits us."

I edged back into the alcove as far as I could. Was Shad in that room? I had followed him off the estate, but I didn't know if he had come here, and I didn't know what to do now. I couldn't stay in the alcove, but leaving its dark protection would be dangerous, too.

My heart cried to the Lord. *Show me the steps to take.*

My answer was a heavy feeling in my chest like the one I had felt in the forest so many weeks ago just before we had met Lib and Miriam at the spring. There had been danger in the woods that night, and there was danger again this night. At that time, I had felt I should run, so I stepped silently from the alcove and darted down the hall toward the back of the house.

I hesitated as I passed the stairs that led down to the kitchens. A lantern was swinging its way up the stairs, and in its light, the face of a boy. I pressed myself up against the opposite wall. I didn't think he had seen me, as I was beyond the lantern's light. I thought perhaps I could escape the house through my bedroom window—it would not be the first time I had slipped through that window out into the night—but when I inched toward that hall, I saw a soft glow of light coming from my room as well.

Who would be in the family quarters, and why? Was Kishkumen offering lodging to all his friends? Perhaps to someone visiting the city just for tonight's meeting? Maybe a girl to replace me? It made no difference who it was or why they were there. It only meant I couldn't go that direction and my options were quickly disappearing.

"A bit unwise to return here, don't you think?"

I bit back a gasp as I whirled toward the hushed voice.

My eyes were well and adjusted to the dark, and I said, "Ammon?"

His white teeth flashed in the darkness. "Where have you been hiding?"

He was leaning back against the wall like we had stopped in the shade on a jaunt through one of the Zarahemlan gardens.

"What do you mean?"

"Jershon? Melek? Bountiful? Gid? Where've you been? Because you haven't been in Zarahemla. We would have found you."

We.

"Why do you work with Kishkumen?" I asked, taking care to keep my voice low. I glanced down the hall toward my room. Was the light getting brighter? "You're a nice boy. Too good for him."

Ammon looked down at the floor. "I'm probably not as good as you think," he said, keeping his voice to a murmur.

I studied his profile for a moment. Ammon was my

cousin. We had taken lessons together, studied the religious scrolls together, grown up together. If I had any relation that was like a brother to me, it was Ammon. And yet, his unexplainable loyalty to Kish had kept me from going to him when I had run from here. He was fascinated with Kish, almost unnaturally, and I hadn't trusted our kinship. He seemed reluctant now, vulnerable, but I still didn't trust him.

"Why aren't you in that meeting?" I asked.

"I left it to retrieve the food. I thought I saw someone in the shadows, so I came to check it out. I'm supposed to be bringing up the spirits now."

"You let him treat you like refuse. Why do you associate with him?"

"You don't understand. You never understood."

"I never will," I interjected.

"It's not about how much you like people, Olivia."

"It's about what you can gain from them. I do get it." It was about games and winning them. I glanced down the hall again. "Do you know who's in my room?"

His eyes met mine and he came off the wall. "Why would there be someone in your room?"

Just then, the light went out, and we both froze. Would the uninvited guest come back through the house, or would he — like I had planned to — make his escape through the window?

I counted my heartbeats and stilled my breaths, but when it became apparent that no one was coming our way, I said, "I have to go."

"You know I can't let you leave," Ammon said.

Our eyes met again. "You are the son of Pahoran. You have a duty to protect me!"

I started to edge away, but he caught my arm.

"Our definitions of protection may differ, but returning you to your betrothed is the right thing for you. You can't live alone. Who will provide you your fancy things?"

I yanked my arm away from him. "Definitions of protection? What happened to you?"

I searched his face in the darkness, but he was no longer that boy I had grown up with.

"My father was murdered!" he growled. "That's what happened to me."

He didn't seem to want comforting, but I said, "I'm sorry for that, Ammon, for your loss."

He scoffed. "You're sorry? *You're* sorry?"

"Of course," I said. "Ammon, I am. You don't think I had something to do with it, do you?"

"No, but I know your father did."

I shook my head, even though a tiny part of me had sometimes wondered about it. "No," I said. "You're wrong. My father loved your father."

He took a step closer. "And I told you, it's not about whether you love someone."

"It's about what you can gain from them," I said softly, realizing that he was not going to just let me walk out of here. He had too much to gain from returning me to Kishkumen.

"Ammon, come with me."

He was silent a moment, but he scoffed. "That won't work again, Olivia. Even if I could let you leave, I couldn't go with you."

"You could." I paused. "You want to."

His silence stretched much longer, but in the end, he yelled, "Kishkumen!"

Whoever was speaking in the front of the house stopped.

A low murmur began, and I heard chairs scraping across the floor. Someone was leaning against the doorframe, and he stepped back to let Kishkumen through the door. A splash of light from Kish's lantern lit Shad's face there in the hall as he made way for Kish, and our eyes met.

When his lantern light fell on me, his grin grew slowly, but the light of his lantern was no match for the fire in Shad's eyes.

He strode toward me, but he seemed annoyed that I was not watching him in fear. He glanced back over his shoulder to see what had my attention, but Shad was no longer there. He had fallen back into the darkness or blended himself with the other men who had spilled from the door, and I was grateful that he had the foresight not to let Kish know of his connection to me. It would not go well for him. Kish would ruin him and hurt his generous family if he knew.

My eyes shifted back to Kish as he drew near. I made myself hold his gaze, and he looked away first—to Ammon.

"Where did you find her?"

"Here in the house."

Kish's smirk was terrifying, but I clenched my back teeth together and stood tall before him.

"Couldn't resist coming back for all your pretty things, hmm?" he said, glancing down my body. It wasn't a question. It was a mockery.

The men behind him were shuffling closer, but he glanced back and put up a hand to halt them. "Ammon's kinswoman has returned from a journey, that's all."

He turned abruptly back. "Take her to the kitchens," he commanded Ammon. The evil in his smile was reserved for me. "I'll deal with you when I have time."

Neither Ammon nor I made a move until Kishkumen and all his followers had shuffled into the reception room again and he was calling them all back to order.

"Come on," Ammon said quietly, and after a pause, "Neither of us has a choice."

He was wrong. There were choices for both of us to make.

I felt his hand on my arm, guiding me toward the stairs. I didn't resist him, for I knew something he did not know. I knew whose kinswoman I truly was.

The staircase was dark, and Ammon urged me toward it ahead of him. I shuffled along, feeling for the first stair, and after I found it, the rest was easy. The air got slightly cooler as we descended and dank, too.

"You can wait in Martha's chamber," Ammon said from behind me.

"There isn't another cook?"

"Kish makes her leave on meeting nights."

That explained the silent kitchens.

"Ammon?"

"Yeah?"

"Please tell me...I've heard things...Is my father still in prison?"

He scoffed. "Your father is where he deserves to be. Stay here by the door. I'll light my lamp."

The door to Martha's chamber creaked open and light filled the doorway behind the broad-shouldered silhouette of a man and fell upon the floor at our feet.

"That won't be necessary, Ammon. I already lit one."

CHAPTER 23

Shad's face was blank—completely unreadable, as the lantern was behind him and his face was in shadow.

I didn't know if he was angry with me for being in my father's house or if he was angry with Ammon, or perhaps completely unperturbed at all, but I knew absolutely that I could trust him.

He is made strong to protect women, not hurt them.

"Livi, come here."

I made a move to join him across the room, but Ammon's hand shot out and gripped my arm again.

"What are you doing down here?" Ammon asked, but didn't wait for Shad to answer. "Olivia…Livi?" He glanced between us. "Do you know him?"

"He is my kinsman."

Ammon frowned.

"Livi, come here."

Ammon was still holding my arm, and when Shad spoke, Ammon gripped it tighter. I tried to wriggle away from him, but despite his slender build, his hand was like a vice.

Shad took one step forward and spoke slow and clear.

"Take your hands off my betrothed wife."

"What?" Ammon was so surprised his voice was nearly a squeak. "Your betro—"

"Now."

I know the woman who raised him. I know his father and his brothers. Shad could not inflict these bruises even if he was very angry with you.

Shad's voice was dark with leashed rage, and I finally understood Keturah's words. Shad could tear this room and everything in it apart, and I would remain standing in the middle, completely unharmed.

I thought of that day at the stream with Keturah when she ministered to my wounds, of giggling with her about Shad's muscular arms.

Do you want to know a secret? When I met Gideon, the muscles were the first thing I noticed, too.

I nearly giggled again, but I said, "Ammon, do not fear Kishkumen more than you fear Shad."

He jerked back, inadvertently letting go of my arm. "I don't fear anyone."

I nearly scoffed at that. He had shown himself to be completely spineless.

"Livi," Shad said, but he didn't need to tell me a third time to come to him.

I hurried across the room, skirting the preparation table and baskets of goods on the floor.

"We're leaving," Shad told Ammon. "You'll leave, too, if you know what's good for you."

"No. Wait. Go if you want, but Olivia's not going anywhere."

"Agreed."

All three of us turned to see Kishkumen had come down

the stairs and was standing in the doorway of the kitchen.

"Let's make this quick," Kish said. "I've got business to attend to tonight."

Except for the fire in his eyes, Shad had seemed calm till then, almost casual, but his right hand slowly balled into a fist.

With Kishkumen there, Ammon seemed to stand taller, and they both moved slowly toward us as if they intended to pounce on us like jaguars.

"Wait in the pantry, Livi," Shad said.

"I can help."

Of all the reactions he might have given to that, I didn't expect him to smile as if my offer of help was somehow humorous. But he didn't look at me. He kept his eyes on his enemies. "It's okay, Livi," he said softly. "Gather some food for a journey. We're leaving tonight."

I made my steps quick so I wouldn't be within Kishkumen's reach for even a moment and rushed into the pantry. It was as dark as it had been when I had come through it an hour ago, but I knew there to be a torch just inside, and I reached for it. I lit it from the low embers of the hearth. There was little more than just heat there now, deep in the coals, but the torch was made to burn, and I blew two small embers into a flame.

Turning, I saw Shad dodging Ammon's fists. I watched for a small moment, but Shad looked completely capable, so I let him do his work, and I went to do mine.

I placed the torch in a sconce at the far end of the pantry. Naomi would raise her brow at a room this size filled with food. It was nearly as big as her whole house. I smiled at the thought of Naomi, but as my hand fell to the tubers and grains, I remembered filling a bag with food on that terrible night I had left home. I had selected the most delicious foods, the perishable foods—sweet breads and berries and pies of meat. I had known I needed food, but not what kinds of food were nourishing and best, and not how to preserve it and prepare it to eat. So many things Naomi had taught me!

I turned when I heard a low chuckle. Kishkumen was leaning on the doorframe with his arms crossed over his chest. The torchlight glinted off his hair but made his features shadowed and indiscernible.

"I suppose you think you're going to just walk out of here," he said. His smile was more of a leer, and his laugh was more of a warning.

"I did last time." I grabbed some wrapped cheese, slid it into the bag with the other items, and cinched the ties, ready for travel. I hugged the bag to my chest like a barrier between us. Behind Kish, I could see Shad was still fighting Ammon. I leaned around for a better look.

"You're not going to help him? I thought you were friends."

Kish glanced back and shrugged. "Ammon is no trained fighter, but he can keep your would-be hero busy long enough for us to…" He bit his lip and let his eyes roam over me. "To finish what we started."

As he turned back to me, Ammon crumpled to the floor and the main kitchen fell silent. The hairs on the back of my neck rose when it stayed silent.

"You see?" Kish said. "Your little cousin is an annoying inconvenience sometimes, but he can make himself useful, too."

He hadn't seen Ammon fall, but had Shad fallen too? I tried to see around Kish again, but I only saw Ammon's body, slumped and still, on the stone floor.

"Shad!" I called out, hating the urgency in my voice, but there was no answer.

Kish chuckled again. "It was nice of him to try," he said. "Your Shad. But you see..." He took two steps closer. "He can't take you away from me again. No one will have what was meant to be mine."

I stared at him for a moment. God had brought me to Zarahemla to be here in this moment. Surely, He didn't want for me what Kish seemed to want.

My heart cried out to God, and inexplicably, my thoughts went to my engraved wooden chest filled with jewelry upstairs. I must have glanced toward the ceiling because Kish followed my gaze.

"Even your god can't save you this night, Olivia," he said and began to close the distance between us.

Now is the time to play your games, I told myself. *Now, more than ever!*

I offered Kishkumen a seductive smile, letting my lips curl slowly up. "How fortunate that I do not need saving," I said as I bent to set the bag of food at my feet. Kish was near enough to touch me, but instead of recoiling in disgust like I wanted to, I lifted my hand to the adornment that held my hair back — the beautiful wood and obsidian one Keturah had given me — and I let my hair fall, slick and full, around my face.

Kish stopped as he took in my invitation, and his eyes filled with a bright, unholy glow.

"I missed you," I lied, looking away from him in a repulsion that I hoped to pass off as shyness. Surely the mix of boldness and timidity would entice him long enough for me to —

"Aaagh!" he yelled as the little blade of my barrette dug into his skin.

287

I lifted it and swung again. I could feel the resistance of his flesh as my small weapon dug deep into his arm. I drew it back and swung a third time.

His furious eyes stared at me for a moment in disbelief before he lurched forward to attack, but his feet caught in the bag of food on the floor between us. He lost his footing and fell headlong into a solid cutting block. When he was on the ground, he lay still.

I took a breath, my eyes trained on Kish to see if he would rise, but my eyes shot to the door when I heard another chuckle. Elias stepped through the doorway and considered Kish's inert form on the ground.

"I may have to send someone to complete his work for him tonight," he mused, "but I can't say watching you knock him out wasn't the highlight of my day."

I smiled tentatively at him, but I knew he was, like Kishkumen, not a man who deserved my smile. I knew he belonged to Kish's despicable group as much as Ammon or any of the others who had attended tonight's meeting did.

I quirked an ear upward. No footsteps. No rumble of low voices. The meeting must have ended. The men must have all gone from the house.

So, it was me and Elias.

Perhaps we could finish what we had started, too, back in the house of Alma.

"Thinking to take what is mine behind my back." Elias tsked and administered a kick to Kishkumen's stomach that made me wince. I wanted to scamper away as I had done in the cut bank in Melek, but there was nowhere to retreat, so I made myself raise my chin and take a step toward Elias.

It was just another game, and I could win it.

"What did he take from you?" I asked.

Elias snickered. "Kish couldn't control you even with your father's help. He was clearly not man enough to secure the political sway we need, so I informed him of the change in strategy and instructed him to burn that betrothal contract." His smile—an infectious one I had once admired—was truly terrifying. "Well, he couldn't burn it fast enough." Elias shook his head. "Kishkumen," he mused. "So eager to please. So spineless in the end."

I gripped the barrette I held in the folds of my skirt. "What do you mean?

He took three steps closer. "You don't think I've forgotten about our plans, do you, Olivia?"

From the corner of my eye, I saw a shadow slip into the room. I forced myself not to look past Elias to the boy I hoped was there in the dim cellar of what was once my father's house.

"Of what plans are you speaking, please?" I asked. "We have had no agreement between us." Indeed, I barely knew him as more than an acquaintance.

He reached into a pocket and withdrew a scroll as he stepped closer. I could have reached out and touched him, and what was worse, he could have reached out and touched me.

"That ridiculous contract of Kishkumen's?" He wiggled the scroll between his fingers. "Its replacement."

I didn't know what was on that scroll, didn't really want to know.

"Then it is fitting that it come to the same end," I said. I grabbed the torch from the wall and shoved it toward his chest.

Elias dodged the torch with a quick step back, but the scroll fell to the stone floor between us. I grinned triumphantly as I watched the flame curl it into ash.

289

Elias growled and charged forward. His reaching hands grasped only air when he was caught from behind, lifted off his feet, and thrown away from me. His surprise turned to rage when he turned and saw Shad in the flickering light of the torch.

And then, as easily as if he had done it every day of his life, Shad proficiently laid Elias flat on the floor with one fierce punch placed expertly between his eyes.

We stood for a moment. Shad caught his breath and stretched his fingers as if they hurt. I held the sizzling torch aloft. The scroll burned on the floor between us.

Shad tried to stomp the fire out, but I said, "Let it burn."

He glanced at me, then reached down to gingerly grab the burning paper and fling it into the pile of embers in the hearth. He took the torch from me and affixed it back into the sconce.

"I'll get the lamp," he said as he turned toward the kitchen.

"Wait!"

When he turned back to me, I flew into him and wrapped my arms tight around him. I might have kissed his neck. Perhaps I surprised him, but after a moment, his arms came around me, too.

"It's all over, Livi. It's all over," he soothed. "But we have to go. They will wake up before long." He set me gently away from him and went to the kitchen for the lamp.

I bent to retrieve the bag of food and had to untangle it from Kishkumen's feet. As I did, I noticed a bracelet tied there at his ankle. It was made from the blackest obsidian, and I recognized it. My father had one similar to it. Though he had seldom worn it, jewelry was not something that could be kept secret from a curious and entitled little daughter like I had been.

"Don't touch that," Shad said as he came back into the room.

I drew my hand away and looked up. "I know what it is," I admitted. It was the bracelet he had described to me back in the woods of Melek. I had never wanted to admit it, but it meant my father did deserve to be in the prison and he did deserve whatever fate befell him there.

Shad held out his hand, and I let him help me to my feet. Then he took the torch from the wall and plunged it into the embers of the hearth, and the room fell into darkness. Except for the light we carried with us, all the light was gone from there now.

"Come on," Shad said. He held up the little lamp before us and led me to door.

We emerged at the back of the house. The night was quiet and still around us. Shad led me through the familiar streets of Zarahemla holding aloft his lantern, but when we heard a patrol of soldiers, he put the light out. We ducked into a deep doorway and waited in silence.

I thought of that long-ago night he had found me in the crumbling building. I had been so scared — of the mice, sure — but more scared of what my future would hold. My heart had been crying out to God in a way my lips did not know how to, and Shad had appeared in the doorway.

I brushed his fingers, wanting to feel him there in the darkness next to me. His warm hand wrapped around mine and held on tight.

When the soldiers had passed and we could no longer hear the scuff of their footsteps and their peevish complaints, Shad moved out onto the street again.

"Tell me where we're going," I said, hanging back.

He paused. "The government building."

"I'll take you the back way."

Another pause. "There's a back way?"

"I grew up on these streets. Follow me."

I was surprised when he didn't balk or argue, just silently followed me into the tight alley between buildings. The ground was moist, and the alley would narrow before we came out of it, but we would be very near the government building in just a few minutes. My way would save us nearly a half a mile of weaving through streets and dodging patrols.

I wondered what business he could have at the government building. Surely Helaman wouldn't be there. All the important men of the government would have been gone home hours ago.

As we approached the back of the large stone structure, Shad took the lead again, and I followed him around the side to an alcove where two men waited, still and silent, in the night.

I couldn't see clearly who they were, but I recognized Kenai's voice when he said, "Your brothers are on the north side. We followed Darius to the place of meeting—the silos—and then we came here to get into position."

"Is Darius here yet?"

I felt Kenai shrug and the other man sigh. Was it Micah? "We haven't seen him. There's some delay."

"We were delayed, too," Shad said. "Kish has no doubt realized he will have to come alone."

"That should make Dare's mission simpler, but the faction won't fall unless Dare can find out who Gadianton is," Kenai said. "And Kishkumen seems to be the only one who knows. Darius has to get the name before anything else happens."

Micah spoke up. "He might not have the chance. There is already a delay. Something has not gone to plan."

"That might have been me," Shad admitted.

Kenai straightened. "Did you have trouble getting Livi?"

"No trouble. Just an extra guest or two."

Kenai grunted.

"I'm going to get into position."

Kenai grunted again, and Shad pulled me away into the night. We slipped along the edge of the building until we came to the front. Shad slowed and peered around the corner. From here, he would be able to look out over the Grand Plaza. I wanted to ask him what he saw. I wanted to ask him what was going on. The place of meeting? Who was Darius meeting, and what were they doing here at the government building so late in the evening? There were so many things I didn't know.

The only thing I did know was the real name of Gadianton.

I had heard it whispered more than once in the halls of my father's house. He was handsome and likeable. I had liked him once, too. Young and charismatic, he picked his friends well and turned them into followers. No one would ever suspect he led a faction that plotted against the government.

CHAPTER 24

A few crickets chirped, but other than that, the night was very quiet. I knew that Darius's kinsmen were here, and I didn't think they were the only ones. The way Shad had talked to Kenai and Micah, and the way Gideon had talked earlier made me feel very much that this whole evening had been planned—even choreographed. They all had a place and a purpose.

Shad stopped in the dark shadow of a protruding stone staircase. He positioned himself so he could see the Grand Plaza around the steps, and he positioned me so I was tucked as far back as possible and could see nothing.

All was silent for many long moments. Finally, I heard the low call of an owl, a call I knew to be a favorite of Gideon's.

Shad tensed and drew back a little closer to me.

"What is it?" I asked, ever so quietly.

But he just raised a hand to shush me as he peered over the stone stairs.

My heart began to race. My ears were suddenly hot, a heavy lump formed in my throat, and I knew I could not go one more minute without telling Shad who Gadianton was.

I eased forward and touched the hand that had shushed

me, and I hoped he would trust me like I trusted him.

"Elias," I whispered.

For a moment, Shad didn't seem to have heard me, but he slowly turned his gaze to meet mine in the moonlight, and I remembered that first moment I had seen him in the moonlight in the old, abandoned house, how I had seen goodness in his eyes and trusted him.

"Elias is Gadianton. After his father before him."

"How...? Are you sure?"

I squeezed his hand in response, for I could hear the voices of two men approaching through the plaza. We both froze as their voices grew louder.

"Give me your knife," one said.

There was a long pause. "What? Haven't you brought your own?"

Just as I ducked under Shad's elbow to see what was going on, a shadow darted across the open plaza toward the two men. It looked to be a woman with long hair flying behind her. She drew a weapon from her back as she ran, and Shad must have seen it too because he let out the piercing call of a margay, a sound I had only heard in the forests near his home, never here in the city.

Before the call had finished echoing through the stone plaza, one of the men was unmoving in a heap on the ground.

I watched as the other man checked for a pulse, then retrieved something from the fallen man's hand. A knife. Moving quickly, he turned, gathered the woman with no more than a glance and ran out of the square, calling to her over his shoulder, "Are you always going to be disobedient?" The girl sheathed her blade and ran after him.

I huffed. "Disobedient?"

Shad lifted his arm and peered at me under his elbow.

"I guess you're in good company. That was Ava, and she certainly wasn't supposed to follow Darius here — not tonight of all nights."

"Good company? I'm never disobedient!"

He huffed. "You have a habit of not staying where you are supposed to be."

If I had stayed where I was supposed to be, I would be married to Kishkumen by now. I would never have met Shad's family, never learned to weave or to make bread or yogurt. If I had stayed where I was supposed to be, Jashon and his kinsmen would never have brought me here to Zarahemla to see the betrothal over.

My eyes found the fallen man on the plaza. It was Kishkumen. I had last seen him in a tangle on the floor of Martha's pantry. I had left him there, the same way he had left me so may months ago.

"Well, which is it?" I asked Shad. "May I go where I wish to go, or shall I stay where you wish me to stay?"

A corner of his mouth turned up. "Go wherever you want, Livi."

"But if I do that now, is that not submission to your wishes?"

He turned fully to me and placed his hands lightly at my waist, and his voice was low when he said, "Would that be such a bad thing? To stay where I want you to stay?"

"Shad."

We both turned at the sound of Gideon's voice.

"Time to get Livi back to the Estate. There will be soldiers here any minute."

Shad's grip on my waist tightened. "Come on," he said.

"Gid's right. This is no place for a girl like you tonight."

A girl like me. Spoiled? A trifle disobedient? Afraid to confess she was a follower of Christ? I didn't think Shad meant any of those things, and I chose to take his words as a compliment. A girl like me. A fighter. A girl who had traded her dignity for her honor.

More men had filled the Grand Plaza, abandoning their hiding places to see for themselves what had been done. A boy with dark eyes inspected the fatal wound, and when he looked up, I could see his eyes were dark because they had been tattooed that way. A lighter boy I thought might be the guard from the West Gate, the one who had murmured good luck to me when we'd arrived in Zarahemla, searched the square around Kish's body, but no one tried to save him or call for a healer. I supposed they deemed it unnecessary and too late.

Shad watched me observe the men. "Death is never our first choice, but if Kish had killed Helaman with Dare's knife, it would have been very bad for Dare. The knife is quite distinctive. Everyone knows it belongs to him."

"But is Helaman here? It's so late."

"No. He is safe on the Estate waiting for word of tonight's events." He paused and scanned the plaza. "That's where you need to be."

"I know why it was necessary. I know that Helaman's life was not safe and that Kishkumen has taken lives before."

"It is a hard truth," he said and ran a hand down my hair.

I closed my eyes at the feel of his hand. "You made the call of the wildcat," I said. I had seen enough changing of the guards on the farmstead to recognize it for what it was. "You warned him."

"The owl was designated as a warning. The margay..."

298

"An alarm?"

He let out a breath. "Yes, more like an alarm. But come on, we have to get you back to the Estate where it's safe."

I nodded. I had thought the call of the margay was a warning against the girl with the weapon behind him, but instead, it had been a signal to Darius to abort his mission and escape at any cost, that it was no longer imperative to elicit the information he needed from Kish.

Shad took my hand and led me across the square. We were nearly to Kishkumen when he said, "You don't need to look, Livi," and he put himself between me and the gruesome scene on the stones.

I pulled him to a stop. "I think I should see."

I thought I saw disappointment in his eyes, but he acquiesced, and I ducked around him again to see that Kishkumen could no longer hurt me. It might take a while for it to truly sink in.

I was aware that Shad was waiting, so I didn't spend long looking at the man who had caused me so much pain, who had urged my father along his path of insurrection. I looked up. Kenai and Micah were making their way back across the square. I saw the brothers, Zeke and Jarom, leaving the plaza from the south end where it seemed they had been hidden. Gideon and Jashon lingered over the body for a moment longer, but turned and followed us out of the Grand Plaza.

"How fast can you get us back to Helaman's house?"

I thought through the path. There were a few shortcuts, but some of it did have to be traveled on the main roadways.

"Ten minutes, faster if we run."

He glanced at my nightclothes.

"I have my boots on."

"Then lead the way," he said.

Gideon and Jashon followed us through the narrow alleys until we were near my father's house, but when we would have passed it, Shad pulled me to a stop in the shadows and held a finger over his lips. I didn't need to ask why. I saw them, too.

Ammon and Elias stumbled down the steps of the front entrance. Ammon held up a small torch, and Elias rubbed his temple with the heel of his hand.

We stayed hidden and watched them shuffle in the direction of the Grand Plaza.

"You're not going to apprehend them?" I asked when they had turned a corner.

"On what grounds? Your word is good with me, but the courts will want proof. We'll have to wait until we have it."

"Did the courts have proof on my father?" I bit out.

Shad sighed. "I believe they did, Livi."

I squeezed his hand in apology. What had happened to my father was his own fault, not Shad's. My head had accepted it, but it would take longer for my heart to believe it.

When we approached the gates at the Estate of Alma, Shad hailed the guards.

"Is Dare inside?"

They opened one side of the gate. As we all slipped through, one of them murmured, "He's come and gone," and then they closed the gate tight behind us.

Shad turned to Gideon. "I have to make a report." He glanced at me. "I have information that cannot wait. Will you see Livi back to the guest house?"

"Of course," Gideon said.

Shad stepped closer to me. "Helaman will want to talk to you tomorrow, surely."

"About Elias? I will help however I can."

He turned to go in the direction of Helaman's family home, but paused, stepped back, and kissed me. His lips were warm, and I felt a small cut that Ammon had given him. I knew he was in a hurry, but his lips were slow, and even when the kiss ended, he lingered for a moment before trotting off in the direction of the big house.

Gideon and Jashon walked me back to the guest house without a word about the kiss, though my cheeks burned hot when I saw their identical smug smiles. It was nearly the fourth watch, and I thought of Lamech back home in Orihah, maybe waking to watch the sunrise. I thought of Gideon's teasing on the journey to Melek and of Jashon's assessing eyes at the waterfall.

"Let's all try to get some sleep," Jashon said as we approached the building.

But Liam was standing in the doorway, very clearly waiting for word of the night's events. His eyes darted between the brothers, and Jashon read the question there.

"He's making a report to Helaman," he told his father. "It is done, and he is safely through it."

Liam only nodded stiffly but I could see the relief in his eyes when they finally fell on me.

It might have been me, it might have been him, but we embraced before I entered the house.

"Sleep," he said into my hair, and I laughed.

"I think you might have been up all night, too," I chided.

Characteristically, he didn't say anything to that, just drew away and let me precede him inside. Kenai and Micah had already arrived and were standing in the great room, as were Jarom, Zeke, and Kalem. They all glanced over when we entered, but Kenai was telling Kalem of the events of the night.

"And was it as we suspected?" Kalem asked.

Kenai hesitated, but said, "Darius had to take the life of Kishkumen."

Kalem grimaced and looked at the floor. The rest of the men were somber as well.

"Kishkumen took my father's knife," Micah said, his eyes bright and filled with fire. "He intended to kill Helaman in cold blood and let Dare take the blame."

Kenai ran a hand through his hair. "The options disappeared quickly once they were in the Plaza."

Jarom spoke up. "But someone made the call of the margay."

"Who made the call?" Kenai asked, and they all looked blankly at one another.

"Shad did," I said. "Because the name of Gadianton had already been learned."

I lifted my chin when they all turned to me.

"I told you. I learned many secrets in the halls of my father's home."

They mulled that over, the same question in all of their eyes. *Who?*

"A friend of my cousin's," I told them. "Shad is revealing his identity to Helaman. I wish I had known you were looking for Gadianton, but I didn't. Truly, I thought it was no more than some kind of title his father placed on him, a distinction of some kind. I didn't know there were meetings and members and levels and initiations."

"Initiations?" Kalem asked, taking a step toward me. "Of what sort?"

He wondered what his son had had to do.

I felt compassion for him. "That, I don't know," I lied, because I did have some ideas. "But I would certainly guess they were of the dangerous and immoral sort, and if Darius passed the initiation tasks, he had to be very cunning and very convincing."

Kalem's jaw tightened, but he nodded. I suspected he knew exactly what sort of tasks one must complete to gain entry into the Gadiantons.

He looked to his sons. "Let's rest. We've a long journey on the morrow."

The impromptu meeting ended and the men began seeking their bedrolls there in the big room. I did likewise and went toward my room. As I passed Gideon, Micah approached him.

"Will you sail?" he asked simply.

Gideon was bent, preparing his bed, but he sat up on his knees.

"You've had Hemni to get everyone to the West Sea, but I'll have to run to Orihah for Keturah and Gabriel. If we make it in time, we will sail."

I could see that Micah was pleased, but I knew this would separate Gideon from his family, probably forever.

I was very fortunate to still be in my nightclothes, because I fell into my bed and barely registered the fine linens before falling into a deep sleep.

It was well past dawn when I awoke, and everyone was gone except Jashon and Liam.

"Are they all sailing north?" I asked as I rubbed the sleep from my eyes and picked at the simple breakfast that was still on the table. "Did Martha bring this? Why did no one wake me? Where is Shad, please?"

"Yes," said Liam.

"And no, it was Deborah," added Jashon.

"And because you needed rest," Liam continued.

Jashon chuckled. "And he is still abed." He gestured to a form on a pallet in the corner of the room.

I watched him sleeping for a long moment.

"He should have gone home to his own bed." I looked back at Jashon. "To his little house in the city."

He and his father glanced at each other. "You've been there?" Jashon asked.

"It's safer here," Liam said.

"I slept one night there when he first rescued me," I told Jashon. Then I turned to Liam. "And you are quite right. I imagine the whole of the band of Gadianton as well as the Nehors will be looking for rogue members today."

Jashon rubbed at his eyes. "They have probably gone to ground and utterly disappeared."

I chewed a few bites of my breakfast. "I take it Gideon is taking his family north?"

"He is," Liam said simply, but was that pride in his voice?

"He wanted to say goodbye," Jashon put in, "but in the end, we all determined to let you sleep. Shad said you had quite the ordeal last night."

I glanced over my shoulder at his sleeping form. "It wasn't such an ordeal. A little snag, that's all."

They glanced at each other again.

How could I tell them I didn't want to relive it by relaying it all to them? I didn't want to admit how naïve I had been to think Kishkumen was pulling all the shots when there had been so many clues that Elias was emerging as a leader among his friends. I didn't want to say what I suspected, that the night Nephi had saved me from his advances was the night Elias's father had bestowed the leadership on him. He had given him rights and responsibilities, and I had a great, gnawing fear that he had intended for me to be part of his initiations that night. I shuddered to think about it, and I didn't want to tell them any of it.

"Shad said you were very brave."

I took a breath. "I was." Why deny it? Why be overly modest or play coy? "Your family taught me to have faith in myself and in my God, and to know what power protects me. If that is brave, then I was." I cleared my throat. "When are we going home, please?"

CHAPTER 25

I hurried out of the kitchen with the bundle Martha had given me. I would see her again, someday when Shad brought me to the city for a visit. But I had to hurry now because it was time to leave.

As I passed the family entrance to the Estate of Alma, I paused for a moment. It was ordinary and small, some might call it narrow, but going through it had saved me twice.

"You're leaving."

I turned to see Nephi. His long strides were cutting a path through the grasses of the garden. He tossed his hair from his eyes and grinned at me.

"No. I mean, I am, but not through this door."

He drew up and turned a little so I could see the large pack on his back.

"Are you coming with us?" I asked.

"Not this time," he said. "This is for you."

"For me? What is it?"

Instead of answering, he set the bag down and went to his heels. Glancing up at me as he undid the tie, he seemed a little unsure of himself. He pulled back the flaps and moved so

I could see what was inside.

I leaned forward to get a look. "My things!"

The patterned fabric on top was distinctive, and I knew immediately what he had done. I fell to my knees, dived into the bag, and felt the soft silks and linens, cool and smooth against my fingers. I felt the soles of shoes and heard my jewelry tinkle as I rifled through the contents.

"But how?" I asked. "When did you do this?"

He rubbed the back of his neck. "The night Kishkumen was found in the square. I went to your house. I remembered you said you missed your things, and I thought I could retrieve some of them for you." His smile was sheepish.

My hands stilled in the bag. Did he know how dangerous that had been? Did he know he had chosen the worst possible night to be at my father's house? Did he know the man they had found murdered in the Grand Plaza had appropriated my father's house and had been there that night?

"Not my best idea?" he asked uncertainly when he saw the look on my face.

I threw my arms around him and hugged him tight, grateful he was safe, and yes, grateful for my things!

I pulled back and looked into his face—his impossibly hazel eyes and his handsome, crooked nose. He had done this thing because he thought I was pretty, and for the first time, I was glad to be pretty, to inspire goodness instead of inciting dark and immoral thoughts. His friendship was as true as his heart.

"Thank you," I said as sincerely as I could.

When we came around the bend in the path, I saw Shad with his father and oldest brother through the mists of the morning. Jashon nudged Shad and gestured toward me. When

Shad looked up from his travel gear, he grinned, and I couldn't help a smile in return.

Shad glanced at Nephi, and I said, "I'm afraid Nephi has brought you more to carry."

Shad cocked his head to the side in a question I didn't answer except to say, "Gifts for your mother and sisters."

Nephi set the pack down and clasped arms with Liam, Jashon, and Shad, but before he could bid us farewell, his father emerged from the big house across the estate. He made a straight path for us, so we all waited for him to make his way over.

Helaman was broad and strong like his father had been. I did remember him from when I was a young girl. He'd had a presence you did not simply forget, and Helaman had it too. When he spoke, you listened. When he commanded, you obeyed. When he counseled, you heeded.

Liam stepped forward and clasped arms with Helaman.

"I've come to wish you a safe journey and thank you again for your son's services." He nodded to Shad. "He has skills not often found in young men of his age, vital skills we needed desperately in this war we have waged against an enemy we cannot see. I hear all your boys have been valuable in this fight." His eyes shifted to Jashon. "You fought with Teancum."

Jashon stood straighter. "In the north. A cunning and brave commander."

Helaman nodded. "I went south with my father for a time, though I never did see battle." He put a large hand on Nephi's shoulder. "I see now I was overprotected, and I fear I've done the same to my son." He paused. "If you've a mind for it, he would like to spend some time in the valley of the Mulekites to begin his adventures abroad."

Nephi's eyes shot to his father's face. Helaman turned to

him. "Go. Pack some things so you don't hold these people up. The sun is ready to rise."

Nephi licked his lips and glanced at Liam, who gave him the barest of nods, but it was a full-blown "yes" coming from Liam. He glanced at me, too, not seeking approval, but seeking...something.

Helaman watched him hurry away. "Don't forget to kiss your mother!" he called after him.

Nephi raised his hand to indicate he heard, but he didn't turn.

"Ardon will be glad to have Nephi in the valley. They've formed a great friendship," Jashon said.

Helaman nodded and smiled wistfully. "It is time he experienced life outside of this estate." He looked around, letting his eyes take in the beautiful gardens and the charming outbuildings. "But the truth is, with the band of Gadianton unaccounted for, Coriantumr's easy conquest of Zarahemla, and the recent upheaval of the judgment seat, I admit I feel he is safer outside these walls."

We were all silent for a moment.

"Do you want me to take Lehi, too?" Jashon offered.

"No." Helaman shook his head. "Thank you. No. But perhaps I will bring all the children for a visit soon. When Coriantumr's men have all passed through the lands."

"You will be welcome at any time."

Helaman sighed and leaned back on his heels. "I suppose I'll go deal with the wrath of my wife now."

Liam actually chuckled.

The sun was fully above the distant mountains when we were finally outside the gates of the Estate. We walked down the long lane toward the city, and I remembered just a week ago when we had traveled this lane with all the other men that had come to protect Darius and Shad — their older brothers and their fathers. The gravel had crunched beneath our feet then, too, and Nephi had decided to get my things from my father's house.

Nephi walked between Liam and Jashon now, carrying the extra pack filled with things from my old life.

When Nephi had packed his travel gear and returned to meet us at the gate, Shad had gestured to the pack full of fine dresses and jewelry and scarves and shoes, indicating that Nephi should carry it to Melek for me. Grinning, he had said, "I could get used to having a little brother around."

But even with the extra weight, there was a hop in Nephi's step.

"We missed the turn for the West Gate," I said, glancing back over my shoulder.

Shad sent me a sidelong glance. "Unless I miss my guess, today is a market day."

I could see the teasing smile on his lips. "How could I have forgotten market day?" I asked.

"A quick stop for a few supplies. We haven't time to browse the shops."

Of course I hadn't planned on anything of the sort, but while the others sought out the food vendors, Shad took my hand and pulled me into an aisle of jewelry booths.

"Here," he said, and I could see he had a particular merchant in mind. "Hello, Cael."

The man turned and beamed, his eyes darting between us. "Shad! You've come at last."

"Is it ready as we discussed?"

"Indeed. It's wrapped, but would you like to inspect it?"

Shad glanced at me and shook his head. "I fully trust

311

your judgment." He handed over some coins, and Cael passed him a small bundle tied with leather cords.

Cael turned to me. "Did the boots fit?"

Realizing this must be where Shad had obtained my longboots so many months ago, I said, "Yes, like they were made for me, thank you."

He nodded sagely. "Sometimes the style is not as we would choose for ourselves, but the fit is just fine."

I thought of the farmstead in the middle of the barley field, of the work required to live comfortably on it, and oh, wasn't Cael right?

"And besides, it's hard to get wrong when you have measurements."

My eyes shot to Shad's. A flush was already creeping into his cheeks, and his mouth appeared to be clamped shut.

"Did you take measurements of me?" I hissed. "While I slept?" But it was such a funny thought, that I broke into giggles.

His lips twisted into a smile, but he kept them closed.

We bid a grinning Cael goodbye and left the market. Shad stopped in a grassy area to wait on the others. It was shaded and there was a bench there to sit on, but he didn't sit down.

"Will you make Nephi carry this present with all the others?" I asked.

"This is a gift, but not for my mother." He passed it to me and waited for me to pull the leather cord. His eyes were bright. He was happy to be giving me a gift, and his expression was so endearing I determined that I would pretend to like whatever was inside the wrapping, even if it was not to my taste.

But I didn't have to pretend.

As I folded back the fabric, I found a leather cord that

matched the binding. I knew what it was immediately and how it would look in my hair. I picked it out of the wrapping and let the feathers fall against my hand.

I had looked at one like this in the market, more than once. I had always talked myself out of buying it. "Next time," I had said to myself several times until one day, there was no next time.

I didn't bother asking him how he knew I had admired this. Those men my father had employed to ensure my safety when I was about in the city, when I thought I was independent and alone—Shad was one of them. I knew it, and instead of being offended at being thought to be helpless, my heart almost burst with thankfulness that, out of all the men of Kish's acquaintance, Shad had been the one given the boring job of following me around.

There were a thousand things I wanted to say, but the thankfulness was a lump in my throat, so I just met his eyes and mouthed *thank you*.

"You know how to wear it?"

That made me laugh. Of course I knew how to wear it. I rolled my eyes and stepped back. Bending at the waist and letting my long hair fall down in front of my face, I set the headband in place. I straightened, and as I adjusted it so the feathers fell just right, I said, "That's the only way to get it in right."

He leaned back for a better look. I could tell he liked it.

"Thank you, Shad. Really. It is exquisite."

He touched my hair. "I'm glad you like it."

I watched him for a moment, the emotions playing over his face, the worry, the hope, and the newness—not of his love, but of being able to show it, to have it returned. I reached up and touched his brow, as if I could ease the uncertainty there.

"But you have given me many things that are more exquisite." At his look of doubt, I said, "A home in the middle of a barley field, a family that knows what it is to love—sweet sisters, teasing brothers, a mother! You have given me of yourself and your faith. You cared about me before I ever knew you." I leaned up on my toes and kissed his lips. "That is all very exquisite to me."

Shad huffed, as if he could not quite believe the things I said.

"You don't have to believe me," I said. "My acceptance of your gift is not conditional upon that."

At that, a slow smile spread over his face.

"You won't miss the city?" he asked.

I looked toward the large stone buildings in the city center, the wooden huts that were built all around us, the people coming and going, and I shook my head, the feathers brushing soft against my cheek. "I have everything I want from this place."

He grinned, probably thinking again of Nephi and the pack filled with my things on his back.

But I shook my head again. "A boy who fell in love while he followed me through the streets of Zarahemla, who kept me safe from the true danger while I flitted about in the market."

His smile faded, but it didn't disappear. He kept his eyes on mine, even when Jashon called from the end of the lane. It was time to go.

"Let's go home," Shad said.

I leaned up on my toes and kissed him again.

"I'll follow where you lead."

ABOUT THE AUTHOR

Misty Moncur wanted to be Indiana Jones when she grew up. Instead, she became an author and has her adventures at home in her jammies with her imagination and pens that she keeps running dry.

Misty is the author of *Daughter of Helaman*, *Fight For You*, *In All Places*, and other novels in The Stripling Warrior series. Her stories are filled with tenderness and humor, and her characters are real, endearing, and memorable. Her LDS fiction titles will inspire you.

Misty loves to read anything with a romance in it, edit, type, stare out the window, and hang with her family. She lives in a swampy marshland and spends her evenings swatting mosquitoes.

www.ingramcontent.com/pod-product-compliance
Lightning Source LLC
Chambersburg PA
CBHW020230180626
46810CB00006B/2128